ADVANCE PRAISE FOR
# *The Spirit of Love*

"Lauren Kate's books never fail to delight, and *The Spirit of Love* is no exception. Equal parts witty and heartwarming, this is a read-in-one-sitting kind of book. I couldn't put it down! Fenny's journey to love, not only with Jude but with herself, is one that will stick with me. Lauren Kate simply never misses!"
—Falon Ballard, author of *Lease on Love*

"Lauren Kate has done it again! *The Spirit of Love* is an utterly delightful and perfectly magical romance that I couldn't put down until the final page. Perfect for romance readers who take their love triangles with an extra dose of whimsy!"
—Ellie Palmer, author of *Four Weekends and a Funeral*

"Lauren Kate's *The Spirit of Love* utterly charmed me! I was swept away by this magical twist on a love triangle, which kept me laughing and clutching my heart in equal measure. At times profound, exploring big themes like finding one's purpose and healing the spiritual fracturing of self, this romance is also fresh, fizzy, and so fun!"
—Melanie Sweeney, author of *Take Me Home*

PRAISE FOR

# *What's in a Kiss?*

A Zibby Owens Summer Reading List Pick

A *BuzzFeed* Best Romance Book to Read in 2024

A *Fangirlish* Best Romance Book of 2024

"A heart-stoppingly romantic exploration of all the what-ifs—told with so much humor and heart that you will lose yourself in the fantasy. Beneath the joy ride of electric tension is a thoughtful commentary on friendship and the consequences of our choices. I loved it!"

—Annabel Monaghan, national bestselling author of *Same Time Next Summer*

"Sweet and funny . . . This second-chance, enemies-to-lovers romance from Kate is sexy and swoon-worthy."

—*Library Journal*

"A sexy and romantic delight about parallel lives, what-ifs, and kisses that cross a multiverse."

—Abbi Waxman, author of *The Bookish Life of Nina Hill*

"Funny and sexy, *What's in a Kiss?* spins a slip of fate into an utterly charming rom-com full of delightful surprises and nuanced family and friendship dynamics. A sweet and smart story of the love found in every lifetime and the destiny we make for ourselves."

—Emily Wibberley and Austin Siegemund-Broka, authors of *The Roughest Draft*

PRAISE FOR

# *By Any Other Name*

One of *USA Today*'s Favorite March Rom-Coms

One of *Forbes*'s Most Anticipated Books of the Year

One of *PopSugar*'s 54 Novels to Read
When You Want a Romantic Escape

"A delightful romp." —*USA Today*

"A smart, imaginative rom-com that had me turning the pages."
—Abby Jimenez, *USA Today* bestselling author of
*Life's Too Short*

"There's nothing better than a book about books, especially when a great love story is involved. *By Any Other Name* by Lauren Kate serves up a behind-the-scenes publishing romance that is sure to delight bibliophiles. . . . Be prepared to finish this one in one sitting." —*Forbes*

"[A] charming, witty tale . . . Among this love story's many charms is one of the most romantic proposals in the rom-com genre." —*Booklist*

## NOVELS BY LAUREN KATE

*What's in a Kiss?*
*By Any Other Name*
*The Orphan's Song*

## YOUNG ADULT NOVELS BY LAUREN KATE

### TEARDROP SERIES

*Waterfall*
*Last Day of Love: A Teardrop Story*
*Teardrop*

### FALLEN SERIES

*Unforgiven*
*Angels in the Dark*
*Rapture*
*Fallen in Love*
*Passion*
*Torment*
*Fallen*

*The Betrayal of Natalie Hargrove*

# The Spirit of Love

A NOVEL

## LAUREN KATE

G. P. PUTNAM'S SONS
New York

**PUTNAM**
— EST. 1838 —

G. P. Putnam's Sons
*Publishers Since 1838*
An imprint of Penguin Random House LLC
1745 Broadway, New York, NY 10019
penguinrandomhouse.com

Copyright © 2025 by Lauren Kate

Penguin Random House values and supports copyright. Copyright fuels creativity, encourages diverse voices, promotes free speech, and creates a vibrant culture. Thank you for buying an authorized edition of this book and for complying with copyright laws by not reproducing, scanning, or distributing any part of it in any form without permission. You are supporting writers and allowing Penguin Random House to continue to publish books for every reader. Please note that no part of this book may be used or reproduced in any manner for the purpose of training artificial intelligence technologies or systems.

Book design by Ashley Tucker
Title page art by TrueArtStudio/Shutterstock (Hollywood)
and Sylverarts Vectors/Shutterstock (cabin)

Library of Congress Cataloging-in-Publication Data
Names: Kate, Lauren, author.
Title: The spirit of love: a novel / by Lauren Kate.
Description: New York: G. P. Putnam's Sons, 2025.
Identifiers: LCCN 2024033352 (print) | LCCN 2024033353 (ebook) |
ISBN 9780593545195 (trade paperback) | ISBN 9780593545201 (epub)
Subjects: LCGFT: Romance fiction. | Novels.
Classification: LCC PS3611.A78828 S65 2025 (print) |
LCC PS3611.A78828 (ebook) | DDC 813/.6—dc23/eng/20240719
LC record available at https://lccn.loc.gov/2024033352
LC ebook record available at https://lccn.loc.gov/2024033353

Printed in the United States of America
1st Printing

The authorized representative in the EU for product safety and compliance is Penguin Random House Ireland, Morrison Chambers, 32 Nassau Street, Dublin D02 YH68, Ireland, https://eu-contact.penguin.ie.

For Anne Velevis

You untold life of me,
And all you venerable and innocent joys . . .
Our time, our term has come.

—Walt Whitman, "Song of the Redwood-Tree"

# The Spirit of Love

 # Part One

# Chapter One

"*THERE* SHE IS," MY FAVORITE SECURITY GUARD SAYS Monday morning as I pull up to the gate at CBS's Radford Studios. "Ms. Fenny Fein, *director*. Look out."

"Big day," I tell Rockwell, reaching through my car's open window to fist-bump him, like I do every morning. Only this morning, nothing feels ordinary. Everything feels new.

It's a plumeria-scented, turquoise-skyed, warm September day in Los Angeles, an auspicious forecast to kick off the next phase of my career.

Rockwell leans forward, scrutinizing me. He gestures at my air-dried, wavy, above-the-shoulder blond bob, then at my unglossed, still-a-little-sunburned-from-last-weekend lips. "Did you do something different with your . . . ?"

"Indeed I did, Rockwell," I say. "I did something very different."

"You've got that boss glow, Fenny. Go in there and get what's yours!"

He opens the gate, and I wave as I drive through.

Rockwell is *partly* right: I am here this morning to get what's mine, to finally fulfill my long-held dream of directing my very first episode of *Zombie Hospital*, the TV show whose rungs I've been climbing for the past seven years.

Today's the day I officially move out of the writers' room and into the director's chair. I've loved writing on *Zombie Hospital*, but once a script is complete, a writer must let go of all she's done, surrendering her pages' destiny to the actual shoot—which can change everything about a scene. To direct is to *be* the show's vision, to make its destiny, to call the shots that add up to its soul.

Is *Zombie Hospital* campy and absurd? Hell yes, and that's why we love it. Is it also hilarious and arch and occasionally resonant with the big question of why we're all here on Earth? It is, and *that's* what gets me up in the morning. That's what makes *Zombie Hospital* my home.

After seven years, one hundred fifty-four episodes, three agents, much schmoozing, and a lot of late-night prayer, I finally get to direct. I feel a little apprehensive, a lot validated, and three hundred percent ready to step into my new role. But the glow that Rockwell mentioned back at the studio gate? I believe that comes from somewhere else. . . .

Have you ever had an orgasm so powerful it rattled the marrow of your bones?

It's one of those if-you-know-you-know experiences, and seventy-two hours ago, I had *no* idea. I would have face-palmed at such hyperbolic language, because I take language seriously.

Cut to now, when I'm attempting to operate a vehicle with *actual* rattled bone marrow. As I wind my way through Radford's forty-acre lot, my mind slips back in time to this past weekend. I know that, technically, I'm here in Studio City, driving this familiar route to my familiar trailer . . . but inside? A part of me is also still *there*.

THE SPIRIT OF LOVE                                        5

In a cabin at the edge of the world. Draped in magic. Fireside. With Sam.

*Sam.* Who I met this weekend at the beach. A giddy smile lights me up as I slam on the brakes in the middle of the lot. I can't remember the last time it was this much fun to think about a guy. I bust out my phone and open a new browser window to see when I can catch the next ferry back to Catalina Island. Back to his cabin, his arms. If I leave after work tonight . . . There's no ferry that could get me back in time for call tomorrow. But then, what even *is* time in the face of that crinkly thing Sam's eyes do when he smiles?

A car horn honks.

"Hey, lady!" a male voice calls from the car I've trapped behind me. "Important people back here, trying to get to important places!"

In my rearview mirror, I see that my car is blocking Jake Glasswell's Lucid Air and I laugh. Jake is the host of *The Jake Night Show* and engaged to one of my best friends, Olivia Dusk. And he is clearly fucking with me.

"Sorry, Glasswell!" I call out my window, putting my Kia EV9 back in Drive, shelving my erotic wanderlust for another time. "I'm moving."

"Fenny. Hold up, I was on my way to find you." Jake climbs out of his driver's side door, opens his trunk, and pulls out a bouquet of zombie-shaped silver helium balloons. "These are from Liv and me."

I put a hand to my heart, touched, as he helps me stuff the unwieldy balloons into my passenger seat. "Thank you, Jake."

"Least we could do to celebrate the new Scorsese in town." He winks.

"You do know Liv and I despise Scorsese, right?"

"Yeah, yeah." Jake beams his dazzling, ratings-reaping smile. "I still think you'd like his early work—"

"I'm more focused on *my* early work at the moment."

"Of course," Jake says. "Hey, how was your trip to Catalina? Did you get that rainstorm you were after?"

I did get that storm . . . and then some. And although the mere mention of Catalina sets my bone marrow rattling again, I can't dish to my friend's fiancé about my naughty weekend.

"It was . . . unforgettable."

"Sounds like a good story," Jake says, with a look that tells me he'll hear it thirdhand from Liv later. "Well, knock 'em undead today—whoops, Liv says I'm not allowed to use that joke anymore."

"You're really not," I confirm.

Jake walks back to his car and gives me a wave as he drives off to his side of the lot and I drive off to mine.

Radford Studios is a labyrinthine lot of eighteen soundstages, where dozens of shows are filming at any given moment. Jake's talk show films on Soundstage 9, *Zombie Hospital* is across the lot on Soundstage 2, and my sister Edie films the weather for KCAL-9's evening news over on Soundstage 18. Sometimes, when Jake, Edie, and I are all at Carla's Café at the same time, the studio commissary feels as tight-knit as a high school cafeteria. I cruise past New York Street, where the exterior scenes of *Seinfeld* were filmed. I pass Steve Harvey, fastening a cuff link on

THE SPIRIT OF LOVE 7

his way to shoot *Celebrity Family Feud.* Then at last, I wind around to the enormous soundstage where *Zombie Hospital* happens.

The first scene I'm shooting today takes place on the Hospital Roof stage. Shot before a green screen, our team of CGI artists will make it look like a bullet-ridden high-rise in a postapocalyptic downtown. The crew has been here for hours, installing lighting, testing sound, and troubleshooting everything that could go wrong once cameras roll. Even after seven years on this show, it amazes me how many people *Zombie Hospital* employs, how many hands cash its paychecks, how many families rely on its continued success. Whenever I feel annoyed about changes to my scripts, I remember my big, weird family. And today, more than any day before, they're depending on me.

I pull into my parking spot and take in the new white rectangular sign proclaiming in gothic *Zombie Hospital* font:

### FENNY FEIN, DIRECTOR

I close my eyes, not because I don't want to stare at that sign for hours, but because closing my eyes lets me feel my sister with me. Edie and I are so close sometimes my brother-in-law calls us symbiotic. Right now Edie's at her Silver Lake home on the other side of town. She's probably wearing our mom's old pink bathrobe, strewn with half a dozen burp cloths, navigating the daily mayhem of three kids under three. But she's thinking of me, too. I can feel it. And she's proud.

I wouldn't be here if it weren't for Edie. Hard to say exactly where I'd be. When I doubt myself, Edie assures me that I know every *Zombie Hospital* character's backstory, side story, and future story, having been a part of the show since showrunner Rich

Stark took a chance on me out of film school. I've worked my way up from production assistant to script coordinator to capital-W Writer to Director. I've studied the geniuses—Barbra Streisand, Maya Deren, and Agnès Varda—and watched Mira Nair's and Jodie Foster's MasterClasses. I've absorbed all media available by, on, and adjacent to Greta Gerwig. I've prepped and re-prepped, storyboarded and un-storyboarded every inch and instant of the scenes I'll be shooting today. If there's an angle I haven't considered, it doesn't exist. I've interviewed six intimacy consultants, all of whom I'd like to bring with me on future dates. Now all that's left for me to do is kick off my new career direction with that single, thrilling word:

*Action!*

Taking out my phone to text Liv, I manage to get myself completely tangled in the balloon bouquet I'm wrestling out of my car.

**Me:** Best balloons, thank you love!
**Olivia:** This is Lorena. I'm on Liv's phone. Screw the balloons, tell us about your orgasms . . .

I tap the exclamation mark response. Lorena is Olivia's mother, and cohost of their advice podcast *Call Your Mother*, which saw a sudden surge in popularity last year when Liv proposed to Jake during one of their recording sessions. What had been a cult favorite among a couple dozen fans turned into a subscribership much wider and more proportionate to Liv and Lo's gifts.

THE SPIRIT OF LOVE                                    9

For some reason, Lorena follows her text with a GIF of Jeff Goldblum smirking from his seat at an award show. Like I won Most Orgasms on a Beach.

Of course, she's referring to the vibrator Olivia gave me on Friday before I left for Catalina Island, back when everyone, including me, assumed I was embarking on a simple solo camping trip to center myself before this week's shoot. I haven't yet told my friends what really happened at the remote campsite called Two Harbors. Sam simply cannot be summed up in a text. That story will have to wait until tonight, when I meet Olivia, Lorena, and our friend Masha at the bridal shop for champagne and Olivia's final wedding dress fitting.

A hand reaches into the balloon bouquet and pulls me out.

"I need you."

Meet Aurora Apple, *Zombie Hospital*'s leading lady and one of the most charismatic, incompetent snobs ever to strike a pose. In Hollywood's game of No Degrees of Separation, Aurora used to cohost Jake's daytime talk show—pre-Olivia, back when Jake and Aurora both lived in New York. Sometimes I think the entire entertainment industry is just one big show mixed together.

Aurora is a nightmare, but she's our nightmare, so I do what I can to help her. She doesn't know how to refill a prescription, use a dryer sheet, or issue holiday bonuses to her numerous staff—she keeps both an erotic masseuse and koi-fish-whisperer on retainer. But train a camera on Aurora's face, and she'll pause the earth's orbit with her pitch-perfect line delivery.

"So," Aurora says, "if someone were to leave their THC

gummies in their scrubs, and someone else's piece-of-shit dog got into them, should someone call a vet? Also, for my scene today, is this right: I'm supporting the kid's transition back to humanity, but also, from a medical perspective, I'm like, skeptical?"

I take them in order of importance. "I'll send Tank to urgent care," I say, referring to Aurora's on-set rival, Miguel Bernadeau's Pomeranian. "As for your scene, yes, you're right—that's a very nuanced understanding of your character's dynamic with Buster."

"Thank you!" When Aurora beams, it's so dazzling that you almost think the nightmare's over. She takes my arm in hers, and the two of us, and my balloons, waft toward my trailer. "One more thing."

I await her next inane demand, but Aurora surprises me. She holds out a small wrapped box.

"Good luck today!"

"What's this?" I'm stunned. For the entire year she's been on set, Aurora has treated me like the assistant I used to be six years ago, even though she joined the show well after I'd moved up to full writer. When I lift the box's lid, I find a Swarovski diamond director's clapper board with my name etched on it.

"This is so nice. Thank you!" I hug Aurora, incredulous.

"You thought I wouldn't remember. But I did."

"Aurora?"

"Mmm?"

"I think I need to say this out loud to someone, to get it off my chest before the shoot. And you're . . . here, so here goes—"

# THE SPIRIT OF LOVE

"You're the one who put my silk bra in the microwave?" She points a finger at me.

"No—what? No. I met someone this weekend. His name is Sam." Simply saying his name aloud makes me tingle. "And we had this—"

"Mind-blowing sex?"

"Yes!"

Aurora slaps me hard across the face.

"Ow! What the hell, Aurora?"

"Better?"

I touch my stinging cheek. As the pain fades, a new clarity emerges. "Yes. I think so."

Aurora nods. "I'm glad you got boned. Your pores really needed it. But I need you *focused* today. Dialed fucking in. We all do. You read?"

I nod, wincing. "I read."

"Good. Action, bitch!" she sings as she bounds away.

Rubbing my cheek, I approach the trailer of Buster Zamora, *Zombie Hospital*'s ten-year-old child star, who can easily go toe-to-toe with Aurora on the diva-style demands. But working closely with Buster last year, I stumbled upon a secret: All he needs to take the edge off is fifteen minutes of meditation first thing in the morning. I see him now, eyes closed, sitting on a vintage Oushak rug spread on the fake grass of his trailer's front yard. His chest rises and falls with his breaths as his guru, Jane, handpicked by me and budgeted throughout this season, leads him through the low chanting of his mantra. Jane gives me a thumbs-up, and I exhale. If Buster is grounded, today will be much easier.

I invite myself to feel grounded, too. This weekend was a roller-coaster—a wild and gorgeous ride—but I'm here to work now, and I'm calm and collected. Maybe it was Aurora's slap. Or maybe I'm just the right person for this job. I tell myself I'm ready to meet any challenge today with dignity and patience.

I dash up the steps to my trailer, decorated with *Zombie Hospital* posters and preschool portraits of my nephews. I have forty-two minutes until call, and after I check my teeth for raspberry seeds from the smoothie I inhaled in my car, I'll take out today's sides and review my plans for our scenes.

There's a knock before I even make it to my mirror.

"What is it, Aurora?" I call.

The door flings open and our production assistant, Ivy Rinata, appears. Her long brown braids are damp with sweat around her hairline, and she's out of breath. Strange. I've made the mistake of taking a "Highway to Hell" Orangetheory class with Ivy before, and she never once got winded, so this a little alarming. Where exactly did she run from, and why?

"Ivy, you good?"

"Did you lose your phone again?"

"No, why?"

"Didn't you get Rich's messages?"

I look down at my silenced phone, presently lit up with eight—no, nine—texts, all from my least favorite producer, and all sent within the last two minutes.

"What's going on?" I ask, a lead anvil bouncing like a pinball in my gut.

"Follow me."

AS WE JOG across the set in silence, I wonder *What the fuck?* on repeat. Rich wasn't always my least favorite producer. Once upon a time, he hired me to be his assistant, fresh out of UCLA film school, and I actually liked working for him. I never liked *him*, per se—my sixth sense always shouted *Boundaries!* around Rich—but the job was just what I wanted. The ropes. Me learning them.

For two years, I drafted his emails, poked fun at his ridiculous coffee orders, watched every film he insisted was "canon," and then galled him with my critiques. In turn, he did a halfway good job of mentoring me and also gave me tons of free tickets to premieres and concerts and plays. He spoke about the "Fenster Future," when he said I'd be running this town.

But then, right around the time my fellow assistant pals on *Zombie Hospital* started either getting promoted or being recruited by other shows, I stayed right where I was—in line at Starbucks, waiting on a nitro stevia mocha with Rich's name Sharpie'd on the sleeve.

I know I could have jumped up the ladder to another show myself. I had lunches and Zooms during that time, offering me more money and creative freedom than I had in my current job. But *Zombie Hospital* has always fit me in a way that felt personally significant, reflective of my life and passions. Plus, I'd already put in two years of hard, driven, quality work. I didn't want to schedule that meeting with Rich to press him for a promotion, but it was well past time when I finally did.

"Fenster," he'd assured me. "I put in for that months ago. But you know, the budget was completely fucked last year, so the network was like—" He mimed a jerking-off motion. "Your raise is literally the first thing I'm splurging on after the new fiscal—"

"It's not just the raise, Rich. You know I want to direct."

"Fenster Future. I'm all about it." He put up his hands as if he had willed this into reality on the spot. "Let's just chill for a beat, okay? It's all happening. Everything will come."

I chilled for several beats. But nothing happened. Nothing came. Not until three months later, when I went over Rich's head and set up a meeting with HR. I made my case with hard evidence in the form of two years' worth of performance reviews, script notes written, and budgets drawn up. Two weeks later, I got what I wanted. Or at least, it was a start. I was moved to the lowest rung in the writers' room—and squeezed into a corner of permanent annoyance in Rich's tiny mind.

Since then, he's only gotten worse. Smarmier, shallower, and so open about his suspicion that I have "just never liked him." It's unusual for Rich to call me to his office first thing in the morning. It certainly doesn't bode well. I try to prepare for a few unfortunate eventualities—is one of the cast members sick? In legal trouble? Is an advertiser nervous about something in an episode? Is CBS canceling us?

Hah. No way.

Still, the thought is unnerving. I can't imagine not working on *Zombie Hospital*. People love to hate our show because its melodrama can veer off the charts, but for me, *Zombie Hospital* is really about what's worth living—and dying—for. For me, this show is personal.

# THE SPIRIT OF LOVE

I don't talk about it often, but when I was ten years old, I almost died. I glimpsed the other side . . . and then I made a choice to come back. A choice that forever changed me.

Edie and I had spent the first days of January that year on the ice of Barton Pond, near where we grew up in Ann Arbor, Michigan. She was on her skates, and I was testing out the new camcorder I'd gotten for my birthday. We were obsessed with our mom's DVD of *Beaches*, and Edie would skate circles around me, off-key belting out "Glory of Love" from Mayim Bialik's audition scene.

We stayed out too long on a day too cold, and we both caught the flu. The illness glanced off Edie, and after a few days she was back at school. But I got bronchitis, and then pneumonia, and then on a rainy Wednesday morning, my mom couldn't wake me.

An ambulance was called, paramedics deployed, an ER room burst into. And although I was unconscious, I saw it all.

I watched it from beyond myself. I was floating ten feet above my body, free from the flesh and bones that I had, until that moment, taken for granted *was* me. I had no idea there was more.

More not just to me, but to everything.

I could look out toward infinity, the cosmos, toward the overwhelming, indescribable beauty that I suddenly understood awaits us all . . . or I could look down at where I'd come from. At the doctors desperate to save my body. At my mother, sobbing against the door of the ER. At the nurse's ashen face when my monitor flatlined.

And then I looked at Edie, sitting in a waiting room chair, holding my camcorder in her lap. Her eyes were closed. She had chocolate on her shirt. Maybe she was praying, I don't know. I couldn't reach her, couldn't make her see me, couldn't let her know I was there.

Edie. Her pink gloves and blond pigtails and chewed nails. Her nose the same as mine. The camcorder in her lap, holding hours of our laughter. I looked down at my sister, and I suddenly knew more clearly than I'd ever known anything before: She needed me. Because Edie was two years older, I'd always thought it was the other way around. But no, *she* needed *me*. I was being given a choice: eternity now, or my sister.

The clarity I felt in that moment was absolute. And in an instant, I was back, waking up inside a tired body, looking into Edie's eyes. My sister and I had always been close, but that was the moment when I knew her on a cellular level. When I could feel how our cells are made of stars.

Edie put the camera in my hands. She turned it on. I held it to my eye and said, "Action."

That's how they found us, the doctors, nurses, and our parents: Edie with her head thrown back, eyes closed, finally nailing the notes of "Glory of Love," and me, fresh from the afterlife, filming her from my hospital bed.

The power of that experience has stayed with me. Choosing love and connection in this life, not despite but *because* there's so much more awaiting us . . . I believe in that. No matter what the critics say about *Zombie Hospital*, I get the sense that our viewers agree with me.

So whatever Rich's problem is today, I'll do well to keep the big picture in mind.

But when I step inside his office, the other six of the show's

THE SPIRIT OF LOVE                                          17

producers are leaning against various walls, like actors in a college play, and I know something is very wrong.

"Fenster!" Rich says, sitting at his desk, beaming a spotlight of white teeth at me. Having read all his emails in the years I was his assistant, I know he has hair plugs, but Dr. Goldman on Wilshire does extremely high-quality work, so I may be the only one in on the secret. Rich is handsome in that expensively preserved, shield-your-eyes-it's-too-much kind of way. "How was Cabo?"

"I was in Two Harbors."

"Where's that again? Hey, I got those chocolate macaroon things you like from Erewhon." He picks up a mason jar from his desk and rattles the cookies inside.

"Now I see why you sent the nine texts."

He howls a laugh. "This is why I love talking to writers. You thought that up on the spot. Do you want to sit? Sit down." Rich points to the empty chair across his desk. I glance at the six other people standing in the room—among them producers I like moderately to far more than Rich. Kelly, Ben, and Adele all nod for me to sit.

I do, and now I'm facing Rich. It's not a good situation for my blood pressure, which thrums in the side of my neck. "So, what's up?"

"Oh, you've got a little something . . ." Rich taps between his front teeth, leaning forward, squinting at me. "What is that? A raspberry seed? It's huge. Hey, Jenny?" he shouts in the direction of his office door. "Jenny? Can you get Fenny some floss? That's funny—Jenny, Fenny. All my assistants should rhyme."

18                                          LAUREN KATE

Before I can protest, Rich's assistant rushes in bearing a translucent plastic box.

"I'm fine," I insist, trying not to be mortified, wedging my thumbnail between my teeth.

"She doesn't speak up for herself," Rich tells Jenny about me. She tries not to cringe when she hands me the floss.

I use it in full view of the producing team, and finally the seed dislodges.

"Thanks," I mutter.

"Fenny is very grateful, Jenny," Rich translates.

As his assistant retreats, Rich makes no attempt to hide the fact that he's checking out her ass.

My lip curls and I manage to lock eyes with Adele across the room, who shakes her head in disgust but says nothing. I know we have to pick our battles, but honestly, why is he allowed to be the instigator of so many of them?

"So, here's what's jiggling," Rich says to me, interlocking his hands on his desk. "I have some truly incredible news."

"It will knock the cover off your balls, Fenny," producer Ben chimes in. Ben never lets anyone forget that he was once drafted by—and played one season for—the Minor League Baseball New Hampshire Fisher Cats, because he speaks in baseball metaphors eighty percent of the time. At least, I hope this one's a baseball metaphor.

"Okay, what's the incredible news?" I ask.

"We got Jude de Silva!" Ben practically shouts, knees out in deep plié, both hands clenched in fists.

I look to Rich. "Who's Jude de Silva?" The name rings a bell, but . . .

# THE SPIRIT OF LOVE                    19

Rich looks at Ben, and the two of them share a laugh like they're embarrassed for me. "Uh. *Shane Is Scared? Brujo of the Maypole?* Only the breakout classic on everyone's lips at Cannes last year."

"Ugh, I hated *Brujo of the Maypole*," I say. And I watched that movie on an airplane, which everyone knows drastically lowers one's threshold for entertainment. The movie was not only in love with itself, it was so nihilistic I felt the climax was making fun of me. But what does this have to do with our show?

"Jude de Silva," Rich says, "is the auteur behind two of the most unflinching *and* hilarious horror films of the decade."

"Scorsese can't do an interview without raving about the guy," Ben adds.

I roll my eyes. "And?" There's a part of me that knows what's happening, and there's a part of me that refuses to believe it.

"He's going to step in and direct this season while you punch up the scripts," Rich says with a smile that makes me want to puke.

"It's a joke, right?" I stammer. "This isn't real."

"It's unreal how lucky we are," Rich says. "Truly blessed to have Jude joining us. The guy's a genius."

"And don't worry," Ben says. "He's fully caught up on the character arcs."

"Fully," Rich agrees. "Jenny wrote this great one-sheet to prep him—"

"A one-sheet?" I hear myself say. *Zombie Hospital* has a five-hundred-page series bible, a comprehensive collection of meticulous character backstories, setting choices, and enough future plotlines to launch a dozen spin-offs. It's essential information to everyone on this show and damn compelling reading to boot. I know because I've written most of it.

"Jude read the one-sheet," Ben continues, "and an hour later . . . I mean, I defy anyone to speak with more authority on the characters. He got *all* the humor. I mean, stuff I didn't even know was funny—"

"I'm sorry," I say. "I'm still a little confused."

"Fenny," Kelly speaks bluntly from her position on the wall. "Jude de Silva is replacing you." She sighs. "You're not directing anymore. At least, not for the first three episodes. You'll be rewriting the scripts to Jude's approval."

There's a moment of silence in Rich's office as I wait to wake up from this nightmare.

Rich takes a long, loud slurp of his nitro latte. The reality of my situation lands. I might as well be back in line at Starbucks.

"I'm supposed to shoot in thirty minutes!" At least I don't sound like I'm about to weep. I sound furious, on a war path, like I'm about to tear out Rich's hair plugs.

"Things have changed, Fenster," he says. "It's not coming from me, I promise. This was dropped in our lap by the network. But don't worry, next season has your name all over it."

"*This* season had my name all over it, Rich. I have a contract—"

"Full of clauses allowing precisely this to transpire," Adele, the lawyer-producer adds with a frown. "I'm afraid it's all completely aboveboard."

"Which board?" I say and stand up. "People use that phrase all the time, but I've never seen the board everything is always above. Have you, Adele?"

THE SPIRIT OF LOVE 21

I knock over my chair, stumble over its legs.

"Fenny—" Adele says.

"Could it be," I continue, "that no one has seen this board that every backstabbing lie is *above* because the board is buried under a million miles of fake smiles and broken dreams?"

"Wow," Rich says. "I wish I'd recorded that."

Suddenly, the only thing I can think to do is run out of this office, away from all these people, and hopefully backward in time.

So that this whole conversation didn't happen. So that I'm still on the brink of living my dream. So that maybe I'm still back in Sam's cabin.

"Dude!" Rich says, rising from his chair, too, his arms spread wide. "Just in time! Get that trailer all set up?"

I look up from my chair leg tangle and see the dude Rich is addressing.

He's in profile, tall, thin, mid-thirties, with tortoise-shell-rimmed glasses, very short dark brown hair, and a well-groomed beard. He's handsome enough that he might be an actor, but he's wearing a suit, which no one does on this set.

And then he turns and his eyes meet mine. My world goes quiet. I stare at him. He stares at me. His eyes are deep brown, slightly downturned at the corners, and familiar, set beneath a remarkable pair of brows.

As we lock ourselves inside this gaze, my entire stomach drops into my feet and then seeps into the core of the earth, cracking open the planet and splitting it down the middle. I'm not one for hyperbole . . . but today, all this feels like an understatement. Because . . .

This guy is . . . *Sam*? My Sam. From the cabin. From this weekend. From the storm. From my heart.

I trace his features with my eyes. I'm not sure . . . but then I'm *so* sure.

No.

Yes?

How can this be?

He looks different. He looks older. He buzzed his hair and lost his tan and quite a bit of the muscles I so enjoyed exploring. And nothing makes sense, but I know a few things with absolute diamond clarity:

I kissed those lips yesterday morning.

I felt that nose nuzzle my neck.

Those hands were all over my body for at least four different orgasms.

From the look on this dude's face, I'm not crazy. He's thinking about it, too.

"Fenster," Rich says over my shoulder.

"Don't. Call. Me. That."

"Allow me to introduce—"

"What are you doing here?" I demand of Sam, my voice a shivery whisper.

Rich's hands come around my shoulders. "Excuse her, man, she's had a bit of a shock this morning."

"What's with the suit? And the glasses?" I ask Sam, shaking off Rich's paws and walking toward Sam. I squint at his chin. "Is that a stick-on beard?"

"Uhh . . ." He stammers a laugh. For the first time, his eyes

THE SPIRIT OF LOVE                                    23

break from mine and move to Rich. He points at me. "Is she okay?"

Rich puckers his face the way he does when someone suggests we order lunch from El Pollo Loco. "She's . . . uh . . . hey, Jenny, how about some Pellegrino in here?"

I take Sam by the shoulders, grip him hard. "Don't look at Rich. You answer me."

His eyes lock on mine again, and he looks like he's seen a ghost. His skin pales, and his voice trembles when he has the fucking balls to ask me, "H—have we met?"

"My fault! Where are my manners today?" Rich inserts himself between us, taking my hand and trying to place it in Sam's. The hand I know. The hand I like so much. The hand I want to tear from his body right now. I pull away.

Have we *met*?

"Allow me to introduce," Rich says grandly, "Ms. Fenny, whom I handpicked for the show, what was it, four, five years ago? Out of that high school intern program?"

Through my teeth, I say, "You hired me on the spot, after sitting in on my master's thesis defense at UCLA, almost eight years ago."

The whole time I speak, I'm glaring at Sam and speaking on behalf of women everywhere who have to put up with shit like this.

"Okay, Fenny-with-the-master's-thesis," Rich says. "I'd like you to meet Jude de Silva, known genius and *Zombie Hospital*'s new director."

*Three Days Earlier . . .*

# Chapter Two

"QUITE THE REMOTE DESTINATION," MY CAB DRIVER says as his Toyota Yaris sputters to a stop at a cliff's edge. We're in deep desert wilderness, on an island where I have exactly zero bars of cell reception, so I have to take his word for it when he says, "This is where I leave you."

"Best ensemble cast of the last quarter century," I say, reaching for my things.

"Huh?"

"*This Is Where I Leave You*—it's a movie. Never mind," I say, climbing out of the car. Sometimes I forget that not everyone speaks film references as a second language.

I lift up the director's viewfinder I'm wearing on a lanyard around my neck. The detached lens creates helpful borders, removing distractions the audience won't see. I picked up this one in a five-dollar bin at the Fairfax flea market a few years ago— the same morning I read an article that said Steven Spielberg swore by his viewfinder when prepping for *E.T.*

Even though so far I've only worn my viewfinder on solo hikes to practice, I consider it lucky. I can't wait to wear it on Monday for my first day of directing.

I peer through it, blinking into dazzling blue ocean and then down at the steep slope of a trail that mimics a Hollywood career in decline. I frame the shot and imagine myself on the beach I can't yet see below.

Letting the viewfinder drop to my chest, I stretch and breathe in salt air, refreshed after the cramped, hour-long car ride from the ferry terminal. Down this rocky path, at the water's edge, lies Parson's Landing, my home for the weekend, a prized jewel of a campground nestled in a pristine oceanfront valley. It's an off-the-grid lair at the remote edge of an island so biodiverse (sixty species found nowhere else on Earth!) that it's known as the "Galapagos of North America." This is the site where I've selected to spend the next three blissfully solitary days prepping for Monday by pondering life's biggest questions.

Like:

Can we choose the moment of our death?

How many lives do our souls get?

Do zombies' mortal existences flash before their eyes when they become undead?

Do zombies have sex dreams?

"The nearest provisions are a six-mile hike," the cab driver says out his window, gesturing south, toward the tiny town of Two Harbors, where I read there's a general store, a bar, and a rustic twelve-room inn. "You have everything you need?"

He's looking at me like I couldn't possibly be prepared.

"Does anyone ever have everything they need?" I say, shouldering my backpack.

"Maybe not," he says, "but most people bring more stuff than that." He points at my gear, puts the Yaris in reverse, and soon he's just a cloud of dust.

THE SPIRIT OF LOVE                                      29

I'm alone. Just like I wanted. Just like I planned. The September breeze brushes my skin, fills my lungs, and reminds me I'm alive.

I pull out my Panasonic AG-DVC30 camcorder, old and awash in excellent juju. My parents gave it to me for my tenth birthday. I shot my earliest films with it, on the frozen pond behind our Michigan home, where Edie used to ice skate.

I promised to document this weekend for her. She's worried about me being out here by myself, which is convenient because it takes the worrying off my plate.

With my camcorder filming, I start down the path.

" 'Be not afeard,' " I say, quoting Caliban from *The Tempest*, " 'the isle is full of noises, sounds and sweet airs, that give delight, and hurt not.' "

Every time I drop a Shakespeare reference into *Zombie Hospital*, Rich cuts it, but I know the ghosts of my first drafts linger on the page, in the actors' eyes, at the edges of the screen.

I pan my camcorder from the calm ocean, up along the scraggly brush, then to the side of my path. I pan up some more and gasp. My lens autofocuses on a majestic deer—a huge buck, with six blond jagged points. When I realize he's standing ten feet away, I almost drop the camera.

But I need the camera, because if I put it down, there will be nothing between this deer and me. My heart races as the buck steps toward me.

"I'm friendly," I stammer. "And I'm leaving."

The buck takes another two steps in my direction, and I straighten my spine, steeling myself for a charge, a lunge, antlers like chef's knives piercing my chest.

I reach into the front pocket of my backpack, where I keep a bottle of mace. It's two years past its expiration date, but it's all I've got.

That's when I notice the others. They're everywhere, stretching beyond the muddy crest of the hill above me, a herd of deer. Their numbers are astonishing, vast. And every one of them is looking at me.

I drop the mace in my backpack.

And I run.

As fast as I can, down the path to my campsite, looking frantically over my shoulder at the stationary herd of deer. I realize halfway down that I have filmed this whole thing. If the herd changes its mind and decides to stampede me, mourners can run this footage at my funeral, interspersed with scenes from Yorgos Lanthimos's terrifying *The Killing of a Sacred Deer*. Either that, or I'll just show the clip to Edie next week, and she and her kids can crack up at the antics of crazy Aunt Fenny.

Finally, the bottom of the trail opens onto the pebbled beach. It's stunning, an inlet of turquoise water lapping a honey-colored pebble beach, embraced by a proud and ragged mountain coastline. I've lost the deer. I've won, or at least survived. I exhale fully, and when I inhale again, the air smells briny and clean with a hint of wild fennel.

I drop my backpack, kick off my rain boots, tug off my socks, and pad toward the water, wincing only slightly at the pebbles underfoot.

The sun's over my shoulder. It's three in the afternoon. Time to set up camp. White wooden markers dot the beach, num-

# THE SPIRIT OF LOVE

bered one through eight. I've reserved campsite seven, although it appears—incredibly—that I might have the whole place to myself. I look to my left and my right, a little thrilled, a little stunned.

Three days alone with my thoughts. Three days to prepare for Monday. When I'd planned this trip in my bungalow on the crowded canals of Venice Beach, I didn't dare allow myself the fantasy of total privacy. That would be too perfect, too exactly what I need. I love when life works out like this.

I check out the unusual rock sticking out over my campsite. Carved of glittering, dark gray sandstone, it juts out at an angle that seems to defy gravity. Staring at it for a minute, I realize it's shaped like a hooded cobra's head. In terms of spiritual and physical protection, I couldn't ask for a better canopy.

I unroll my tent, which I borrowed from Edie, who seems to have neglected to hose it down after her two toddlers and three German shepherds camped out in it in their backyard for most of the summer. It's mildewed and spotted with various species of stains, and the stakes have been gnawed into near oblivion. Pitching this tent will be like squeezing into a pair of college-era jeans. I know, ultimately, I can do it. But I'm glad there's no one around to watch me try.

I drive one nubby half-stake into the ground and move to secure another. When all are finally done, I smile and chuck my things inside. Then I turn toward the beach and look hopefully toward the horizon. It holds what I've been yearning for: a mackerel sky, named for its thin, fish-scale clouds, harbingers of rain.

Yes, we're in for a storm tonight. It's one of the main reasons why I came here this weekend, to get inspired for the upcoming storm scene in the climax of *Zombie Hospital*'s season opener. Shortly after sunset, Edie assures me that the wind will pick up, and Parson's Landing will get approximately a quarter inch of soft but steady rain.

I plan to be in a raincoat in my hammock, reading books under an umbrella, absorbing every restorative drop in preparation for next week's shoot. Very soon, this moody, windswept beach is going to be just what I need, just what I imagined.

I string up my woven green and white hammock between two palm trees. It was a gift from Masha and her husband, Eli, brought back from their honeymoon in Sicily last summer, and this is the perfect venue for its debut. I walk along the beach and dip my toes in the cold water, watching pelicans dive for fish.

Kneeling down, I train my viewfinder on a heaping bed of kelp. Lustrous green and craggy with barnacles, I hold the frame as the tide rushes in, then back out, leaving a sizzling lace of white foam. With my free hand, I lift a length of bullwhip kelp and pop the wet bulbs between my fingers. It feels like I'm popping the ocean's bubble wrap, like the ocean is a fragile gift delivered to my door.

And in a way, it is.

Back at my campsite, I fire up my battery-powered hot plate, set my kettle on top, and pour in a can of Wolfgang Puck's beef stew. I bite into an apple, crack the seal on a pint of Uncle Nearest whiskey, and pour a finger into my *Zombie Hospital* promotional coffee mug. Then I take out my phone, open the Final Draft app with the shooting script for next week's episode, and imagine myself directing.

BY EIGHT O'CLOCK, the sun has set and the beach is cloaked in fog so thick I can't see the water. My blond hair has gone full Simba, barely fitting inside my raincoat hood. I'm flopped in my hammock, framing the light rain in my viewfinder, inspired by the endless, velvet fog. The weather gives the island an ethereal glaze, where the veil between life and death is thin, where zombies might be real, where the world beyond this one might be almost within reach.

Wind ripples across the beach, carrying a misty drift of harder rain. In the distance, thunder cracks. I sway in my hammock, my clasped hands a pillow under my head. I think of *Zombie Hospital*'s child actor, Buster, somewhere out there, on the far side of this forty-mile stretch of sea. Is he wondering, like I am, what it will take for him to give the performance of his life next week?

What *will* it take? That's always the question. An actor gets to wonder. A director needs to know.

The rain falls more steadily, drumming the pebbles on the shore. Goosebumps dot my arms. It's getting colder. I think back to the pneumonia that hospitalized me when I was ten. I should get into my tent and dry off. I spill out of the hammock, soaked. A gale of wind assaults me as I struggle back across the beach. It's strange that Edie downplayed the ferocity of this wind. Her tendency is usually to oversell a storm's potential. I duck inside my tent, take off my raincoat, and towel off. I click on my lantern and pull out my camcorder. Maybe I'll film myself practicing a pep talk for Buster, to see what ideas flow. I draw my sleeping bag around my shoulders.

The tent poles bend sharply as the wind around me howls. I make sure they're secure, then I pick up my camcorder and press Record.

"Hey, Buster, it's me. I've been thinking about your performance, and—hold on . . . *What the hell?*"

Someone—something—is unzipping my tent!

My free arm darts out to freeze the zipper, to tug it in reverse and keep myself sealed in here. To keep whoever that is out there.

The zipper unzips again, a swift hand's width this time, before I catch it and meet it with equal, opposite force.

"Let go!" I scream as the terrifying tug-of-war ensues. Whoever's out there really wants to get inside.

Suddenly, there's a horrible shredding sound as the zipper falls away from the tent fabric.

A bright light blinds me, and a blast of rain assails my face.

"Aughhh!" I scream, scurrying backward.

"Aughhhh!!!" the light screams back, louder and deeper than me.

Wet sand slams into the back of my skull. It takes me a moment to realize I've fallen out of what's left of my tent. I'm defenseless, vulnerable, and blind.

"Damn, you okay?" a low voice with a hint of southern twang asks as the garish light disappears. "Ma'am?"

I blink up at the figure crouching beside me. He wears an orange helmet with a miner's light attached, and somehow his hand is holding mine. I'm about to whip away my hand when he pulls on it so gently, I don't realize he's helped me all the way up until I'm standing in front of him.

# THE SPIRIT OF LOVE

A flash of lightning affords me a better view. This might be the largest human I have seen up close. He's far north of six feet tall, with broad shoulders and rippling forearms.

He finds my lantern on the sand and holds it up, illuminating us both.

He's handsome in an extreme way, and that's really not what I need right now. His soaking raven hair wings out from the back of his helmet. His eyes are a melty chocolate brown, downturned at the corners, set beneath a robust pair of brows. His mouth is full and slightly open, showing two rows of straight white teeth.

"Are you hurt?" he asks as rain hammers us with biblical force.

"Not as hurt as you're about to be!" I say and jerk my hand out of his. "Who the fuck *are* you?"

He smiles. And there are dimples. Great, now I'll need to put up my dimple shield. They've been known to mess with my head.

"Catalina Search and Rescue," he proclaims.

"Not interested."

"I'm . . . not soliciting. I'm here to save your life."

I laugh. "I don't need to be saved. I don't need to be searched, nor rescued. I need to be left alone!" I grab my lantern from him and spin away to look for my raincoat and my camcorder. "And I need a tent that zips!"

The rain is freezing, hard, and mean. My sister can really be full of shit sometimes.

"Let me help you," Search and Rescue says, turning his miner's light back on. His voice is honeyed, even when shouting over the rain.

Now soaked to the bone, I wrap my arms around myself and nod at the ruins of my camp. "Yes, you're off to a wonderfully helpful start."

A gust of wind almost lifts me off the ground. S&R catches me with both arms. In the fraction of a second that he's holding me, my body betrays me. Despite the situational impossibility, something inside me acknowledges that he's giving end-of-summer-college-fling-best-sex-you've-ever-had vibes.

"Let go!" I decide to tell him. "You are wrecking *everything.*"

"Look," my brave and bumbling hero says. "I have one job, and I take it seriously. In extreme conditions, like this storm, events often fail to unfold according to plan—"

"Who wrote that?"

"Wrote what?"

"You memorized that nonsense, I can tell."

"It's not nonsense," Search and Rescue says, sounding almost hurt. "And allow me to remind you, ma'am, that I'm responding to *your* distress signal."

"Stop calling me ma'am!" I say, backing farther into the rain, playing off how I've just tripped over my hammock in the dark. "I assure you that I became distressed only after your arrival."

Search and Rescue's fantastic eyebrows furrow. He's cute when he's confused, which is lucky for him, because I'm guessing it happens a lot.

"A flare went up eleven minutes ago," he says, looking around as if suddenly he's doubting his side of the story. Which he should.

"Dude, the last time I packed any flare was when I waited tables at BJ's Brewhouse."

THE SPIRIT OF LOVE                                    37

He stops walking and rubs his bicep, thinking. "Maybe we should start again."

"Do you want me to get back in the tent?" I deadpan.

"I do owe you a tent," he says.

"And a priceless, irreplaceable camcorder," I say. "And a weekend of spiritual restoration. And—"

"We can tally it all up later." For some reason, he's smiling at me now. "Right now, it's time to seek higher ground. This storm is getting unfriendly—"

"Look, cowboy, I *wanted* this storm. I called it in. Not only that, but I was in a flow before you bodice-ripped my tent."

"You called in *this* storm?" he shouts over earth-rattling thunder.

"Okay, *a* storm!" I shout back, wiping my face with my hand. "Not this one necessarily. This one is . . . a lot. Perhaps more than I anticipated."

"That's the whole point of my speech! Which I wrote, by the way."

"Yeah, well, Search and Rescue needs an editor."

"The name is Sam," he says. When he turns his head, his profile in the helmet, with rain streaming off it, is something I wouldn't mind capturing on film. Very quickly, while Sam is looking at the steep path up from the beach, I lift my viewfinder to my eye and frame him. It would make a beautiful shot.

"Do you see that rock formation?" Sam shouts over the rain. "The one that looks like a serpent's head?"

"Of course." My protector. My good omen.

"Listen," he says, holding up a finger.

I do. "All I hear is rain."

"That prehistoric natural sculpture is about to become a contemporary rockslide. Any second now, the levee up the trail is going to give way. So, flare or no flare, I'm not asking. You either walk with me up that path to my Jeep so I can drive you to Two Harbors—"

"Here comes the authoritarian threat—"

"Or I toss you over my shoulder and carry you. I'd prefer your consent, but saving your life comes first."

For a second, I picture this: Sam actually tossing me over his shoulder. Something warm pulses inside of me, which I dispel with a laugh that turns into a full-body shiver.

He notices, and a moment later, his vest comes off his huge chest and drapes around me. It should be soaking wet and freezing, but his body heat has kept it warm. There's no masking my gratitude.

"Thanks."

"I can heat my Jeep's interior in three minutes," he says. "I can have you checking into a fireplace room at Banning House in under twenty. I'm out of your hair in twenty-one."

I gaze up at the path I'd trekked down so optimistically only hours earlier. I look down at the beach and sigh at the sight of my busted tent. "Just let me find my raincoat and my camcorder."

"There isn't time."

I ignore him, flinging aside impractical underwear and storm-soaked books. I find my raincoat and put it on. But I don't see the camcorder anywhere.

*Where is it?*

A sepulchral groan sounds above me. As I look up, it's sud-

THE SPIRIT OF LOVE                                    39

denly a little too easy to imagine myself being taken by a real-life rockslide, swept away like a feather on a wave.

Then giant arms are scooping me up and Sam's voice is in my ear. "We're getting out of here, ma'am."

"I said stop calling me that," I say, even as his strong arms and firm chest are putting me in an almost grateful state of mind.

"Then perhaps you should tell me your name?" he says.

"The name's Fenny," I tell him, just as the serpent's ancient hooded head crumbles onto the sand.

## Chapter Three

THE LIGHT ON SAM'S HELMET FLICKERS AND THEN DIES twenty feet into our trek up the trail.

"Top-notch rescue," I say, still in his arms. "Didn't they teach you to charge your lantern in hero school?"

"We'll be fine," he tells me, still climbing. "It only takes eighteen minutes for night vision to kick in."

"Fantastic. I'll just scream until then."

He laughs, surprising me. "You're funny. And light as a feather. Anyone ever tell you that?"

"Not since the last time I was rescued."

"Now you're making me jealous."

"Shut up." I roll my eyes. At least he can't see me smiling in the dark.

"Almost there," he says. "Uh-oh. Oh no."

"Oh no, what?"

Up the path, a torrent of water, mud, and rocks rushes toward Sam's legs. "I was hoping we'd make it to the Jeep before the levee broke."

This is the levee he predicted would break while I yelled at him on the beach. If he hadn't shown up, hadn't tossed me over his shoulder, this avalanche would soon be landing on my tent,

# THE SPIRIT OF LOVE                                    41

smothering my campsite, smashing me and all my possessions. I'd have been sent straight out to sea.

"Oh no," I whisper, tensing in his arms as he presses against the current. For the first time tonight, I feel truly afraid.

"Don't worry," he says, so warmly and softly that I turn to meet his eyes. I still can't see him, but I want to. "I've got you."

I can hear in Sam's voice how he isn't afraid. It eases my mind a little.

"Hold on!" he shouts, as the mudslide slams into his thighs and stops us in our tracks. I feel his spine bow backward like a fishing pole, then straighten. He presses on.

"Dude," I say, impressed.

"Learned that one in hero school."

"What were you, valedictorian?"

"Sorta." He dodges passing boulders and uprooted trees, moving nimbly, holding me tightly, never faltering. Not once. It's as if he possesses a preternatural power, like the monster in Mary Shelley's *Frankenstein* trotting across the Alps for weeks or Pedro Pascal's *Mandalorian* never loosening his intergalactic grip on Baby Yoda.

Angry new rivers swirl around us, carving the earth with violent force. Sam pauses, grunts, lunges forward—until we're all the way up to the top of the trail. I'm almost disappointed when he sets me down near the cliff's edge, the same place where my taxi driver dropped me off this afternoon. Water courses over the tops my rain boots, flowing inside and freezing my ankles.

The island feels oddly empty, except for the two of us and the storm. The legion of deer is nowhere to be found. I wonder where they go in apocalyptic moments like these. I wonder why I was the only camper on that beach. I wonder what the flare was that Sam thought he saw. The light that sent him down to me.

He pulls a ring of keys from the pocket of his jeans and presses the Unlock button for his Jeep. I don't see the car, but I swipe my soaking hair out of my eyes and try to smooth it down, suddenly aware that in a moment we'll climb into his Jeep, straight into an overhead lighting situation—and something tells me Sam will be looking like tennis legend Taylor Fritz crossed with Charles Melton and Tom Bateman . . . whereas I will look like something from the *Star Wars* cantina scene.

Having written dozens of erotically charged apocalyptic episodes of *Zombie Hospital*, I'm happy to discover that, despite what that cranky *Variety* TV critic wrote in his review, I've actually been onto something: The end of the world *can* be a turn-on.

"Sorry about this," Sam says, turning in a slow circle. "I must have parked a little farther off the road . . ."

I follow as he strides inland, away from the cliff, still holding out his keys, still pressing the Unlock button. A sudden blast of wind blows me sideways. My feet slip in the mud, and when I stagger to catch my balance, my foot finds only air.

"Sam!" I cry out.

His arm is quickly around my waist, pulling me against him, where it's warm and far more solid than the ground. For the second time in five minutes, he saves me.

"You okay?" He studies me. The longer we stare at each other, the more brightly his eyes exude this *warmth*, like someone backstage is turning up a light inside of him. It makes it impossible to break his gaze. Something inside me says, *Keep looking until you can put this into words.* What I'm feeling in my chest is almost playful, strangely happy—entirely at odds with everything else about this situation. My entire night, and possibly my entire weekend, has been upended.

"I . . . I think so?" I am, because of him.

"What happened?" Sam asks.

"There's a drop. I didn't see it."

"There's no drop here. I know this route like the back of my skull."

"Wait. What?"

"Oh wow," Sam says, halting as if he's just run into an imaginary door. "Oh *crap*." He turns his head to me, then back in the direction he'd been facing. "Look."

He bangs on his helmet, and a weak stream of light flickers long enough to illuminate a deep ravine below. At the bottom, a hundred feet beneath us, I see the dented, upside-down reflection of a word:

**JEEP**

For a moment, we just stand in the pouring rain and stare. The miner's light goes black again.

Sam finally says, "I guess there is a drop."

"Yeah, maybe you should check in on the back of your skull."

"Let's get out of this storm."

"How?" I ask, shivering. "Your Jeep is totaled. And isn't it six miles to Two Harbors?"

"I know something closer."

WE TRUDGE SO long in darkness, up and then down and then up steep and muddy slopes, that eventually I lose track of time. When finally the downpour dwindles, so does the temperature. My teeth chatter. The chill penetrates my bones. The only part of me that's warm is my left hand, in Sam's, which he uses now to gesture up ahead.

At a cabin that stands at the end of a path cut through tall grass and wildflowers. It looks like something out of a fairy tale.

It's modest and charming, built of rough-hewn logs. There's a porch, a tin roof, two large windows downstairs, and a tiny window up top—near the chimney, from which curls an undulating arm of smoke.

"Who lives here?" I ask as we approach the cabin. "The Seven Dwarves and Jason Voorhees?"

"I do," Sam says, eyeing the place with a look of pride. "It belongs to the Conservancy—they handle the land trust of the entire island—but I get to hang my helmet here while I complete my training."

I clear my throat. "Training?"

"All right, you got me. You're my first rescue," Sam says, like it's a huge compliment.

"*What?*"

"Success, though, right?"

I scowl. "You were a virgin. Now it all makes sense."

"What makes sense?" he asks, looking wounded.

"You *did* show up looking for someone else," I say, teasing

THE SPIRIT OF LOVE                                    45

him. "And when it was time to go home, you forgot where you parked your car."

When Sam laughs, his eyes crinkle and he looks down at his feet, nudging the wood stairs with the toe of his boot.

"Yeah, well, now I'm inviting you to stay the night," he says. "So, we must have done something right."

This comment silences me as we step onto the porch of the cabin. It feels like a lifetime since I wasn't feeling rain. Sam still holds my hand. We seem to notice this fact simultaneously. His fingers slide loose. Something subtle and enormous shifts now that we're not touching.

He points at where he's standing on the porch. "This is where I was when I saw the flare."

I look into the sky, imagining his perspective. Then down at the beach, the sliver of it that's visible from here. It feels so far away, where we first met. Another world. Whatever it was that Sam mistook for a flare, I realize I'm grateful it happened. I'm alive because of him. And more than that, I'm intrigued to find myself here. But I'm unsure what happens next.

I hear a creak behind me and realize Sam has opened his front door. He stands at the threshold and gestures inside.

"You coming? Or you want to hang out with your storm some more?"

In the zombie TV drama, this is the part when the audience would be screaming, "Don't go in there, you moron!"

But I'm no dewy ingenue. I'm a waterlogged queen of plot and motivation, and here's the important thing:

I have nowhere else to go.

Here's another thing:

If I were directing a scene in which a strapping young stranger needed to convey that his invitation of hospitality to a slightly less young woman was a sincere and simple offer of protection, then this man's gentle-giant posture, the earnest set of his jaw, and the kind, alluring sparkle in his eyes is how I would direct the actor to play it.

When it aired, the fans at home would scream, "Go in there, girl! Go get it!"

And I'm not just saying this because I'm freezing and soaked to my core. I'm saying it with my director's hat on, and I take that shit seriously.

But first, I really do need to bring up the elephant on the porch.

"Look," I say, pulling back the hood on my raincoat. "I work with hot people every day."

"Congratulations?" He smiles. Damn those dimples.

"You destroyed my tent on a desert island with no other shelter within walking distance. Therefore, I have to stay with you. In this trope of a cabin. Where there'd better not be only one bed."

"I'm waiting for you to get to the part about me saving your life."

"Maybe you did and maybe you didn't."

"Maybe I definitely did." He takes a step toward me and laughs under his breath.

I find that I'm holding mine. "It's nothing I haven't lost before."

"What does that mean?" Sam asks, tilting his head. "You've been . . . dead?"

THE SPIRIT OF LOVE                                        47

"Never mind." I look away. I can't believe I just said that. I never talk about my near-death experience with anyone but Edie.

"Fenny, are you trying to tell me you're not going to sleep with me tonight?"

"To put it bluntly, yes."

Sam studies me, a small smile turning bigger on his very smooth lips.

"Not that I have to explain myself on that particular front," I continue, "but I don't even know your last name, or where you're from, or how many more hours you have yet to log to be an actual employee of this island, or if you like dogs, or have any allergies, or your favorite movie, or what your mother's name is, or what kind of afterlife you believe in."

"Afterlife?"

"Yes. Generally, this is a thing I would need to know about someone before . . . but none of that is happening. With us. Is what I'm trying to say."

"I respect that." Sam nods, his smile now a little teasing. "But you presume I'm the kind of man who'd just sleep with any gorgeous woman he rescues from certain death?"

"I—I don't presume," I stammer. "And you know, my death wasn't exactly *certain*—"

"That's the word you take issue with? Not *gorgeous*?" he asks softly, seeming to take all of me in with a single nod until I feel warm inside. "It's good when a gorgeous woman knows she's gorgeous."

"I didn't say that—"

"You're shivering," he says, concerned. "How about we just go inside, dry off, and maybe have a cup of tea?"

"Okay."

Sam enters the cabin and I follow. He crosses the room, strikes a wooden match, and lights a thick white candle. The humble exterior of the cabin hasn't prepared me for what the candlelight reveals. The vast, open, two-story space looks like Frank Lloyd Wright and Norman Rockwell were hiding out together. A geometric heirloom quilt is draped over the couch. A primitive oil portrait of a Catalina Island fox hangs on the wall. The kitchen is vintage and iron and not too shabbily equipped. Built-in Douglas fir bookshelves stretch from floor to second-story ceiling, complete with a custom ladder that rolls on metal tracks.

A fire fades in the elaborate fireplace, which is decorated with intricate carvings.

"Holy shit," I say. "Who built this place?"

"It was bare bones when I moved in. The kitchen was trashed but mostly the same. I did everything else."

"You . . . *did* that fireplace?"

"I carved it. It's based on a design by William Blake. The figures represent each of the four seasons."

I look closer and I see it. Sam's hand-carved personifications of the phases of the year—a plump baby for spring, a laughing young woman for summer, a strong matriarch for autumn, and an austere witch for winter.

"You're telling me that you built *all* this"—I turn from the fireplace to gesture at the cabin's many warm and inviting features—"in your *spare* time?"

"You make it sound like I'm permanently and forlornly holed up here with my chisel."

THE SPIRIT OF LOVE                                        49

"Who said anything about forlornly?"

"Yes, I like woodworking, but I also like hiking and fishing, cliff-diving, zip-lining—"

"You must have a lot of free time," I say. Most people say this sentence as a dig, but I'm honestly envious that Sam has time for so many fascinating hobbies.

He lifts a shoulder casually. "I just call it living."

"I'm sorry, I'm still processing all this. You built the bookshelves, too? And the ladder?"

"I'm pretty proud of that."

"Have you read all these books?"

"Of course not."

"Do you intend to read them?"

"Why else would I have them?"

"And you're just going to leave here when you're done with training?"

"God, I can't wait."

I really didn't need to know that my knight in flooded armor is also a Jesus-level carpenter. My gaze falls on a built-in wet bar with wine bottle cubbyholes and a knotted pine shelf holding half a dozen bottles.

"You build that wet bar, fancy pants?" I ask.

"In less than a week."

This island, this weekend, and this man continue to surprise me, to pull the floor out from under me just when I thought I knew where I stood. I'm more surprised than anyone when I turn to Sam and say, with a hint of challenge in my voice:

"Let's see how fast you can make a highball."

# Chapter Four

"I'LL MAKE COCKTAILS, YOU MAKE YOURSELF COM-fortable," Sam says, nodding over my shoulder. "The bathroom's there."

He presses a thick terry-cloth towel and a stack of folded clean clothes into the crook of my arm, then turns away from me and tosses two logs on the fire. A glorious gush of heat fills the cabin.

Why do people ever camp?

I close myself in the bathroom and gaze into the mirror. Gorgeous? Hah. I look like the cosmos gave me a swirlie. I try to smooth my wet hair, finger-combing the chaos. My face is bare and pale, and my lips are purplish blue.

But Sam did say the word, no less than four times. The most I could get out of my ex, even on date night when I was really trying, was a tossed-off, thoughtless *hot*. Sam and I are still basically strangers, but the dynamic between us has definitely shifted ever since . . . well, since he carried me up a cliff. I'd felt something in his arms. Is this standard S&R on the island, or is Sam going above the call of duty?

I take off my raincoat and my Moz T-shirt. I hang my view-finder on Sam's towel rack. I kick off my rain boots and peel off

# THE SPIRIT OF LOVE

my cutoffs and underwear. I pull the towel around me and examine the clothes I've been loaned.

The socks are thick gray merino wool that banish the goosebumps from my calves. The boxers are enormous and thought-provoking, printed with dogs playing poker.

The word *doggystyle* flashes in my brain. I splash my face with water.

I put on the extra-large white T-shirt and reach for the thick black concert hoodie from a Taj Mahal tour. I read the dates and cities listed on the sleeve, all from twelve years ago in South America. How old would Sam have been twelve years ago? Surely not more than twelve himself. And not, I'm assuming, rocking out to the blues in Buenos Aires. He must have picked this up at a thrift store in Avalon.

When I put on the hoodie, it smells like him. How am I already familiar with his scent? It's hickory and cloves and petrichor. It makes me want to crawl under the thickest covers and drift away to sleep. With him.

But first, sweatpants. I cinch them up as tightly as I can. I look ridiculous, like when Tom Hank's kid-self goes home at the end of *Big*, and I'm too comfortable to care.

I study the items on Sam's bathroom counter. The bar of Irish Spring in the dish next to sink. Peppermint floss with the cap left open. I click it closed. I give his aftershave a whiff and trace the scent of cloves.

I hang my wet clothes on the shower rod, take another look in the mirror, and slip back into the main room, where the fire blazes.

"Sam?" I call, walking into the kitchen. I take in his cereal boxes—Kashi and Cocoa Krispies. I clock the single bowl and spoon in the sink.

"Your drink's waiting on the bar," he calls from somewhere up above. Impressed, I lift the highball off the counter and take a sip. Of course, Hunky Brewster makes a mean drink. Why would he build a custom wet bar if he sucked at making cocktails?

A moment later, Sam bounds barefoot down the stairs. He's changed into a gray T-shirt and jeans. His dark, wavy hair is down now, loose, cut just above his chin, and tousled slightly dry.

He runs his eyes over me. "Everything fits."

"Thanks," I say. "I feel a lot warmer."

"You know," Sam says mischievously, "I work with warm people every day—"

"Shut up." I laugh, and he does, too.

"I changed the sheets on the bed upstairs," he says. "I'll sleep down here. How's your drink?"

"Inspired."

"Usually, I add a drizzle of honey to my highballs, but I must have just run out. Are you hungry?"

I wave him off. "I had some soup earlier—"

"Not what I asked," he says, moving toward the back of the kitchen, where I notice a slow cooker is plugged in. When he lifts the lid, an exquisite aroma seizes my senses. It's garlic and wine and tomatoes and thyme, all tangled together.

"I can cook exactly two dishes," Sam says, placing a steaming bowl in front of me.

"I hope this is one of them," I say.

THE SPIRIT OF LOVE                                      53

"Boeuf bourguignon," Sam says, making a bowl for himself. "Bon appétit."

We carry our bowls into the main room. He flops onto an old knit plaid recliner with its stuffing bursting out. I sit on a supple leather couch, sinking into the deep brown cushion with an audible exhale. I place my highball on his clearly homemade coffee table, on a coaster resting on top of a Pelican Shakespeare copy of *The Tempest*.

"Good script," I say. "Are you reading it?"

Sam nods. "Living here, it makes a different kind of sense."

"'I must eat my dinner,'" I say in a low voice, quoting Caliban from the play. When I taste the stew, I moan. It's rich and savory with meat so tender it melts on contact. A second bite brings the exotic umami pop of wild mushrooms.

Sam closes his eyes, lifts his spoon, and picks up later in Caliban's monologue: "'And here you sty me, in this hard rock, whiles you do keep from me the rest o' th' island.'" His eyes pop open. "I never imagined I'd find the right audience to show that off." He winks at me. "How's the stew?"

"Truly delicious," I say, trying not to make a big thing about the fact that he's just casually quoted Shakespeare back at me.

"All in the spirit of Search and Rescue," he says. "You thought you didn't need it."

I nod, acquiescing. "I can admit when I'm wrong. It's funny, I had beef stew tonight for dinner at my campsite. The canned version. I thought it was fancy because I got it at Gelson's and it had Wolfgang Puck's face on the label, but after tasting this, I'm going to proclaim him disqualified from making stew."

"No! This is his recipe!" Sam says, laughing, using his spoon to point. "My mom sent it to me when I moved here. Along with an apron, which I caught on fire the first time I tried to cook it." He shrugs. "Finally figured it out."

"Yeah, you did. What's the other dish in your repertoire, Wolfgang? Duck à l'orange?"

Sam shakes his head, dabbing his mouth with a napkin. "It's a very simple grilled fish—there's not even a recipe. Just salt and lemon. But I do prepare it over an open fire, and the trick is knowing how to get the flame just right, and then there's a whole scaling process . . . I'm boring you."

"Not at all," I insist, but Sam is perceptive enough to notice the shift in me. It wasn't boredom; it was something closer to regret. Because I'd like to experience his grilled fish, but tomorrow, once this storm blows over, we'll go our separate ways. We're only here tonight because of the most bizarre series of events.

"But yeah," Sam continues, "everything else in the kitchen, I'm hopeless at. I burn toast, wreck mac and cheese. I'm also somehow terrible at making tea, so it's a good thing you wanted something stronger."

He has a way of saying things so earnestly they sound like sarcasm, but I'm starting to see that they're not. I've never met anyone so naturally open. It's like he doesn't know another way to be. I think of myself as someone who tells the truth when I speak. But so often, I choose not to speak, to keep the things I mean inside.

Sam doesn't seem to have that reflex. We're definitely from two very different worlds. I wonder if working in Hollywood has made it harder for me to speak the truth to others.

# THE SPIRIT OF LOVE

Sam raises a mug toward mine.

"Cheers," he says.

"What's in your glass?" I ask.

"It's called a Phoebe Snow," Sam says. "Dubonnet, brandy, and absinthe, strained over cracked ice."

"Someone needs to get you your own HGTV show."

"I don't know what that is," he says, shaking his head.

"No one does."

"Tell me, Fenny," Sam says. "What were you so busy working on at the beach that you didn't want me to save your life?"

By way of answering, I deliver *Zombie Hospital* character Dr. Josslyn Munro's world-famous tagline: "The Hippocratic oath applies to zombies, too."

Sam blinks, clearly having no idea what I'm talking about.

I stare at him, sure he's messing with me. "Seriously?" I ask. "*Zombie Hospital*? You've never . . ."

More blinking. Sam clears his throat. "I'm sorry, I'm trying to stay with you, but . . ."

"It's a big hit television show," I say. "A juggernaut."

"That explains it," he drawls. "I haven't had a TV in a while. Too hard to hook up cable or internet out here. But I don't mind. There's plenty to watch and think about. So, that's your job? You work on a TV show about zombies?"

I nod. "Zombies are life."

"And what exactly do you do?"

"I'm a . . ." I pause here, searching for the right word. There's the one that's described my profession for the past seven years, and the one that describes my profession starting on Monday. "I'm a director."

56 LAUREN KATE

"*Director*?" Sam says. The light in his eyes is unexpectedly satisfying. Like even though he's never seen the show, he gets what this means. Not only that, he seems excited on my behalf. He lifts his mug and says, "Congratulations! Wow. I would love to hear what that's like. When I was a kid, I used to think, someday . . ." He lifts a shoulder, looks around the cabin. "Nah. Maybe in another life. I'm still barely getting started here at Search and Rescue."

"To tell you the truth," I say, "my first shoot is on Monday. Until now, I've been working as a writer on the show. So, I guess we're both on the brink of doing what we always wanted." I meet his eyes, as warm as the fire beside us. "When you came along and saved my life," I grant him and he smiles, "I was trying to get my thoughts together for Monday's shoot."

"Are you shooting here?" His eyes light up. "On the island?"

"No, back in LA on a soundstage. I just came here to clear my head. Though this would be a stunning place to shoot something. Someday."

"It would be. I could show you around. There's so much beauty here most people never get to see. Hidden treasures everywhere, if you know where to look. There's this mind-blowing reef. We could go tomorrow—"

"That sounds amazing. But I have to prep for Monday."

"Right. Of course." He smiles like I didn't just shoot him down.

"Boring, I know."

"Not at all. I'm fascinated. I should have known."

"Known what?"

THE SPIRIT OF LOVE                                      57

He tips his head. "You give off the air of someone with a really spectacular career."

"You, too—no, wait, that was just the blinding light of your miner's helmet," I tease.

"Whose batteries I'm currently charging, thank you very much."

"Nice. A lucky future damsel in distress shall get the five-star rescue."

"Tell me more about what you're shooting on Monday," Sam says, his southern drawl becoming a little more pronounced with his drink. He sets down his empty bowl and leans closer to me in his chair until I can feel the heat coming off his skin.

I have no idea what time it is. My carefully planned vacation weekend has been washed away. And somehow, I don't care.

This isn't like me. I don't have fun with strangers. Especially Good Samaritan cowboy-types who probably still make their own Mother's Day cards. But even though this is normally when I'd pack up the conversation, I find that I want to stay up talking to Sam, eating his stew, warmed by his fire, nestled in his enormous, soft, nice-smelling clothes.

"Okay, so there's a boy on the show who has to choose life over being a zombie," I say. "I know it sounds campy, but I want to direct the scene like it means something . . . more."

"It's a huge choice," Sam says. "A person would really have to know what they were living for."

"Exactly."

"Do you? Know what you're living for?"

I nod. "My family. I'm really close with my sister and her

kids. You could say I live for them. And a job that challenges and surprises me most days. But also, little things."

"Like?"

I think about this for a moment. "Like the first sunset of daylight saving time from my balcony in Venice. Or catching a fly ball on the intramural baseball team my friends finally convinced me to join. Really luxurious shower gel. The symphony—"

"I've never been to the symphony."

"You'd love the symphony."

"What else?" Sam leans closer.

"Great books."

"Authors. Titles. Go."

"Really?"

"My TBR list needs to know."

I smile and close my eyes. "Lucille Clifton and Colette. Jia Tolentino and Madeline Miller. Elaine Pagels. Riane Eisler—"

I stop when I hear the scratching of a pencil. I look over and he's holding a pad. "Are you . . . taking notes?"

"It's not every day I rescue someone like you."

I tilt my head. "What are you doing out here by yourself, Sam?"

"What do you mean?"

"Most guys your age—"

"Which is?" he asks playfully.

"Twenty-two?"

"Twenty-three."

"I found that to be an awkward age," I say.

"I'm okay with it," he says.

# THE SPIRIT OF LOVE                                    59

"But don't you want to be in bars with single women, saying things like, 'How can you afford yourself?'"

"I don't get it," Sam says.

"'Cause you're so *fine*."

Sam winces. "Wait—*fine* like being charged a fine? Has someone used that line on you?"

"Never mind," I say. "But even if Search and Rescue is your calling, why do it in total isolation? Seems a little heavy on the search and a little light on the rescue."

"Yet here we are." Sam gives me a wink.

I reach for my viewfinder, but it's in Sam's bathroom, not around my neck. I'd like to lift it up right now and study him with no distractions. There's a dusting of freckles on his nose I hadn't noticed until now. He has a slight overbite that's only visible when he's not talking, and his feet, propped up on the coffee table, are more attractive than any feet I've ever seen.

"When I first came here," he says, "I had all these questions. I thought being in nature might answer them."

"How's it going? Have you found any answers?"

"It's more like the questions have receded."

"That's beautiful," I say.

"Maybe," Sam says. "But sometimes I feel like I might be stuck here forever."

"You're not stuck," I say. "You're completing your training. There's honor in that, right? We all have to put in our time before we can do what we're meant to do."

"Or maybe training is bullshit, and you and I aren't learning anything we don't already know."

"I've been on the apprentice track at *Zombie Hospital* for

seven years. Sometimes, that's felt like forever, but in a few more years, I might look back and—"

Sam shakes his head dismissively. "There's only now. Now is all there is."

"Huh?"

"I mean it. Why waste another moment searching for what we already have?"

"Are we still talking about our jobs?"

"No," Sam says, leaning in toward me, staring at my lips. I look at his. Pink and smooth, highly kissable.

I lean a little closer, too. Definitely feeling the *now*.

"Do you hear that?" Sam says suddenly, turning away. "The rain stopped. You've got to see this. It's so beautiful after the rain."

Trying not to feel disappointed that what felt like a kiss moment was, in fact, not, I follow Sam to a side door, and we step out onto the porch.

The predawn world sparkles with raindrops. Everything is brilliant, glistening. Sam looks at me and smiles.

"Do you hear it?"

"What?"

"The morning. Here it comes."

"Wait," I say. "What time is it?"

Sam shrugs. "Listen. You can hear it rise."

I try, but all I hear is the softness of his breathing. And then my eyes find the horizon, the ocean, gray and greased with nearly morning light. The world gathers a harmonious silence around itself like a shawl.

THE SPIRIT OF LOVE 61

"Do you do this often?" I ask. "Listen to rock formations? Listen to the dawn?"

"Do you know about the native Moken?"

I shake my head.

"Oh, you'll like this," he says. "You'll bring it out one day at a fancy LA dinner party. The Moken live in Thailand, and in 2004, when a tsunami wiped out millions of homes, the Moken heard the warning. They heard it in the stillness of the water, in the shifting flights of fish. Their entire tribe got out in time. Nature is always telling us something. The trick is to remember to listen."

"I'll remember that," I whisper. "I can't believe we talked until morning."

"Oh, right. Sorry," Sam says. "You need your rest. Big week, right? There's a spare toothbrush in the bathroom drawer."

"Oh. I . . . Of course."

I close myself in the bathroom and brush my teeth, thinking maybe I'll go out there and take back everything I said about not wanting to sleep with him tonight. But when I leave the bathroom, Sam's fast asleep on the couch, looking like Michelangelo's *David*.

I watch him for a moment, young and peaceful, lovely and strong. How intimate and also still unknown he is to me after tonight. Then, as the sun finds its legs on the ocean, I climb the stairs to Sam's loft and tumble into his soft and empty bed.

# Chapter Five

LISTEN. YOU CAN HEAR IT RISE.

The voice swells in my dreams, coaxing me from deep sleep. Where am I? How did I get between these silky sheets? Did that storm, that hike, those eyes—did any of that really happen?

I'm still tired, and these sheets are delicious, but a guilty feeling spreads like a storm cloud in my stomach, and I'm not sure why. I roll onto my side, stretching diagonally, arms over my head. When my fingers curl around his bedpost, the guilty cloud shifts into a shiver that dives between my legs.

I decide not to imagine him sleeping here. But does he take off his shirt before he climbs in? Does he sleep on his side, his stomach, or his back? Edie says you can tell by the creases in a person's face. But Sam's face is so smooth, maybe he sleeps hanging from the rafters like a bat.

How much heat comes off his skin when he's dreaming? What other women have lain here? Why is it so easy to imagine Sam's face between a woman's legs, his shoulders flexing as she writhes?

A green tendril of jealousy curls around my chest, which makes me roll my eyes. I *cannot* be jealous of imaginary women having twenty orgasms in a row on a random stranger's face.

But *is* he a random stranger?

# THE SPIRIT OF LOVE 63

Yes. Although he may not have felt like one last night, he is. I know next to nothing about this man, which means I can't do what my body's begging for.

I sit up in bed—God, this bed—and pull back the home-made curtain covering the small loft window. Daylight ava-lanches into the room.

I check the analog clock on the dresser by the bed. Holy hell, it's almost noon.

I pad toward the wooden ladder leading down from the loft. I try not to notice that Sam's bedroom is enchanting—clean and spare and sparkling—but I do:

A book of *New York Times* crossword puzzles and tortoise-shell reading glasses on a glass tray by the bed.

A mahogany box on the dresser, left open so I can see the corner of his driver's license—a pornographically good picture, along with a set of keys and a wind-up watch with a leather strap.

Behind the box, a framed Polaroid of what must be little boy Sam. He looks around five years old, and he sits in a forest on a fallen tree, between his stunning mother and a father he's grown up to look like.

Descending the ladder, the smell of burnt toast finds me. I don't see Sam in the main room, only charred bread slices on the top of the trash. It makes me smile to imagine him burning them. Toast isn't one of his two dishes. This scorched breakfast is evidence of his honesty.

And evidence that I'm in trouble, gazing into the trash with a goofy smile on my face. I can't be seen like this. I can't *be* like this.

I move to the bathroom, where I find my dried clothes,

folded—yes, horror, even my paisley thong, tactfully tucked into the pocket of my cutoffs.

I put my clothes back on, fold his, and use the spare toothbrush again. I like his toothpaste. I like knowing what he tastes like when he goes to bed.

Through the window that looks onto the back porch where we'd listened to the dawn, I see him, and the man is doing one-armed pull-ups—shirtless—on a metal bar. His body glides, outside gravity, muscles flexing.

I wish I weren't eight years older with a skepticism that makes me feel warm and wise in Venice but uselessly cold on Catalina. I wish I didn't have a new career to launch, an industry to dominate.

I wish he'd asked me to stay.

But because life is what it is, I scrawl the following note:

Sam,

Had to run. Heaps of zombie work to do today. Thank you for the S&R.

—Fenny

I write quickly, not letting myself second-guess my phrasing or I'll be here all day. I can't risk Sam turning around to complete his reps on the other trifurcated arm, because he might see me, and I might see his pecs, and my paisley thong might quickly hit the floor.

I take one last look at him, fan myself, and slip out the front

THE SPIRIT OF LOVE                                           65

door, grabbing my shoes as I go. I carefully close the main door behind me, but the screen door—I hadn't realized—squeaks like Fran Drescher's voice on *The Nanny*.

"Fuck," I mutter, then freeze, trying to discern if he heard.

"Fenny?" his honeyed voice calls from so close, he must be inside the cabin. He must be a single wall away. "Is that you, sleepyhead?"

How can he sound so intimate, like we've been friends—or more—for years?

"I fucked up the toast," he says. "But I was thinking . . ."

He trails off. What was he thinking? Should I stick around long enough to find out? No, I should go. I *could* stay. I *should* go. I would stay, if only—

"Oh," he says, quieter now. And I know he's found my note.

Which makes it official. And so, finally, I run.

Down the steps and down the path lined by tall grass and wildflowers. Through the woods, which bear no sign of last night's storm. My eyes sting with regret as I take the fork in the path that leads down to the beach. When I reach the ravine where Sam's Jeep slipped off the road, I stop and stare.

The mudslide we waded through last night got worse, because half of his car is buried in it. Totaled. For a moment, I see him inside the Jeep, tumbling down. I wince and rub my eyes, shaking away the vision.

He's healthy and hale, safe in his perfect cabin.

I sigh and stagger downhill to the beach. The water is calm, gently lapping at the shore. It's like the ocean's pretending nothing happened here last night.

Walking toward my campsite, I see that the serpent head rock—which I am fairly certain I watched crumble to the sand last night—is . . . there. Just as it had been when I first arrived.

"What *is* this?" I demand of Catalina Island. "Are you fucking with me?" I kick the base of the serpent rock.

I don't know why I'm angry, or who I'm angry with. I sit on the beach and cradle my head in my hands. I inhale, feeling a word forming in my mouth. A word I'm scared to say.

"Sam." Hearing his name gives me goosebumps. "He was . . ." I pause to find the words. "Like a dream . . . except . . . I held his hand." I look at my palm, remembering how his fit in mine, remembering the warmth.

A long, lazy wave splashes my feet. In place of present serenity, I see last night's water, rampaging over black and broken stones. Then I blink and all that's gone, just calm sea and the sun beating down on my shoulders remaining.

Ever since I read *Alice's Adventures in Wonderland* in eighth grade and then watched the PBS version eight hundred times, I've hated the trope of "It was all just a dream." My English teacher tried to defend it—"No dream is ever *just* a dream," he said—but I don't buy that. We don't turn to fantasy to be reminded that it's fantasy. We turn to fantasy because we *want* it to be true.

Okay, then. This is my reality. It's not the vacation I wanted, but you never get the vacation you plan. You get the vacation you get.

I find my Sicilian hammock, matted in sand and popped bullwhip kelp. My tent is on its side, the zipper shredded. I'll have to buy Edie a replacement. I peer inside and find my back-

THE SPIRIT OF LOVE 67

pack and my books, my phone—either waterlogged or dead—and my sleeping bag. That means my camcorder must be here, too.

I crawl into the tent and search on my hands and knees. When I don't spot it, I empty the contents of my backpack onto my sleeping bag. Pens from past vacations pour out, but my camcorder doesn't.

I roll up my sleeping bag and push it outside the tent. The one thing that matters to me is nowhere to be seen. My hands sweep the tent floor. I feel nothing but pebbles, sand, and despair.

I crawl outside and walk in circles around the rocks and prickly pear cacti. I walk up the steep path and turn around to get a better view of my campsite. I look through my viewfinder and beg it to help me.

No camcorder, anywhere.

*Let it go,* I try to tell myself, but I can't. Edie brought that camcorder to the hospital the night of my near-death experience. It was the first thing I touched when I came back. I never should have brought it here. I never should have been so careless, never should have let it out of my sight. Now I've lost it forever.

I look at my sodden possessions. Even if I manage to hike to town and book a room, I'm not going to ground myself in work tonight. It's a lie that work is why I fled Sam's cabin. I fled because I wanted to stay *too* much. But what am I so afraid of, really? Not Sam rejecting me; I'm old enough to handle that. Then what? That I don't know his mother's name or what he's allergic to? That his cabin and his lifestyle and his body and his kindness late last night felt *too* appealing?

I recall the adage "If it seems too good to be true, it probably is." I disagree. That at any moment, life might become too good to be true is what gets me out of bed in the morning.

So then . . . what's my problem? What am I waiting for?

The decision makes itself. I grab what I can of my things, stuff my tent inside the beach's trash can, and then, for the second time this morning, I take off running.

I run up the rocky path, past the place where the taxi dropped me off, past the fork in the road, past the trees and clumps of cacti I'm starting to memorize.

I slow to a walk when I near the cabin. I need to catch my breath, still my heart, and gather myself as much as I can.

I hear a male voice up ahead. I can't make out the words, but then—

"Ragweed, Sarah . . . yes."

When he rounds a corner in the path, Sam breaks off talking and we both jump at the sight of each other.

"Fenny!" His brown eyes light up like a small town on the Fourth of July.

"Sam." I look past him. "Were you . . . talking to someone?"

"No." He shakes his head. "Yes. Myself. I mean . . . the idea of you."

"The idea of me? I thought you said 'Sarah—'"

"Well." He clears his throat. "I was brainstorming. Ways to convince you to spend the day with me."

"Will Sarah be there?"

He glares playfully at me. "Probably not. What are you doing here? Did you leave something at the cabin—or were you on your way to convince me to spend the day with you?"

I bite my lower lip, knowing he's got me.

# THE SPIRIT OF LOVE                    69

"Do you *like* me, Fenny?"

"Are you in the fourth grade?"

"That's an honest question from a grown man, even though I think I know the answer."

"I'm considering trying it out."

"Try again."

"I don't know . . ."

"What's so hard for you about saying how you feel?"

I take a step toward Sam. He takes my hand, and we both stare at it for a while. He swings it. Slowly, I use it to pull him toward me. He lifts his other hand to tip my face toward his.

"I never do this," I say.

"That's okay." His lips hover right above mine.

"I need you to know that I'm not a fling person."

"Message received. But also, I'm getting a strong intuition that you *could* be an amazing fling person."

"No." I drape my hands around his tall, strong neck. "I like to plan and research and cross-examine and—"

"In that case, Dripping Springs."

I blink. "What?"

"You wanted to know last night. That's where I'm from, a little town in Texas. My mom's side goes back four generations there. Thirty-two, that's how many hours I have yet to log in my Search and Rescue training, even though"—and here he winks at me—"you and I both know I'm qualified to handle anything."

"TBD on that," I warn, but I'm smiling.

He smiles back. "I like dogs, but I love birds."

"You love birds?"

"Birds are wonders, but don't distract me, because I've got this memorized in order. Ragweed, I'm allergic. I take Zyrtec in the spring. My favorite movie is *Fearless* or anything starring Jeff Bridges."

"Respect."

"And Sarah—"

"That's your mother's name."

"That's my mother's name." He nods. "And about the last thing you asked me on the porch."

"The afterlife," I remember. *Don't fail this one, please.*

Sam scratches his head. "I can't say I've thought about it much before. My world is quiet by design. But since last night, I've been feeling . . . I don't know. Like there's more out there that I want to see. Like you. So. Do you want to spend the day with me now?"

I squeeze his hand and grin. "I do."

# Chapter Six

"IF YOU GO BACK TO LA WITHOUT SCREAMING YOUR face off on my homemade zip line," Sam says to me later that morning as we enter a grove of cedar and eucalyptus trees, "were you even here?"

In preparation for the day ahead, Sam has instructed me to wear closed-toed shoes, a strong coat of sunscreen, and a bathing suit under my clothes. He's decked out in fitted black swim trunks, a well-worn pair of gray New Balances, and a sleeveless gray tank that's been washed so many times it's practically translucent. Which makes it practically perfect. The sight of his tanned, bare shoulder flexing as he lifted the backpack he brought with us was something I feel I should have paid admission to see.

"Did you just say *zip line*?" I ask.

"It's more than a zip line," Sam says. "It's my masterpiece."

"Your fireplace isn't your masterpiece?" I ask, adding in my mind, *Or your butt?*

"My fireplace is good for warmth and contemplation. But this zip line, Fenny. This zip line lets you slip the bonds of Earth and dance in the skies. This zip line touches the face of God." He glances at me. "Or whatever you believe is out there."

"Out there or in here?" I ask, thumb to my heart.

I stop speaking when we reach the wooden platform that abruptly ends the trail. Beyond it lies an endless expanse of scary sky. The platform is nailed into a crook of branches in a stately cedar tree. A few feet above my head, two thick steel ropes have been tied around the trunk of the cedar. They run parallel to each other, stretching out into an unknown downward distance, ending somewhere unseen.

A silver pulley is attached to the ropes above my head.

"Oh, hell no," I say and start back the way I came.

Sam laughs and puts his hands on my shoulders. There's that soft, penetrating look in his eyes again, the one that signals to my brain, *Trust him.* "There's nothing to be afraid of. I've ridden it a thousand times. Look at me." Sam gestures at his fantastic body. "Not a scratch."

It's hard to refute that he's anything less than physically perfect.

"These ropes are made from galvanized steel," he says. "I could send a hundred Fennys down them at the same time, and these ropes wouldn't flinch."

As he unknots the pulley, I gaze down from the platform into the abyss. I cringe at the jagged boulders only twenty feet below, at the drought-parched cacti covering every visible piece of disappearing slope. Vertigo darts around my chest, scorching a path of fear. I'd rather not show up to set to direct my first episode wearing a full-body cast.

"Where exactly does this end?" I ask.

"Sooner than you'll want it to," Sam says. "The ride is less than two minutes, but about three seconds in, you enter an endorphin-flooded state you'll crave for the rest of your life—"

THE SPIRIT OF LOVE                                      73

"Ooh, another flood. How *fun*."

"This is the kind of flood we want," Sam says. "Not that last night wasn't."

He smiles. I gulp.

"And right before the end, the pulley slows enough for you to put your feet down and walk."

"And where will this slow walk occur?"

"It's a surprise," he says and hands me a helmet.

"Where's your helmet?" I ask.

"I only have one helmet," he says. "I've never done a . . . duet."

"Never made the beast with two backs?"

"Not on a zip line."

"Well," I say, feeling my cheeks turn red, "I'm honored."

"Me, too. I'm really excited to do this with you."

I'm not used to guys like him, who speak so plainly, whose compliments don't come out coded in self-protection and self-promotion. It makes Sam seem even younger than twenty-three. It's like he hasn't been hurt yet. Maybe that's what makes him so sure I won't be hurt today.

It's contagious. He's contagious. I put on the helmet and snap the chin strap in place.

"All you have to do is hold on to me. And lift your feet a little."

"Unless I die of a heart attack."

I grip the galvanized steel rope and stare out at my wide-open future. I wish I could call Edie or Olivia or Masha right now and have them tell me that this is okay. Or maybe I wish I simply could know all by myself that my intuition could speak up louder, more clearly, that it could guide me toward what I'm supposed to do.

"Now is all there is," Sam whispers in my ear as he lifts me in his arms and puts his cheek against mine. He kicks off the platform, and we fly down through cedar branches, my boots barely clearing the boulders just beneath the platform.

"Ahhhhhhhhh!" I scream.

I can feel Sam's smile in my cheek. He's got his knees up, making his lap a seat for me to sit in. His firm body presses hard against my back, my ass. When I lift up my knees to settle into him a little more, he groans.

I realize I'm riding an Adonis down a mountain. When the ocean bursts into view, wild and blue and endless, I become aware that I don't want this to end.

This feeling alone is worth coming back from the dead for. I can see how albatrosses go years without touching land. I can see why stars stay in the sky. I want to do this every day.

We begin to slow naturally, and I look down and see a brilliant white blanket of ultra-secret beach. Sam and I jog together as our feet touch down on sand. Twenty feet ahead is a stately pine tree with a tire nailed to it as a cushion. We come to a stop before we need the tire, and I exhale deeply. I'm buzzing with adrenaline.

I gaze in wonder around me. This pristine beach is a tenth the size of Parson's Landing. Whereas at my camp the shore was pebbly and strewn with boulders, this one is made of fine, white sand. Lizards dash here and there. Cluster lilies bloom. There's even a C-shaped cove, shaded by boughs of pine that hang low with sap-heavy cones. This place is indeed a surprise, the best one I've had in a while.

"Did you love it?" Sam asks.

It's a big word. *Love.* I try not to overuse it, but in this case, it applies.

"Yes," I say. It brings out Sam's dimples like morning brings out the sun.

"Good," he says, "because there's more. Come on!"

We kick off our shoes and bound toward the water with an abandon I haven't known in twenty years. It's like I'm eleven, and school's out, and nothing stands between me and summer but a heartbeat and a smile. Sam stops at a wooden post tethering a canoe and what appears to be a tarp-covered Jet Ski.

"Are these yours?" I ask.

"Which one should we ride first?"

I run my hand over his canoe. "Nice gunwale."

"You know your canoes."

"I have one like this at home."

"I take it out at sunset," Sam says. "That's when the whales sing."

"I can't say I've ever heard a whale in the canals of Venice."

"What do you hear?"

"Families eating dinner. Teenagers getting stoned. Dogs chasing squirrels up palm trees."

What I don't tell Sam is that I've only used my canoe once, at Olivia's and Masha's insistence, on the night I closed on the house it came with. Our tour of my new neighborhood's canals was soothing and tranquil and deeply Venetian. We toasted with champagne, and I promised myself I'd pick up that paddle at least a few times every week. But somehow, eighteen months after I moved in, I'm embarrassed to say I haven't found the time.

"I bet you don't have a Jet Ski in Venice," Sam finally says.

"That would violate section sixty-three fifty of the LA Municipal Code."

"We have a winner!" He flings back the cover on the Jet Ski. I watch his body move as he prepares our watercraft, checking various gauges and earnestly turning several knobs.

"There's so much I want to show you," he says. "So much I want you to see with your director's eye. I know you're going to want to come back here and shoot some of these places someday. I can almost guarantee it."

"I can't wait."

"There's a bald eagle's nest on a cliff about a mile north. You can only see it from the water. Nothing has prepared you for the cuteness of a baby bald eagle."

"Do you name the babies?"

"Rogaine and Propecia."

"Because they're *bald*?" I ask, then burst out laughing. "Wow."

He winces. "You'd kick me out of the writers' group for that one, wouldn't you?"

"The writers' room? No way. We'd take you out for beers. That's comedy gold. Or at least bronze."

"I bet it's fun. Working on your show. I bet you're good at what you do. I bet people look up to you."

"It is fun, and . . . thank you." I feel a little embarrassed that he's put his finger on my insecurities so quickly, but mostly, I'm grateful for his kindness. My defenses are crumbling around this man. Maybe his being the physical paragon of the male species has something to do with it? Maybe it's because when my eyes catch on his full lips I feel like I'm going to turn inside out?

"You snorkel, right?" Sam asks. "Wait 'til you see this reef I'm going to show you. We can picnic there. I brought food! Sometimes I think about getting scuba certified—"

"When was the last time you had a visitor, Sam?"

"Have you ever spearfished? Your face is saying no, but when I put the shaft of that polespear in your hands, you'll know what to do."

I almost laugh—because the sexual innuendo is getting a little ridiculous—but when Sam meets my eyes, I see that he meant it not as a ha-ha joke, but a flirtatious and very direct one. And my stomach flips.

"Now get over here," Sam says, as if he knows all this. "And take off your clothes."

"What?" I gulp.

He lifts the seat of the Jet Ski to reveal a waterproof compartment. "We need to store them here. Otherwise, they'll get soaked."

"THIS IS MY favorite place on island to snorkel," Sam calls over the waning motor of the Jet Ski. The sun is high in the sky, and my arms are wrapped around his waist. My cheek is pressed against his sun-warmed back and also aching from the grin that hasn't budged since we first kicked up a wake.

Somewhere past the unfathomably darling baby bald eagles

and the ancient cave hollowed into the northernmost face of the island, I stopped asking myself, *Who is this guy?*

He's Sam, and he probably only happens to women like me once in a lifetime. Which is why I've decided to say yes to all he offers. He wants to show me what's beautiful about his world? Who am I to say no? It turns out, there's a lot to see.

Sam cuts the motor as the Jet Ski draws close to a cluster of rocks. I can almost taste the salt on his skin, but it would be weird to lick him, right?

"You gotta meet my friends the garibaldi by the reef," he says. "They're going to love you."

"Do we just jump in?" I ask. I've never swam anywhere so remote and pristine. He was right about letting me in on Catalina's best secrets.

"You can wear your life jacket if you want," Sam says, "but the water here is super salty, so you practically float on your own."

I watch as he unclips his life jacket and drapes it over the handlebars of the Jet Ski. The muscles I hadn't wanted to let myself see from the front this morning now gleam in the sun. His chest contains my dream amount of chest hair—lots—and he wears an oval-shaped stone charm on a chain around his neck. It's hard to take my eyes off him.

"Do you want to swim, or should we just stare at each other?" he asks with a smile. "Honestly, I could go either way."

I blush and drop my eyes, but I like the feel of his on me as I unclip my life jacket until I'm wearing just my red bikini.

"Staring contest it is," Sam says.

"No," I laugh. "Let's snorkel. I need to meet your friends the garibaldi so they can give me the dirt on you."

THE SPIRIT OF LOVE                                    79

He shakes his head. "They'll never tell. You have no idea the dirt I have on them."

While Sam reaches into the compartment under the seat for the snorkeling gear, I face the water and dive in.

The cold braces me and fills the space around me with buoyant light. I can't remember the last time I totally submerged myself in the ocean. It feels inaugural, like I'm ushering in a new season of life. I break the surface, grab some air, and wipe my eyes to look up at Sam. He's watching me. He's smiling.

"Fenny?"

"Sam?"

"I'm glad you stayed," he says, and before I can answer, he tosses me a snorkel set. "Keep staying, okay?"

My face mask stretches as I grin. "Okay."

I feel a pulse of water come toward me when Sam dives in. He meets me underwater, hooking his fingers through mine. His mask magnifies his eyes, which makes meeting his gaze even more intense.

I want to spit out this snorkel and kiss him like he's my oxygen source. But he's tugging my hand toward the reef and then the two of us are flitting between schools of luminescent fish.

Reaching the reef is like crossing into another world, a hive of activity—golden garibaldi, turquoise sea anemone, pink and golden coral clusters. I've been to Catalina Island half a dozen times, but I've never snorkeled here. I never knew all this wonder was hidden away.

When we've snorkeled enough, Sam shows me where to climb the rock next to the Jet Ski. He takes out his backpack, unfolds a small blanket, and starts unpacking a picnic he's made.

"I've got turkey on white or . . . turkey on white."

"You said you could only make two dishes," I tease, taking a big bite. It's just bread and meat and mayonnaise, but it's unequivocally delicious, as beach sandwiches always are. "You used just the right amount of sun, salt, and snorkel-induced hunger."

"Your palate is very sophisticated," Sam says after a bite. "Those are the secret ingredients."

I'm happily chewing my second sandwich half when Sam pulls out a nylon bag and starts assembling something made of narrow aluminum poles.

"What's happening now?" I ask.

"We're fifty percent through with lunch," he says, "which means it's time to start thinking about dinner." He twists one aluminum pole to fit inside another.

"Is that what I think it is?"

Sam holds out what appears to be a two-foot-long dart with a trigger attached to one end. "You're about to throw your first spear."

He places it in my hands and then leans behind me to help me position my fingers.

"I've never done anything like this before," I say, feeling the electric sensation of warm water dripping off his skin and onto mine.

"All you have to do is see the fish, picture me grilling it tonight on our secret beach, and pull this trigger. Easy."

Sam holds the spear as I slip back into the water and lower my mask again, fitting my snorkel in my mouth. He hands over the spear carefully. I dip beneath the surface. I'd feel more confident if I had my viewfinder to frame the shot of all these hali-

# THE SPIRIT OF LOVE

but gliding before me, but my viewfinder is tucked away with my clothes under the seat of Sam's Jet Ski. Besides, it probably would not love the salt water, so my snorkel mask will have to do.

*See the fish*, Sam said. Easy enough; they're everywhere. *Picture me grilling it tonight on our secret beach.* I try to imagine Sam's face lit by the glow of a campfire, and a warm swirl passes through me. What will it be like between us when the sun sets and the stars come out and there's still just one bed in his cabin? I can see us laughing. I can see us inching closer to each other. I can see the moment when I decide I can't wait anymore to kiss this guy.

I pull the trigger, and the next thing I know, I hear Sam's whoop above the surface, shouting "Bull's-eye! That's my girl!"

SUNSET ON THE secret beach. We showered back at his cabin and changed into warmer clothes. I'm wearing Sam's Taj Mahal hoodie, which I'm hoping he understands is now mine. We took a second thrilling zip line down the cliff. I'm watching Sam, who builds a fire with his hands.

"So, you've found your passion for zip-lining," he says, his heather gray hoodie unzipped just enough to reveal a tempting triangle of dark chest hair. "And jet-skiing. And snorkeling and spearfishing and watching me build this fire. Very soon, you're going to be overwhelmed by my grilled fish. I don't think you're going anywhere, Fenny. I think I get to keep you."

I run my fingers through the sand, wanting to touch him, wanting to close every distance between our bodies. "It's tempting."

"Just tell me what else I have to do. Or . . . tell me how back home competes with all this."

"You mean, my life?"

"Yeah," he says, scooting closer so he's right next to me, so our knees are touching, our shoulders brushing as we gaze into the fire. "What do you love about Venice? What do you love about your job?"

I think a moment. "What excites me about directing is helping the cast bring out the best version of their characters. It requires really getting to know the actors and what they want, both in and outside their roles. Like, most people think the one kid star on our show is a diva, but once you get to know him, he's really more like a gangly Buddha. Looking close enough to see that in Buster shows me how to lean in. It shows me how to shape episodes around what he's already great at doing, which maybe no one else has noticed—"

"Fenny."

"Uh-huh?"

"I'm loving hearing about your work," he says, his voice dropped to a whisper, "but right now I need you to shhhhh."

"What?"

"Shhhhh," he says, leaning closer, putting one hand on my chin, and looking into my eyes. He puts a finger to his lips. Is this the moment? Have I finally waited long enough to meet his lips?

He tilts my chin a few degrees to the left.

"Look," he whispers.

There's a hummingbird six inches from my face. Sam and I both grow completely still to watch the creature sip nectar from

# THE SPIRIT OF LOVE

the bud of a magenta thistle flower. We stare at its wings, blurred in phosphorescent motion. We watch its throat pulse as it swallows greedy gulps. We watch its eyes focus on each bud before it plants its beak in the stamen. We listen to the whir of its tiny, ferocious life before our eyes. It's one of those things that you know, even as it's happening in the present tense, that you'll never forget, no matter how far in the distance your future stretches. And when Sam squeezes my hand, I get the feeling he's thinking exactly the same thing.

It feels like eons pass before the hummingbird has had its fill, and when it flies off and disappears into the fading light, the moment is gone too soon.

"Tell me Buster competes with that," Sam says.

# *Chapter Seven*

"WHAT'S THE STORY WITH THIS GUY?" SAM ASKS, reaching for the viewfinder I wear around my neck. It's after sunset on the secret beach, and there are more stars out in the sky than I have ever seen. We've eaten every delicious morsel of the halibut I speared and Sam grilled, and we've drained the last drops of a bottle of white wine. It feels like Sam and I have known each other all our lives, yet also like we're just getting started.

"It's a viewfinder," I tell him. "You hold it up to your eye to see what the camera will see, to frame a shot in your mind before a crew takes hours setting up." I lift the lanyard from my neck and drape it over Sam's. "Try it."

"Is it expensive? I don't want to break it."

"I got it for five dollars at a flea market. There are a million more where this one came from."

"A million more that haven't been touched by you." Sam puts it to his eye and looks at me. "Oh, yeah. Great shot."

"Don't frame me," I say, embarrassed, pushing gently on his hand. "Frame something artful and unexpected. Like the wine bottle we should have brought two of."

"Nah. I don't see anything but you." He gets closer, close enough so I know he's framing just my face. "I like this thing. I feel like it lets me see more somehow."

# THE SPIRIT OF LOVE                                        85

"Yeah," I say, understanding. "That's it."

Sam lowers the viewfinder from his face and reaches into his sweatshirt to pull out the chain I'd noticed him wearing earlier. "I've got a viewfinder, too. This one's called an adder stone."

He holds up the stone between his thumb and forefinger. It's ebony black, the right size and thickness for skipping, except for an unusual hole, about the diameter of my pinkie, just off center of the stone.

"Did you find it here, on the island?"

He nods. "I've got this coffee table book called *Stones* in the cabin. I looked up this one and it says that, in Celtic legend, if you look through an adder stone, you're supposed to be able to glimpse another world."

I run my fingers around the stone, sandy here and smooth there. I dip my pinky in the hole, touching Sam's palm on the other side.

"Does it work?" I ask.

"Let's see." Sam raises the stone toward his eye, but I put up a hand to stop him.

"Hold on," I say. "This is directing 101. Before you try to glimpse another world, first you need to establish the one you're in now. For comparison."

"Good idea, director," Sam says and smiles. He shifts on the blanket so he's sitting cross-legged, facing me. He takes my free hand in his. He closes his fingers around mine and the adder stone.

"So right now, in this world," he says. "I'm looking at Fenny. A cool lady I picked up yesterday on the beach. Literally."

I groan, but Sam squeezes my hand to keep me from pulling away.

"If you're embarrassed now, buckle up." He laughs to himself, gently biting his lip for a moment, thinking. "So, Fenny . . . she's a lot like my favorite island: a great natural beauty. Don't groan." He warns me. "You're just listening right now. I'm establishing a world."

"Maybe just get to the new one—"

"I'm getting there," he says. "I'm taking my time. As I was saying: Fenny. She's a stubborn camper. A sneaky little houseguest. Absolute zip line freak. Spearfisher extraordinaire." His eyes drift over me and soften in the firelight. "I like her hair. I like those flecks of gold in her brown eyes. I like her tiny feet. She's a great fucking kisser—"

"How would you know?"

He takes his time looking at me. "You think you're the only one who knows things?"

All it takes is seconds for him to close the four inches between us, but the moment his lips find mine still manages to stun me.

Sam's mouth is firm and warm, his lips are velvet soft, and his hands are huge, but as they pull me to him, they're as gentle as a whisper. The contradictions within this man beguile me as his teeth tug on my lips. Heat builds between us, and I pull him close for more until it's frenzied, hot, and both of us are gasping.

"Told you she was great," he says, out of breath.

He softly kisses both of my cheeks and then presses his fore-

THE SPIRIT OF LOVE 87

head to mine so the tips of our noses touch, which somehow feels even more intimate than the kiss.

"That stone is powerful," I say in a shivery voice.

"Oh, wait!" He laughs. "I forgot about the stone. I didn't even get to the good part yet. Shit, where'd it go? We've got other worlds to glimpse."

We finally find Sam's adder stone underneath my thigh. He closes it in his hand and refocuses on his task in a way that is sweet and funny.

"So you remember all that stuff I said before?" he asks.

"Great kisser. I remember."

He nods. "Still true. That's Fenny: here, now. But see, Fenny's also got another thing going on." Now he lifts the stone near his face, closes one beautiful eye, and with the other, he looks through. Toward me.

I don't know what's coming, but I hold my breath and wait.

"Ah," he says, "Now I see her in her *other* life, that fancy *Zombie Hospital* life. It's fast. She's paddling around Venice in her canoe."

"Ha."

"Very busy, all day long, beautiful people to deal with, her mind moving in a thousand directions." He pauses, as if he really can see this. "She's an important person on set. The show doesn't work without her." For a moment, his voice dips and he almost sounds sad, but it fades quickly, everything in him turning light again. "She's making—yes, I see it—*art*." He draws down the stone so I can see his face. "Was I close?"

I couldn't take anyone else seriously if they used those words to describe my work. But I actually think Sam means what he just said. Partly because of how out of the cultural-zeitgeist loop he is, and partly because somehow, he seems to see me the way I never realized I wanted to be seen.

I know the show is campy, *and* I know it's also, occasionally, art.

I know I used to place the latte orders, *and* I know the show doesn't work without me.

And somehow—more than any other person in my life—this guy knows it, too. That, or else the stone really does have magical powers.

But I think it's Sam. How is it that he's exactly what I needed this weekend? The solo camping trip I'd planned would have been peaceful, but it wouldn't have made me feel this alive. It wouldn't have reminded me—like Sam is doing right now—who I am. Who I want to be.

I lean forward and kiss him. He kisses back like the kiss was his idea, his hands on my back, pulling me close. His lips are tender, firm, and I love the way he smells. God, I am *so* attracted to this man. I could crawl into his lap and kiss him into next summer.

"You should try now," he says, pulling millimeters away and draping his chain with the adder stone over my neck and resting his forehead against mine. He's still wearing my viewfinder. "Maybe we trade for a while."

I sit back, rolling the stone between my palms. "Okay, I'll play."

"Establish the world," he says. "Don't forget that part."

"Never," I say. "So here in front of me sits Sam."

THE SPIRIT OF LOVE                                    89

"Hot name. What's he like?"

"The first thing you need to know about Sam is that he saved my life."

"*No*," he gasps.

"Indeed," I say. "Almost died trying. There was lightning and a rockslide, and we lost a car and a camcorder." I sigh. "It was all a little touch-and-go for a minute. But then . . ." A smile creeps in. "We warmed up to each other. A lot. His cabin smells good, and he makes me laugh. I usually reserve laughing with people who have known me for at least four seasons."

"Really?" he asks. "Why hold back? You've got a great laugh. You should be sharing it with the world."

"Because . . ." I start to say. I find that my body isn't close enough to him, so without thinking, without even time to second-guess my boldness, I crawl into his lap.

And get instantly rewarded by strong, warm arms around me and legs that make just the right shape for me to sit within.

"That's better," Sam murmurs, and his breath tickles my neck.

"I agree."

"Now, back to why you don't laugh enough."

"Laughter feels vulnerable. It comes easy when I feel safe," I say, looking down at the stone in my hand. "It comes easy with Sam."

"Are you saying he makes you feel safe?"

"I think so." I nod. "I like his stew. I like his fireplace and his highballs. I really like his eyebrows, and what happens to this muscle"—I run my finger down the skin just below his shoulder blade—"when he does a one-armed pull-up on the porch."

"Thank God. I was hoping you saw that." He lets out a breathy laugh. "Fenny?"

"Uh-huh." We're staring deep into each other's eyes, and I'm not sure I'll ever move.

"You forgot to mention how fucking great Sam is in bed."

I gulp. I'm tingling with desire for this man, and I feel like he can smell it, because there's this new look in his eyes that is primal and focused and hungry.

I slowly pull off my sweatshirt and feel his intake of breath. My T-shirt comes off next. I grab for his shirt, practically tearing the thin fabric. Our chests meet, and I can feel his heartbeat, racing like mine.

"I never do this." My voice comes out in breathy pants.

"So you've said," Sam whispers, kissing a trail down my neck.

"Oh, God," I breathe. "I bring it up only because it's . . . important . . . that you know . . ."

"Know what?" He cups my breasts, squeezing them exactly as hard as I like it.

"That this is . . . different. That I don't . . . at other times . . . with other guys . . . that I am capable of . . . restraint."

"Okay," he says, putting his mouth to my nipple now and making me moan. His eyes and his hands run over my bare skin. Everything about this is too much to take in, and he's still wearing his pants.

He pauses, looks up. A beat passes.

"What happened?" I ask.

"Did you want me to say that I never do this either?" Sam asks.

"Oh, no! That's not what I meant."

THE SPIRIT OF LOVE                                    91

Sam stares at me intently. "Here's the thing. All that matters to me is this. You. Right now. In this moment. You're wonderful. You're warm, and bright, and lovely."

We roll onto the sand, me atop him, straddling his broad chest. "That's a big thing with you, isn't it?"

"What is?"

I can feel him between my legs, so it's an effort to stay on track. "*Now*. The now, as a way of life."

"Now." He nods and draws me to him. We kiss again. "What else is there?"

"You're right," I say, in momentary, blissful surrender. His hands are on my hips, tugging down my cutoffs, and then reaching inside the waist of my underwear until his strong, soft hand is right where I need it.

"I can't imagine anything but now," I gasp as his fingers work miracles. "Sam."

"Say my name again."

"*Sam.*"

"Ask me to do anything for you. I will."

"Kiss me."

"Too easy." But he kisses me in a way that makes it feel anything but easy. "Ask me for more. Ask me to move mountains. Ask me to come back from the dead."

"Alternately, you could just fuck me until we both explode."

"You're right," he says, laying me down in his arms on the blanket. "Good idea. I'll move mountains tomorrow."

He stares into my eyes, his gaze as open as the sky. He's propped up on his forearms, holding my hands in his. "Are you ready?"

"I can't wait," I breathe and use my hips to guide him in.

When Sam fills me, the pleasure is so intense, I cry out with abandon.

"You're so sexy when you scream," he says into my neck.

I scream again. I can't seem to help it. With every thrust Sam makes, the intensity of my pleasure, our connection, builds to the point that it's impossible to not scream.

"God! Yes! You feel incredible!" I hear my words. They're what I feel, but I can't believe I'm saying them. I'm being louder and more honest than I've ever been before while having sex. Part of it's the isolated setting, but ninety-five percent of it is Sam. His hands. His hips. His heat. I let loose every ecstatic noise I never knew I had within me. I don't keep anything inside. I arch my back and look toward the sky. Toward God and whatever else is out there or in here. I feel as close to everything as breathing.

Sam's hands in my hair draw my face back down to his. I think he's going to kiss me, but instead he says, gazing deep into my eyes, his lips grazing mine as he speaks, "I would drop everything for this. For you."

AFTERWARD, WE LIE on the blanket, his fingers tracing patterns on my arm.

"I have to be honest," Sam says. "I've never come so hard in my entire life."

"Me, neither," I say. "I can still feel it. Like it's ringing in my bones."

"I think I'm paralyzed."

THE SPIRIT OF LOVE                                         93

I run my hand over his groin and feel a twitch. "There's still some movement. The prognosis is positive."

"Thank you, Doctor," he says and kisses the top of my head. "Do you want to sleep out here or hike back up to the cabin? There are benefits to both."

"Lay them out for me."

"If we stay here, we don't have to break this spell, and I'll be ready to go again in another ten minutes."

"Seriously?"

He tosses his head. "Eight to ten minutes, roughly."

"Damn." I laugh. "And if we go?"

He rolls to face me and brushes my hair out of my eyes. Am I imagining the shadow crossing his expression?

"This may be a benefit only to me," he says, "but if we sleep in my bed, I'll be able to picture you there every night after you leave."

"Can you picture me there if we have morning sex in your bed?"

He thinks a moment and then nods. "I believe I can."

"Then let's not break the spell just yet."

He nestles closer, and a moment later, Sam's asleep, snoring softly and adorably.

*In twelve hours*, my brain starts to go, and I stop it. *Not yet. Not yet. Be here, in this now, with this gently sleeping wondrous man. This is the last night with him you're going to get.*

The adder stone around my neck showed it all—my busy life, which I'll return to.

I never looked through the stone at Sam. We were interrupted.

Quietly I reach for it, trying not to wake him as I sit up. I gaze at him and then I hold up the stone and wait for magic. Insight.

I wait.

He looks the same. No secret, second life. I wonder if he needs to be awake for it to work. And then I almost laugh at how seriously I'm taking this stone's magical powers. Because of course Sam made up what he said, about the life he glimpsed through the stone. He only said things based on what I'd already told him. It isn't magic, just storytelling.

I am in the business of making up stories, but for some reason, looking at Sam sleeping, my mind is completely blank. Either he fucked all the narrative creativity out of me tonight . . . or else he's perfect, here, just as he is, and I don't need to picture him anywhere else.

I *want* to though. I want to know more about him. What else he does when I'm not here. What his plans are for Thanksgiving, and what kind of car he'll get to replace his Jeep.

He stirs and the soles of our feet touch, and it feels intoxicating. In his sleep, his lips tick up in a smile. I smile and take his hand. His eyes flutter open and he reaches for me, pulling me back into his arms.

"Where are you?" he asks.

"I'm here."

"But you're also somewhere else." His fingers trace my brows, the curve of my cheek. "Your thoughts. Where are they? Work?"

"Maybe."

"What else?" he asks, sleepily. "Stuff you need to do back home? Get your air-conditioning serviced? Buy the dog food?

THE SPIRIT OF LOVE                                          95

Make a date to break up with your boyfriend now that you've reached nirvana with a master sex god?"

I nudge him. "No boyfriend. Dog passed away last year. And it's my water heater that needs servicing. But I wasn't thinking about that."

"Good. Were you thinking about sexual transcendence?"

"Closer." I smile. "That and . . . I do have to leave tomorrow."

Sam is quiet for a moment. I start to think he might have fallen back asleep, but finally he says, very softly, "I'm into this, Fenny. If you ever start to wonder, if you ever question whether tonight was possibly this good? Whether I like you—a lot? Don't. Be as sure as I am right now."

"I'll try."

"There is no try."

"So you have seen a movie."

He kisses me one more time, and then, at last, with the universe's most powerful orgasm still ringing in all of our bones, Sam and I fall asleep.

# Chapter Eight

SHOCKING ABSOLUTELY NO ONE, SAM LOOKS FINE AS hell in a canoe. And yet, I hate the sight of it because we're pulling away from our secret beach and he's taking me to Two Harbors, where I'll catch the ferry home.

It's after noon on Sunday, and my ferry leaves at four. Sam's canoe is loaded with my backpack and the lunch I helped him pack. He didn't have anything in his fridge beyond turkey, bread, and mayonnaise, but why mess with yesterday's perfection? We've also thrown in his last bottle of sparkling wine. We'll both need a little liquid courage, because somewhere along this coastline, we're going to have to figure out how to say goodbye.

I don't know how the morning passed so quickly. Deep in the night—somewhere between my second high-decibel orgasm and sunrise—we hiked back up to his cabin. I protested this move at first but was promised a series of full-body kisses once my head hit the pillow in Sam's bed, and the man did not disappoint. The man has yet to disappoint.

I'm glad I woke up in his bed, to the sight of him watching me. To the sound of his voice asking, "How do I get inside your dreams?"

I'm taking that memory with me when I go. Along with the

hoodie Sam insisted I keep and the adder stone I'm wearing around my neck. It's warm in the center of my heart. These are my favorite souvenirs I've ever picked up. And like all souvenirs, they pale in comparison to the trip and companion they're supposed to help me remember.

Like the smell of his burnt toast again this morning.

Like the whooping ovation he gave me when I achieved exactly one pull-up on the metal bar on his ocean-facing porch before I collapsed, red-faced and aching.

Like him explaining over jasmine tea how he'd carved the fireplace, which evolved into a fireside make-out session.

I like the way my viewfinder looks around his neck as he rows. I've never met anyone who makes me want to mess with the space-time continuum, who makes me want to go back and do two days all over again. Just as they were. No notes. We wouldn't have to change a thing.

How can it be only two days since Sam unzipped my tent, since Sam unzipped me? I feel like we've known each other all our lives. I think this is because I let him see more of me this weekend than I've let other boyfriends see in years of dating.

"You look worried," Sam says as he rows. Our beach recedes behind him, the zip line barely visible. My eyes travel up to his cabin, already too far away.

"I don't want to leave," I say.

Sam stops rowing. "I'll turn this thing around right now. You can stay forever."

I laugh and put my hand on his. "I don't want to leave, but I have to. Tomorrow—"

"I hate that word," Sam says.

"It's a big moment for my career," I say.

Sam looks at the sky. "How can our timing be so perfect in bed, and on the beach—"

"And in this canoe, if you're up for it—"

"Yet so out of sync that you have to leave here when we should just be getting started?"

"I'm trying to be grateful that we got this weekend, instead of angry we didn't get more."

"Is it working?"

"Not yet."

Sam rows on. I reach into the bag for our provisions. I unwrap both sandwiches and offer him one, which he declines.

"You're not hungry?"

"I'm always hungry, but I've got to row if we're going to make it on time."

I lean forward to feed him one bite, then take a bite myself. I used to watch my mom feed my dad on long road trips. They always seemed to find an outsized pleasure in the act. I understand it now. The intimacy of watching him chew, the tenderness of timing the next bite.

I pop the cork on the cava and pour it into two aluminum flutes. We eat and drink like this as the coastline curves and juts. I'm looking at Catalina, but Sam is looking through my viewfinder at the mainland.

"You sure you don't have a boyfriend over there?"

"Let me think," I say. "Oh, yeah! There *is* a guy I forgot about. You should be really jealous. He carves fireplaces and does one-handed pull-ups . . . *at the same time!*"

THE SPIRIT OF LOVE                                        99

"Wouldn't be that hard," Sam mumbles.

I laugh. "There's no way I could be like this with you if I had a boyfriend."

Sam lets out his breath, and I'm charmed by his obvious relief.

"I'm not seeing anyone either," he says.

"Sure you don't have a steady stream of desperate house-wives sailing out from Beverly Hills?"

"Land ho!" Sam laughs but then grows serious. "It feels like a long time since I've met someone I like as much as you."

"It feels like a long time for me, too," I admit.

"Like maybe ever?" he says, holding my gaze, waiting.

"Are you asking about me, or telling me about you?"

"Both."

I swallow. I could say it, and maybe it is true, but something holds me back. "Two days isn't long enough," I whisper instead.

And then, right on cue, the gleaming white Catalina ferry comes into view.

The last time I was on that boat, I was a different person, embarking on a different trip. I don't know how to go home and be the same old me.

Yet tomorrow is a bright new day. I've got nothing but good things to look forward to, starting at nine a.m. I know that once the ferry hits thirty-two knots, that once the Port of Long Beach wraps its arms around the boat, I'll be back in the show biz mindset, back in creative mode.

But for now, I've still got the taste of a gorgeous man on my lips. Parts of me are sore that haven't been for ages. I get to be here, with him, a little longer.

"Tell me about those sunset whales," I say.

"Have you ever heard them sing?" he says.

"I think once, on PBS."

"You should come back. In a few months, they'll be all along this coastline. You can see them first thing in the morning. Sometimes I think I can feel their vibrations through my paddles."

"What do you think they sing about?"

"One says, *I am here*, and another says, *Understood—I am over here*. And finally, one of them works up the courage to say, *Want to be together?*"

"Do you think they ever fight?"

"Orcas bite each other's tongues," Sam says.

"It's not a bad way to shut someone up."

Sam looks at me with his deep brown eyes. There's a long, peaceful pause. "Hey, Fenny?"

I look up at him. "Yes?"

"Anytime you want to do this, exactly this, again? I'm down."

"Yeah? Great." I grin. "Or you could come visit me. Anytime. I think you'd like Venice. It'd be fun to show you around."

I try to picture it—curled up at a corner table at Gjelina, ordering too much pizza and wine. Bringing Sam as my plus-one to the *Zombie Hospital* dinner at the Malibu home of the president of CBS. Making my on-set trailer rock. Brunch at my sister's house in Silver Lake. Dancing with him at Olivia and Jake's wedding later this month. Sam in my bed and my shower. Sam on my roof deck, squinting through power cables at the stars.

# THE SPIRIT OF LOVE                                             101

"Maybe," he says. His eyes aren't on me, and his voice sounds distant.

"Oh," I say, surprised. "Or, yeah, maybe it's easier if I just come back here."

He grins. "Hey! We already know it works!"

"Right."

I feel my brows furrow, but I try not to read too much into this. After all, how many times does Sam have to say he wants me before I let myself believe it?

"We should swap numbers," I say. "I can't believe we haven't done that yet. I actually can't remember the last time I hung out with a guy who I hadn't texted with for days or weeks before we ever met in person. Modern romance, right?"

Sam looks away and keeps rowing. "I don't really do the phone. You know where to find me."

"Okay . . ." I blink in surprise, hurt. I turn toward the ferry, which looms up ahead. I feel embarrassed and want to be on-board it more than I thought possible twenty seconds ago.

Have I been wrong about this weekend? Is my reality askew? I consider that I never saw him with a phone this weekend. Is it possible he doesn't have one? Of course he has a phone.

"And Fenny?" he says. "Please do."

"Please do what?"

"Find me. Again."

Our bow touches the beach in the harbor where the ferry is already loading passengers. It's time to go. And I don't want to go, not with the awkward taste of this conversation in my mouth.

Sam climbs out and drags the canoe farther up onto the

beach. I grab my backpack and stumble clumsily onto the sand. "Thanks for the ride—"

But his mouth is on mine before I can finish. His hands are in my hair, and his tongue is searching for mine. His lips remind me of the tide, steady and yet surprising with the intensity of their pull. I kiss him back, surrendering completely to how aroused this man can make me in a second. I'd do anything for one more time with him.

The ferry horn blasts.

Anything but miss the last boat home and my chance to direct tomorrow. I'm weak in the knees as I pull away.

"Is it just me, or is it seven thousand degrees out there?" I gasp.

"You could come back," Sam says, like a man leaving for war. "You might."

It doesn't need to be this melodramatic. We could simply swap numbers and sext for a month like normal people until one of us says, *Hey, I bought a ferry ticket. Let's low-key hang.*

Only that doesn't seem like something Sam wants to do. And now the loudspeaker at the terminal exclaims that it's last call for anyone who needs to reach the mainland tonight.

Time's up.

"Last chance to stay forever," Sam whispers in my ear.

"Bye, Sam."

"Bye, Fenny." He nods.

I nod back like this isn't agony. Saying goodbye for a day would be hard enough—but not knowing if or when I'll ever see him again, or why he refuses to give me his number . . . it's a form of torture I've never known.

THE SPIRIT OF LOVE 103

But what can I do about it? Other than rush onto the ferry, which is so packed with tourists that there's not a single seat left. I can't even get near a window to take a final look, to prove to myself that Sam, and this whole weekend, wasn't just a dream.

 # Part Two

# Chapter Nine

*I'D LIKE YOU TO MEET JUDE DE SILVA . . .*

Near sunset on Monday evening, after my sudden, shocking demotion, I'm standing next to a two-ton saguaro cactus, watching a doom-shaped dot on my phone. Jude de Silva, known genius, *Zombie Hospital*'s new director, and Sam look-alike is getting closer.

Approximately thirty-six minutes ago, Jude shared his location with me, unprovoked, to "reduce logistical confusion." I've spent the last thirty-six minutes watching him, in avatar form, descend upon my evening.

It wasn't enough for Jude to wreck my day; now he's insisting upon a "quick chat" to curdle my night. He's been blowing up my phone ever since I fled the set at the first reasonable opportunity this afternoon. I assumed he'd be too busy to notice, too much of an utter genius to care . . . but he noticed. And he seems to care.

I can't stop seeing Jude's—Sam's—face from this morning. He'd looked so genuinely excited to waltz in and steal my dream.

*Zombie Hospital's new director.*

Jude is the last person I want to see, but he insisted we do this, so I'm taking some pleasure imagining him in eastbound evening rush hour, coming to meet me in this part of town. I don't know where Jude lives, but for most Angelinos, Pasadena is *very* inconvenient, which was at least one good reason to invite him here. That and I was already here at the Huntington Gardens, still with hours to kill before Olivia's dress fitting at a bridal shop up the street.

But Jude didn't balk when I dropped the pin. He shared his location and got on the 101.

The Huntington Gardens, LA's prized botanical gem, keep occasional late hours in September, winding down their "Summer Evening Strolls" series. When I arrived an hour ago, the tranquil Japanese garden felt too Zen, and the lush rose garden, too superior. When I found myself among the cactuses, the flora finally fit my mood.

Because my rage continues to blossom like an *Adenium obesum*, otherwise known as the desert rose. Which is poisonous.

I figured I could stay a while among the burrs and needles because I'm not meeting my friends at the bridal shop until eight. Olivia made special arrangements to keep the store open late to accommodate my schedule . . . back when I was supposed to direct today. Back before Jude de Silva, director from another vector, pierced my heart and soul.

My palms are damp and my chest feels tight because Jude is close and getting closer. And I'm still so upset I don't think I should see anyone, let alone my new boss and the source of all my rage.

If he wants an apology or even an explanation for what happened in Rich's office this morning, I may accidentally impale him on a dragon fruit tree. The only upside to this encounter

THE SPIRIT OF LOVE                                    109

might be seeing him in natural light and confirming with clear eyes that he's not . . . that he has nothing on Sam.

I smile because that's what happens now when I think of Sam. But the smile soon fades. Sam's so far away, he might as well be a dream. Jude is my *now*, my waking nightmare.

I hear footsteps, and I know it's him. I don't want to look up, but I do. At the sight of him—still in his suit from today, his face fixed on his screen, pursuing my pin—I let out a breath that feels like it's been stuck in my lungs since the meeting in Rich's office. Jude doesn't carry his shoulders like Sam. He doesn't walk like Sam. He doesn't take in the natural world like he's grateful to be participating in it, like Sam.

His hands, though, they're familiar. And I wonder if I went to him and took his hand in mine, if my skin would know the answer. Not that I will *ever* take Jude de Silva by the hand.

When he finally looks up, he seems startled by his surroundings, like he hadn't known until now he was in a botanical garden at all. And then he looks at me. And his dark eyes go soft, a little downturned at the corners. His brow smooths out, like day two of a really good vacation. And there is *something*. I don't know. Something reminiscent of the man I fell for last weekend. He smiles, and my stomach twists the way it does right before a kiss. I have to look away and hope Jude doesn't see the heat rising to my cheeks.

"Fenny."

"Jude."

"I found you." He glances at the saguaro over my head. "So you're into cactuses?"

I raise an eyebrow. "When I'm in certain moods."

"Nature's wisest plant. They never let down their guard."

"Inspiring. Is that a Glennon Doyle quote? Or some team-building trope you're developing for tomorrow?"

"Funny," he says, dry as a desert garden. "I'm not above team-building. Are you?"

"The thing is, Jude. This team—*Zombie Hospital*—it's pretty much already built. We saved you the effort, long ago."

"Right, so I've learned. I got to talk to the rest of the cast and crew today, but I didn't have a chance to connect with you. You left so early."

"Something came up."

*You did, dickhead.*

"Everything okay?" He tips his head, and I have to look away again because from a couple of angles, despite the beard, despite the hair, despite the arrogance, there is something Sam-like about him.

Is this what happens to me when I fall for someone? I see them in everyone, including the worst possible people in my life? Is there a medication to undo this particular mindfuck?

"I can manage," I say.

"Thanks for meeting me here," Jude says awkwardly, looking around him. "It's like a scene in a film noir." He levels his gaze at me. "Should we walk?"

He gestures toward a fork in the path lined with succulents named Silk Pinwheel and Moonlight Jenny. I keep my eyes on the plants and the plaques that bear their names, anything so I don't have to look at him.

A warm breeze rustles through the plants as we walk, carry-

THE SPIRIT OF LOVE 111

ing the fruity scent of prickly pears. We're the only souls in the cactus garden.

"So," Jude says. "We're going to be working closely together. Do you have any questions for me? Do you want to know my background, or—"

"No, thanks. I'm good."

"You're . . . good?" he says. "You have no interest in learning anything about me?"

"I know enough."

"I heard you went to film school at UCLA. That's impressive. I—"

"Please don't," I say. "Just don't."

"Don't what?"

"Don't play the fancy school game. Rich went to Harvard. Adele went to Yale. You probably went to the American Film Institute. No one cares."

"I didn't go to film school. Applied, but didn't get in."

"Can I borrow your pocket square?" I ask.

"Sure," Jude says, reaching into his breast pocket. "Are you alright?"

"I just need to wipe the tears from my eyes. Your story is *so sad.*"

"Got it." He tucks away his pocket square.

"Come on. It's obvious why you're here. An unexpected delay in the shooting schedule for your next film? Perfect timing to take a giant paycheck. You're just another masturbating nihilist with a slight sense of humor."

"You've seen my films? You think they're nihilistic?"

"I don't need you to pretend to care about *Zombie Hospital,* or any of the people who work on it. We already care. We care enough."

"You've got it wrong."

I laugh. "Oh, I can't wait to be corrected."

"I'm a huge fan of the show."

"Bullshit."

"It's true. I—"

"Spare me. Let's just do the work and then leave each other alone after hours to live our lives."

"Right." He nods, as if this is an unusual request he's trying to figure out how to accommodate. "Are you married, Fenny? Kids?"

"Yeah, I've got nine husbands and six kids. They should be around here somewhere."

"What's your life like, outside this cactus garden?"

"I don't have one. The evil fairies won't let me leave."

He's quiet for a beat. Our footsteps crunch along the path.

"I work a lot," he finally says. "Wow, that sounds pathetic."

I sigh, saddened by the fact that lips shaped so much like Jude's spoke to me in a cabin on an island just the other day about a love of hiking and fishing, cliff-diving and zip-lining. Jude must do something in his spare time. What's he hiding? And why on earth should I open up to him if he's this closed with me?

"How'd your other meetings go today?" I ask him. Aurora. Buster. Can any of them be counted on to help sabotage Jude's working experience for me? Would any of them—I wonder— have told Jude he replaced me? Does he know?

He didn't shoot at all today. He took meetings with the cast

# THE SPIRIT OF LOVE                    113

and crew on the soundstage all day long. The word I got from Ivy is that he needed to get his bearings, and that he's reordering my shooting schedule entirely, starting tomorrow.

"The meetings were pretty awkward," he says. "I used a script."

I stop walking and look over at him, his hands clasped behind his back.

"What? I was nervous."

"Hand it over," I say and put out my palm.

Jude sighs, knowing defeat. From his suit pocket, he passes me a crumpled piece of paper. I unfold it and read the rushed cursive:

*1. What's your favorite thing about the show?*
*2. How best can I help you reach your dreams?*
*3. What would you be doing with your life if not this?*

I give him back the paper. "What ingenious questions. Truly genre-defying."

"You're harder to impress than Danny DeVito at a table read. I'm doing my best here, Fenny."

"I'll answer the third one," I say.

"Really? Okay. Great."

Jude faces me, and suddenly I feel a little nervous about what I'm about to say. Then I remember he deserves it. You don't want none, don't start none.

"I'd be a wilderness EMT," I say. "You know? Search and Rescue. Somewhere cool like Catalina Island."

Jude's chin tips up slightly. He clears his throat. He licks his lips. "It feels like you're trying to tell me something. Do you want to tell me something, Fenny?"

"Nope, it just seems like a cool job."

"Uh-huh." He nods, inscrutable. A beat passes when we just stare at each other. I go from wanting him to confess—that what, he ate Sam's heart and stole his body?—to getting lost enough in our staring contest that I forget what we were talking about in the first place. My chest warms. I hold my breath. Finally, Jude looks away.

"Want to know what I'd be doing?" he asks, running a hand through his close-cropped dark hair.

"Why not."

He takes a deep breath and lets it out. "Nothing."

I look at him. Wait for more.

He looks down at his feet and toes the pebble in the path with his brogues. "I was in a bad way when I came to Hollywood. Sleeping on my friend Matt's couch while I made my first film on less than a shoestring budget, credit card debt, and favors from Matt and his friends. I had no experience outside of one film class in college, just this kind of vision for what the film could be."

"So you just willed *Brujo of the Maypole* into being?" I ask, skeptical.

He tosses his head. "Matt showed the rough cut to a producer friend, and we got lucky with distribution. But what I'm trying to say is that directing saved me. I fell in love with it. And I think this is *it* for me. I don't—can't—see another life."

I want more details, but I don't want to ask. Jude has gotten my attention, but I'm still angry. He got such a big break right

# THE SPIRIT OF LOVE                    115

out of the gate and then showed up this morning and took mine, too.

"I'm going to level with you, Fenny. I can tell you're not happy about the direction we're going in. I can't imagine Rich sprung that on you nicely."

Oh, wow. He's going to go there. Am I ready for this? To hear him defend stealing my job?

"Rich isn't known for his bedside manner," I say, leaving the conversation open, leading him to the edge of the cliff.

I realize Jude is right, that I should be mad at Rich primarily. And I am, but I also expect it from Rich. I'm used to it with Rich. And as of this morning, there's so much rage in me that it has to flow out somewhere, and maybe it's like lightning. The tallest thing in the room attracts it.

Jude stops walking and gathers himself, like a man about to make his toast. "To be a writer of your talent and experience," he says, "and to be asked to do extensive rewrites on the eve of principle photography—I can see why you're frustrated."

A *writer* of my talent and experience? No mention of directing. Is it possible he just thinks I'm pissed about some extra work?

"I want to encourage you," Jude says, "to feel free. Try something new. This may sound weird, but imagine these rewrites are . . . a fling. You're having an affair with the script. Something you wouldn't say yes to forever, but for a little while, you'll give it a whirl."

I roll my eyes. "Just grasp that script and spread my legs?"

"Well—I—"

"Let it take me from behind?"

"I was only—"

I roll my eyes again. That's not the way my work works for me. I'm methodical about my research. I don't whirl. I don't fling. I *did* fling last weekend; I took my eye off the ball for forty-eight hours, and look where it got me: my job stolen. I know there's no causal connection between my fling with Sam and Jude ruining the next year of my life. He was already on his way in to wreck it, regardless of how many beachfront orgasms I had last weekend.

I give Jude a skeptical look. "You're the expert on flings?"

"God, no." He laughs. The tips of his ears turn pink. "Actually, my ex broke up with me over this show."

I point at him. "That I would like to hear more about."

"We were watching last year's season finale, and I kept rewinding parts to show her again, to make sure she got the jokes, the references, the cultural vocabulary. She wasn't laughing at anything. She was just . . . eating. Finally, I put my hand over her quinoa salad—"

I burst out laughing.

"Yeah, Lisa did not like that. We had a huge fight, and a lot of other stuff came up, but anyway . . . I think it was for the best."

"You broke up over *Zombie Hospital*?" I'm stupefied yet a little thrilled.

"I take the media I love seriously. And while Lisa was moving her stuff out the next day, I emailed Amy Reisenbach—"

"The president of CBS?"

He nods, like this is no big deal. "I asked if there was ever anything she could do to get me on the show."

THE SPIRIT OF LOVE                                    117

I stare at him. "Sorry, you did what?"

He lifts a shoulder, casual. "I told her it was the sharpest writing I'd seen on network TV in years, and I wanted to get in however I could." He's studying me. He smiles and a light goes on in his eyes. A light that reminds me of Sam because it's . . . kind. "You wrote that episode."

"It was a joint effort," I manage to croak out, suddenly feeling like I might be sick. Holy Catalina. Jude de Silva is here because of *me*.

"Sure," he says, "but you got the credit, which means it was yours originally. I checked. That's why I wanted to talk to you today in particular. I've been looking forward to meeting you for what feels like a long time. Although I have to say, you're not exactly what I expected."

I narrow my eyes. "Meaning?"

"You're younger than I guessed. Also, more . . . female."

"You thought I was an old man because I'm funny?"

"That's not what I mean. I couldn't tell from your name, and IMDb doesn't have a picture." His eyes pan my face, like he's uploading the missing photo with his mind.

"Also," he says hesitantly, "what happened in Rich's office this morning threw me for a loop. What was that about?"

He's looking at me for an explanation, but I don't owe him anything. He should see the loop he threw me for. I'm still in it, shrieking inwardly, begging to be let off. And now I can't even blame him. He clearly doesn't know I was meant to direct this season and he's ruining my life because I wrote a good episode. I brought this on myself.

"Gardens are closed," a green-jacketed security guard says,

rounding a bank of blue agave. He points a flashlight toward a wide path and says, "Exit's that way."

"So ends our film noir," I say to Jude.

"'I steal,'" Jude whispers.

"What?" I ask, startled.

"That's the last line of *I Am a Fugitive from a Chain Gang*," Jude says. "My favorite film noir."

I *love* that movie, too. Edie and I used to watch it with my dad on the couch in our garage, but I don't tell this to Jude de Silva. Even if he's not just here for the paycheck, even if he does claim to be a fan of the show, he's still my competition. Not my colleague. Not my friend.

# Chapter Ten

"WOW, ROUGH DAY?" SAYS THE WOMAN IN THE PANT-suit who opens the door when I buzz at LouLou's Bridal.

"It's that obvious?" I'd planned to make it inside the shop, and hopefully into the comforting arms of my friends, before my total emotional breakdown. But this woman—with her blond ponytail pulled regulation tight and her taupe lipstick matching her taupe uniform—tells me with one look of her pale-blue eyes that she can read me like a billboard.

I spent the drive from the Huntington Gardens to the bridal shop imploding like the big bang in reverse.

Because the reason for my crisis is entirely my fault. I did the thing I've spent my whole life trying to do: I moved someone with my work. The poetic justice is a little absurd.

Sure, Rich and the president of CBS helped out by being douchebags. By sidelining me because they know I'll wait my increasingly long turn. By bowing to the industry's overinflated idea of Jude's worth compared to mine. But the real shock here is that my current situation isn't actually Jude's fault. All he did was laugh at my jokes.

I imagine him in his living room, fighting over quinoa salad and my writing with some beautiful girlfriend. Ex-girlfriend.

And now that I know all this, I have to go back to work

tomorrow, demoted, but I don't even get to hate him for it. Which leaves me feeling a little adrift. If I can't blame Jude de Silva for stealing my job—if I am, in fact, the master of this disaster—then what the hell *can* I blame him for?

It's his eyes I can't stop thinking about—and believe me, I have tried. At sunset tonight, I was sure of it: same color, close in shape, similarly unforgettable brows as Sam.

And yes, I know it's impossible.

Maybe everything that happened today was so shocking, it was the emotional equivalent of a blunt blow to the head. And now I'm concussed and confused, wishing I had amnesia.

Google failed to help me sort it out. She served up plenty of Getty images where I could study Jude de Silva's eyes from the safety of my car. Google was scarcer on images of Sam, whose last name I somehow never caught. His face didn't pop up when I tried his first name + a slew of reasonable keywords.

*Sam + Parsons Landing*

*Sam + Search and Rescue*

*Sam + carpenter + Jet Ski + sex stallion*

In sum, I couldn't do a proper side-by-side comparison, which means I'm having to rely on my memory of Sam.

Similar eyes, but not the same. Sam's eyes are blown wide with wonder and presence, but Jude's eyes . . . *aren't*, on some fundamental level. Even on the red carpet, surrounded by staggering beauty, Jude's eyes look closed to the world's possibilities. Not color-blind. Beauty-blind.

They look different in person. Tonight in the garden, when we were alone, when Jude was telling me he had not a single hobby, he looked at me straight on. And he looked—I don't

THE SPIRIT OF LOVE                                    121

know—a little lonely, a little lost. Like all of us are sometimes. But Jude de Silva's inner world is not my problem. I don't care what's missing from his life; I just want him out of mine.

"Ma'am?" the woman still in the door of the bridal shop says.

"Sorry. Hi. It's just this guy . . . two guys . . . no one."

"Ah," the woman says knowingly. "Repeat after me."

I realize I'm ready to repeat anything this total stranger says. Is this how cults recruit?

"Men," the woman says.

"Men," I say.

"Are the devil."

I laugh, but the woman isn't amused.

"Say it," she says sternly.

"Are the devil," I say, carefully enunciating. "Men are devils."

"Welcome to the fitting," she sings, dancing out of the way. "Champagne is everywhere."

"Thank you?"

"I'm Yas, your bridal stylist. Your friends are in there already." She tilts her ponytail toward the interior of the small shop, where racks of white taffeta make a pure and glowing forcefield as far as the credit card can see.

I step past Yas onto plush pale-pink carpet and inhale rose-scented candles. There are worse places to melt down.

"I've been serving the bride bubbles," Yas calls from a wet bar on the far side of the room. "Can I offer you—"

"A healthy pour for me," I say.

"Fenny!" Masha curves toward me like a fairy in a taupe terry-cloth LouLou's Bridal dressing robe. Her dark curly hair is pulled back loosely in a bun, and her other bun, the one in the oven, is just beginning to rise. I blow her belly kisses. She gives my shoulders a squeeze. "I can't wait to hear everything. *Everything*."

I've been friendly with Masha ever since we both joined the same book club a few years ago. I admired her instantly. Her job as conservator of antiquities at the Getty Villa seemed so cool, and her comments about the book were glib and insightful—a clear indicator of good friend material. But for years, we stayed in an acquaintance holding pattern. Masha's an introvert, and I have introverted tendencies, and sometimes two such likely friends can orbit each other for years without either one making a move.

It took us running into each other at the massive CBS Christmas party last year, where Masha introduced me to her oldest friend, Olivia Dusk, for things to really click. The moment I met Olivia we started cracking each other up with our impressions of old-Hollywood dames. She does a pristine Katharine Hepburn dropping the olive in *Bringing Up Baby*, and no one can beat my Bette Davis landing on a cactus in *The Bride Came C.O.D.* Masha, it turns out, does a mean Myrna Loy—chin up, eyes narrow, pretending not to be absolutely charmed. By the time we started talking about our favorite recent movies, I felt like the three of us had been friends in another life.

We were three undrinkable chardonnays in at that point, so, like the candid poet I am, I announced my everlasting devotion:

"You two," I said. I pointed at them and shook my head as I searched for further language. "You two."

Olivia hugged me tight and said she knew exactly what I

THE SPIRIT OF LOVE                                123

meant. The three of us clicked into a triangle of close friendship, laughing for hours and never looking back.

Now Masha fills my hands with hers and tugs me toward the dressing room. "Olivia? Fenny's here!"

"Right out!" I hear Olivia's muffled voice call. It sounds like she's deep inside many layers of a gown.

"How was the doctor's appointment?" I smile at Masha's belly, which is the happiest thing I've seen all day.

"Eli Junior is auditioning for the Rockettes," Masha groans as she flops down on the couch. "And my feet are so swollen they look like I am, too. But fuck that—how did your first day of directing go?"

I fall face-first onto the couch and feel the largest sob of all time rising in my chest—

"Wait!" Olivia calls from behind the curtain. "I'm stuck with one boob in and one boob out of this dress, but I need to be out there for this download! I want to hear all about the shoot, and all about Catalina!"

"I can help with your boobs," Yas calls, waltzing into Olivia's dressing room.

Masha strokes the back of my head. "Fenny? You okay?"

I hear a squeak. A zip. The casting aside of a curtain.

"Wow, you're good," Olivia tells Yas as she steps into the shop's main room wearing nothing but a slip. "Fenny, what's wrong?"

Then both of my friends are at my side, and although I can't think of a more sympathetic audience, I'm still dreading what I have to say. Because telling your best friends the disastrous details of your life makes the disaster real.

It's all a dream until you say it out loud to someone you love.

"Upsy-daisy." Olivia rolls me over, hoisting me up on the couch until I'm looking into her soft brown eyes. "Take it from the top."

"Did something go wrong on set?" Masha asks, scooting closer. "It was just your first day. I tell Eli this every time he's starting new rehearsals: It takes time to get in a flow—"

"There will be no flow," I say, blowing my nose on the tissue Masha hands me from her purse.

Yas holds out a tray with flutes of champagne. I toss back one glass quickly and then reach for another.

"What do you mean 'no flow'?" Olivia asks. "Wait, you're not pregnant, too, are you?"

The next thing I know, the three of us are curled up together on the couch, sipping champagne and sparkling water. Masha brings out a Tupperware of pierogies. Yas keeps topping us up and then goes back to pinning the bust of Olivia's middle-finger-to-tradition, deep-purple wedding gown.

"I've been replaced."

Masha gasps. "On your first day?"

"What's his name, and where do I find him?" Olivia's face twitches. She's gone into fight mode. "I'm going to make Beyoncé's video for 'Hold Up' look like a bouncy-house party."

"Jude de Silva," I say through my teeth.

"*JDS*?" Olivia says, hand to her mouth.

"Why are you calling him that?" I ask.

"People call him that. The internet. Emmanuel Macron. Jake."

THE SPIRIT OF LOVE                                    125

"Oh, really? Whose side is Jake on?" I dare her to respond.

"Jake had JDS on the show when his latest film premiered," Olivia says. "He has a reputation for being very intense, but actually, he and Jake hit it off."

"Ahhhhhhhhhhh!" I cry and resume my face-down position.

Now the whole awful story tumbles out. I tell my friends about the vision board I made for Buster, about Aurora's gift this morning, about Ivy running to get me, and the horror film that followed, right up to the compliment bomb Jude de Silva detonated two hours ago in the Huntington cactus garden.

"So in a way, he's your biggest fan *and* your biggest rival?" Olivia says, biting into a pierogi and then slyly trying to put it back in the Tupperware and take another. "That's going to be tricky."

Masha busts her pierogi switcheroo, handing Olivia back the half-eaten one. "Mushrooms are good for you."

"I know," Olivia whines. "But I like pork better."

"Or maybe he was lying?" I wonder aloud. "What he said about my writing. Just trying to butter me up so I don't throw a wrench in the works? Oh my God, it almost worked."

"That feels like a stretch," Masha says gently.

"There's something about him," I go on, reaching for more champagne. "Something that's not quite right. Like he's hiding something. Wearing a mask."

"But isn't that why people move to LA?" Olivia asks. "To hide the ugly things inside? To try on endless masks?"

"You're right. Who cares about his secrets," I say, crossing that one off my mental list of bullet points. "The problem is, he has no idea what he's doing. I need to get rid of him. For the good of the show."

"Of course," Liv nudges me. "For the good of the show."

I watch her and Masha exchange glances over my head. I put down my champagne because I need them to take me seriously. I need to focus, to make a plan.

"That's not the worst part," I tell them.

Olivia and Masha look at each other again.

"Jude de Silva also . . . bears an uncanny resemblance to . . . to . . ." I hold my face in my hands.

"To who?" Olivia demands.

"To a man I met this weekend."

"WHAT?" Masha and Olivia say together.

I close my eyes and tell myself I'm safe. I try to transport myself to that beach on Catalina. To Friday night, when I'd been happily sheltering in my tent, preparing for the shoot that wasn't to be. I've lived so many lifetimes since that sundown, but still, it's strangely easy to go right back to the moment when Sam unzipped my tent.

"His name is Sam. We met Friday night, and I ended up staying with him. At his cabin. All weekend."

"Girl, you've been holding out on your friends," Yas says.

"There's more. When we slept together, it melted my bones," I say. "Or maybe my brain. I think something's wrong with me now. Because this morning on set, I really thought that Jude *was* Sam."

Masha nods at me. "Unpack that a little for us."

"Do they look alike?" Olivia asks.

"Yes and no. Jude is older. And their hair and clothes and

THE SPIRIT OF LOVE 127

vibes could not be more different, but somehow I still . . . acted like an absolute lunatic when we met. I acted like he was Sam."

"I used to see my ex everywhere," Yas says. "Cutting me off in his Audi on Crescent Heights and Melrose—"

"You're right," I say. "I'm losing my mind."

"That's actually not what I was saying—"

"There's nothing wrong with you, Fenny," Masha says, putting a hand on my arm. "You just had a big shock today."

"And this weekend, too, it seems," Olivia says. "Meet-cute, *now*. How did all this happen with Sam?"

And so, while Yas helps Olivia back into her thousand-buttons dress, I tell them this story, too. About the weekend, the storm, the evacuation, Sam's Jeep and the cabin, and the beauty he showed me on the island. I keep my eyes closed so I can see him, keep him distinct from Jude. It's easy—it's a warm and happy memory. But when I open my eyes, it feels so far away that it hurts.

"Name, age, occupation?" Masha asks me. "You and I agree, these details matter."

"And what about the first moment you knew you wanted him?" Olivia says.

"Sam. Twenty-three." I wait for my friends to finish whistling. "Catalina Island Conservancy Search and Rescue." I look at Olivia, grateful for her question. "I knew I wanted him when . . . well, first we had a little disagreement over whether or not I needed to evacuate the campsite."

"Go on," Oliva says, sitting down on a stool facing the couch.

"At a certain point he kind of tossed me over his shoulder. And climbed the mountain with me in his arms."

128          LAUREN KATE

"Holy shit," Masha says.

"For a split second, I was furious, but once I felt myself in his arms, everything shifted. I pretended to be just as pissed as ever—"

"I've seen you do that very convincingly," Olivia says.

"But I knew. The chemistry was undeniable. Like, on a carbon level. And then, he just kept surprising me."

"Keep talking," Olivia says, crossing her legs. "This is gold."

"You know the game Scattergories?" I ask.

Masha nods. "Eli and I play it on Tuesday nights."

"Of course you do," Olivia says and turns to me. "Do not tell me you bonded over board games. This triangle already has a Masha."

"No. You know the die that comes with the game?" I ask.

"With all the letters?" Masha says.

"Your man," Yas explains, like everyone but her is an idiot, "has many different sides."

"Yes," I say. "He was this bossy rescue hero man who turned into a gracious bed-and-breakfast host, then a ferocious body-builder, then a gifted artist whose medium is wood—"

"But whose wood, I gather, isn't medium," Olivia says.

"He was such a *boy*," I say, delaying the inevitable sex discussion. "Not just because he's younger. I mean, like, the kind you fall for at first, when you're finding out how it feels to have a crush." I sigh. "He built a zip line."

"For you?" Masha asks.

"We went jet-skiing and spearfishing. We traded viewfinders. His was a stone he found on the beach—" I touch my hand

THE SPIRIT OF LOVE 129

to my chest where I'm still wearing the adder stone, tucked under my shirt.

"Terrific foreplay," Olivia says.

I close my eyes and let myself remember Sam kissing my naked body on the beach. How it hadn't felt ridiculous when he proposed moving mountains. For me.

"When are you seeing him again?" Masha asks.

"I don't know." I don't want to tell them about my final moments yesterday with Sam, the strained and noncommittal way we said goodbye. "Maybe it was just a fling."

Olivia shakes her head. "Fenny don't fling."

"It's true. I don't. Unless, maybe . . . I did? I don't even know his last name."

"Fenny," Masha says, "you know where Sam lives. If you want to see him again, you simply go back to Catalina, knock on his door. He'll be thrilled to see you."

"Olivia," I implore. "Please reason with this raging romantic. She and Eli agreed on the name of their firstborn child before they finished their first kiss."

"Masha believes in love," Olivia concedes, shoulder bumping her oldest friend. "Maybe it's time you did, too."

I put my face in my hands again. "Not cool."

"Look," Olivia tells me, "I know what it's like to feel you've missed your only sail on destiny's dreamboat. I know what it's like to waste *years* blaming that missed chance on *him*. I'm also living proof that second chances are real. And they don't seize themselves. Maybe right now it feels like you'll never see Sam again. Like it was a fling and it's over. But someday, Fen? You, too, could be one boob in and one boob out of a dress you might be allergic to." She sneezes, and Masha fishes out a Zyrtec from her purse.

"I don't know," I say sadly. "I think it's over. Just like my career. Maybe I should quit the show," I say.

"No!" Olivia says.

"You're *not* quitting," Masha says.

"Maybe you take a few personal days," Olivia says, getting an idea. "Just while you sort out your emotions around these very real, complex life challenges. I like this plan because it would also allow you to skip that *Zombie Hospital* travel shoot Sunday and join us for my skydiving bachelorette!"

Masha winces. "That's still the plan for your bachelorette?"

Olivia crosses her arms. "It will never not be the plan. 'Our valor is to chase what flies'!"

"No, you're right," I say. "I can't quit. And I can't miss the travel shoot. Who but me can stop Jude from fucking up everything we had planned for the season opener? No, I'll just have to sit on the sidelines, watching him live my dream." I muster a smile for Olivia. "Otherwise, you know I'd jump out of a plane with you any day," I say, mouthing to Masha behind Olivia's back, *Not.*

The door to LouLou's chimes, and in glides Olivia's mom and podcast cohost, the inimitable Lorena Dusk. She's decked out in one of her mai-tai-shaded ombré pantsuits with an orchid behind her ear.

"Liv, baby!" Lorena says, tearing up, palms cupped to her face. "You look like a princess, honey. I see you at the altar with curls. It's perfect. All we have to do is dye the dress white—"

THE SPIRIT OF LOVE                                    131

"Mom, my palette is purple and green—"

"White is purity, baby. It's tradition. Vir—"

"Don't say *virginal*. That's exactly why Jake and I are eschewing it. We like purple and green."

"Then . . . I like purple and green!" Lorena says. "Your late father, on the other hand, may he rest—"

"Mom!" Olivia says. "Sit down. Talk to Fenny while Yas gets me out of this dress. Tell her Jung's take on synchronicities!"

"What about some champagne for the matriarch?" Lorena calls out, sitting down next to me. "A synchronicity, honey, is an acausal connecting principal. Linked events stronger than coincidence that occur separately in time. They can't be explained, only acknowledged." She smirks. "You know, my daughter only invokes psychological buzzwords when she wants to shut me up, but if you actually want to know—"

"I do, Lorena," I say, clinking my glass sadly with hers. "I need help."

After Masha, Olivia, and Yas help me fill in Lorena on each new cringeworthy angle of my life, Lorena sits for a moment and thinks.

"Classic presentation of erotic conflation," the mistress of advice says at last.

"So what does that mean?" I ask. "How bad is it?"

"Well, I made it up," Lorena says. "But you seeing the same physical features in your work rival as in your recent fling tells me that there's something not quite right about the connection you made with this Sam individual. There's a rift somewhere between you two, something you don't want to confront."

"I wanted to stay in touch," I admit. "I don't think he did."

"What a fool," Lorena says kindly. "So you're superimposing Sam's features onto Jude de Silva, a completely separate person whom, due to professional circumstances, you are already primed to hate. To destroy. Your subconscious is helping you set emotional boundaries with Sam via the physical form of Jude. I'd recommend not shying away from this Jude de Silva. Love him or hate him, there's something he's showed up to teach you."

# Chapter Eleven

"I'M SORRY, FEN, I'VE GOT NOTHING," MY SISTER SAYS the next morning from her sunny Silver Lake breakfast nook. Edie's wearing her pink bathrobe that should probably be washed, and the same goes for her hair, but she still looks like an empress, nursing her seven-month-old son Jarvis with one arm and using the other to internet sleuth on my behalf.

"That's impossible," I say, whisking almond extract, my secret ingredient, into the batter I'm making in Edie's kitchen. It's six a.m. on a Tuesday, an uncivilized hour to descend on anyone, unless they happen to have three children under three who can't get enough of their Aunt Fenny's pancakes. "You're the best online detective I know. Your gift for key words is unmatched—"

"Well, you've finally found a weirdo who can stump me," Edie says, in a cooing baby voice, grinning down at Jarvis. "Yes, she has. Yes. Why did Auntie do that? I don't know either."

I halve and then spoon the pulp from three passion fruits I plucked from Edie's vines on my way into her house. Left to simmer in a saucepan with a bit of sugar, the fruit will reduce to a decadent tropical syrup just in time to serve over the pancakes. I preheat the griddle, add a healthy pat of butter, and think about Sam's cozy cabin kitchen on the two mornings I'd spent there. The smell of burnt toast . . . the clove and hickory scent of him when he wrapped his arms around me.

"He was my kind of weirdo. That's what made the weekend so—"

"Magical? So you've said a few times." Edie looks at her laptop screen. "All I'm seeing about Search and Rescue on Catalina Island is a hiking accident from like ten years ago. Right around the time your young cowboy would have been going through puberty, right? So I don't think it's him."

I frown, dolloping batter onto the sizzling pan. A heavenly aroma fills the air, and I hear Edie's twin two-year-olds Teddy and Frank squeal "Pancakes!" from the living room couch, where they're watching *SpongeBob*. Which means time is running out before this conversation goes from adult to feral.

"What dirt are you hoping to find about Sam anyway?" Edie asks me. "You know he lives off the grid. You're not going to unearth some illuminating TikTok account, or even, like, LinkedIn."

"I need to know if he has a brother . . . or a cousin or another close relative who is male—"

"Why? Can't we just assume those odds are good?" Edie sidles by me in the kitchen on her way to refill her coffee. In her arms, Jarvis grabs hold of my hair, tucking it in a vice grip between his gums. That the three of us can hold this pose gracefully for as long as it takes for Edie to re-caffeinate, me to flip a pancake, and Jarv to get his fix of my hair feels like a testament to our bond. This was the right place to come to solidify my on-set warpath.

"Because I know there's some connection between Sam and JDS."

# THE SPIRIT OF LOVE                                    135

"Other than both of them screwing you in the past week?"

"Other than that. In addition to that." I reach into Edie's cupboard for the chocolate chips, because what better way to send twin toddler boys into a day of preschool than with a battering ram of sugar in their stomachs? "If I'm going to declare war on Jude de Silva, and he ends up being the first cousin of the love of my life—"

"Whoa," Edie says. "Love of your life?"

"I just think I should go into battle with as much knowledge as possible," I say.

"I like the advice Lorena gave you last night," Edie says. "It's far more likely that your brain erotically conflated these two men than that they're close blood relatives. She should patent that term."

"PANCAAAAAKES!" Teddy and Frank dive-bomb into the kitchen to the tune of the *SpongeBob* closing credits. Each twin wraps himself around one of my legs as I frog-walk their steaming plates to the table. Now they clamor up to the breakfast nook, pressing in either side of their mother like Edie is a human pillow. Jarvis, usually chill, begins to wail.

"I didn't forget you, Jarv," I sing, passing Edie a bowl of torn-up pancake bites for the red-faced baby, who tucks into them as his hiccups and sniffles subside.

"You hungry, Ede?" I ask her, making an adult plate, which I'll top with the passion fruit syrup.

My sister closes her eyes. "My sustenance is silence," she says as her children chew.

"I'll leave a plate in the oven for you," I offer. "It'll still be warm when the boys leave for school."

136                                    LAUREN KATE

"Morning, Fenny," says my brother-in-law, coming into the kitchen smelling like aftershave and the cedar shoe-stuffers I got him for Christmas. Todd works the sports desk on the same news channel where Edie works as a meteorologist. He looks at the plate in my hands. "That for me? Looks incredible."

Edie and I roll our identical eyes, but I hand the plate to Todd and make a second one to save for Edie. Todd sits like an island across the table from his wife and three kids. He tries to mime a kiss at Edie, but she's pulling pancake out of Teddy's hair.

"So what's wrong today?" Todd asks me.

"Why do you always assume something is wrong with me?" I ask.

He answers through a huge mouthful of pancakes. "Because you cook when you're angry."

"I do not cook when I'm angry," I say, defensive, and then, turning to my sister, "Do I cook when I'm angry? Are we even talking to him today?"

"No," Edie says, as if just remembering. She levels a gaze at her husband. "Because *someone* thinks it's perfectly appropriate to show his mother our credit card bills."

"For the twelfth time, babe," Todd says with remarkable patience, "I didn't *show* her. She happened to glance. She's a glancer. We know this about her."

"She keeps a letter opener in her purse," Edie says, and I swallow back a laugh.

"Completely unrelated! She's just too nervous to carry mace in case one of her dogs get into her purse, and she once had a thing in a parking lot—"

"Whatever," Edie says through gritted teeth. "I don't want

## THE SPIRIT OF LOVE                                   137

her judging my skin care purchases anymore. Once was enough. And Fenny doesn't cook when she's angry!"

"What's *skin cawe*?" Frank lisps, sliding down from the table.

"It's Mommy's version of *SpongeBob*," I say. "It makes her happy."

I watch as Todd slides into the seat Frank vacated so he, too, can be next to my sister. I wonder how it feels having so many male bodies pressed against you all the time. Does Edie ever want to scream? Build a moat around her body? Run out the door and never come back?

But then I watch as Todd gently lifts the baby from her arms—Jarv has dozed off with a piece of pancake between his lips. Todd removes the pancake morsel, pops it in his own mouth, and with his spare hand, gives my sister's neck a massage, which I can see she deeply needs. She closes her eyes and lets her head drop forward, onto the table.

"Breathe, baby," he says. "I'll have a word with Mom about snooping, okay? It doesn't mean we need to forbid her from entering the house, right?"

My sister huffs as if she'll think about it. Todd kneads her shoulder tenderly. He kisses the side of her head.

"Because Grandma also loves to babysit," he reminds Edie softly. "And iron."

"She does like to iron," Edie says on an inhale.

"Just breathe, love. Let it out."

My sister, now a human puddle, exhales deeply. I realize she might not want that invisible fence after all.

She looks up at me and nods. "You know what? Todd's right. You do cook when you're angry."

"That's cheating, Todd!" I scoff. "The massage?"

"Last Christmas," Edie says to me, "when you were breaking up with Eric because you were convinced he was a conspiracy theorist on 4chan, you made the whole Feast of the Seven Fishes."

"I still think about that cioppino," Todd says, rising from the breakfast table and bouncing the sleeping baby. "I'm simply observing a pattern in which you come over here before sunrise, reduce tropical fruits into syrups, let Edie supportively fuel your rage-fire, and then drive off, tires screeching, on a warpath."

"What," I demand, "is so threatening to men about a little feminine rage?" I turn to Teddy. "You're not scared of it, are you?"

"I like it!" my nephew says, raising his plate to his face to lick it.

"I agree," Todd says, "I wasn't being critical. Your problems deserve a Michelin star."

"Mommy needs more problems," Frank says, and Todd, laughing, puts a finger to the boy's lips.

"Mommy's cooking is perfect, got it?"

I lift Frank in my arms. "Maybe you should start learning to make dinner. See, cooking is like directing a TV show. You ever directed a TV show, Frank?"

"I don't think so," Franks says, grabbing the whisk from my hands.

"Yeah, me neither, but it's all about the vision. You've got to know where you want to go, while keeping your eye out for the secret paths that take you there. You want pancakes with crispy, salty exteriors and fluffy, sweet interiors?"

"Yes!"

# THE SPIRIT OF LOVE                                   139

"That's your vision. Be ready to do a thousand takes before you get there."

"I'm tired," Frank says with a yawn.

"Yeah. That's okay. You'll build up stamina," I say, setting him down to go with Todd to gather his things for school.

When I straighten up, Edie and I are suddenly alone in the kitchen, and she's watching me with those fifteen-months-older sister eyes.

"What?" I ask, not sure I want to know.

"I found him online."

"Sam?!"

"SJD."

"JDS," I correct her. "You're on TV, and you have no idea about anyone who works in the industry."

"Three kids under three, beyatch," Edie says. "You're lucky I brushed my teeth."

"Anyway, I will puke if you mention Martin Scorsese. And don't you dare utter the word *genius*."

"So you've already googled him." Edie's fingers are flying. A second later she cocks her head. "Oh. This is interesting."

"Not to me," I warn her, even though I am curious.

"This is from an interview he did with *GQ* last year—"

I plug my ears, but she just talks louder.

" 'Every film generates a world.' "

"What the hell? That's what *I* think! Have you not heard me say that?!"

"I have, many times!" Edie laughs. "Seems like you two have a lot in common. Maybe you could learn something from this experience?"

"What, like, be his protégée? No way! What happened to the Edie who supportively fuels my rage-fire?"

"Does he even know he took this job from you?" Edie asks.

"What difference does that make?" I reply.

"A sizeable one."

I don't want to tell my sister that Jude seems to have no idea, or she'll snuff out Project Sabotage JDS like a candle, and then what will I do with the excess energy I *should* have been putting into directing?

"Is Jude really the bad guy here?" she asks. "Or is it, more obviously, Rich?"

"They're *both* bad guys! Obviously."

"*Two* bad guys?" Teddy calls from the living room, putting on his backpack. "Oh, no!"

"Kill all the bad guys!" Frank chants.

"That's right, Frank!" I point at my nephew. "I love you. I love your brother. I love the third one who's asleep. I'm late for war. I mean work. I mean war."

"It's WAR!" the twins shout.

"Beware advice from toddlers—" Edie calls, but I'm already out the door, tires screeching.

# Chapter Twelve

"KNOCK KNOCK." I START MY RECON AT THE TRAILER of Miguel Bernadeau, one of *Zombie Hospital*'s original cast members. Miguel has well-meaning but slightly smarmy uncle vibes and has been known to blow a gasket when asked to pivot his plans for a scene. Today I find him dressed in his surgical scrubs, getting his makeup retouched.

I already grabbed my copy of today's sides—the ten-page printout containing the script pages and all the logistical details needed for the scenes being shot. I studied it meticulously for any surprises I could use to my advantage. I noted a number of small rewrites that Jude must have authorized to today's pages. When I spied the new line added to Miguel's scene for today, an idea took root.

"Fenny," Miguel says warmly, meeting my gaze in his vanity mirror. "I'm so glad you're here. I heard something about last-minute changes to the script? After I've memorized the old lines? Between friends, I'm too old and too rich for that *mierda*."

I close the trailer door behind me. "I completely agree, Miguel. The shooting script was circulated Friday. The window for script changes has closed." I pause, like the idea is just now forming in my mind. "I wonder . . . if you and Aurora and I all came together—we know she hates last-minute revisions, too—maybe we could put a stop to this?"

"Amazing," Miguel says in his signature husky voice. "I really only care about my scenes, you know? But you'll relay this all to JDS? Take care of it?"

"I was thinking that it could be more of a group effort. Strength in numbers—"

"Oh. No. I can't." Miguel shakes his head. "I don't want to kick off my relationship with JDS by presenting as a diva. It's been a personal dream of mine to work with a director of his caliber. The man's a genius."

"So I heard." I force a smile. "Yeah, I'll talk to him."

Miguel makes prayer hands at me and mouths *Thank you.* "Just don't make me sound like a dick. I know you won't! You and your way with words."

I stand outside Miguel's trailer and resist the urge to scream. I should have known that conversation would go exactly as it did. Miguel and I are friends and colleagues, but only in the shallowest, most Hollywood of ways—i.e., he's using me just as much as I was trying to use him. I'd planned to go to Aurora next, but who am I kidding? Yesterday, I spotted her asking Jude his preference of three different scales of scrubs cleavage. She isn't going to help me take down JDS any more than Miguel.

Who else on this show has any sway and any spine? I shake my head and come up short.

I take refuge in my trailer, lock the door, and pull down the blinds. I brew some Earl Gray tea. I have enough rewriting to

# THE SPIRIT OF LOVE

keep me locked in here all season, to hole up, to hide out, to never have to see Jude de Silva's directorial genius at work.

It hurts to picture him out there now, behind the camera. The kind of hurt that isn't angry, that isn't on a warpath, that's simply wounded. I covered up that wound with indignation last night when I'd confided in my friends, and this morning at Edie's house, but it didn't lessen the pain. I wish I were brave enough to let someone know that I feel sad and broken. That I hurt. I don't know why that feels so hard. I flop down on my couch and wish its cushions were Sam's arms. I close my eyes and remember how directly he had spoken about his feelings. How inviting it had felt for once to do the same. I remember the warmth of his skin; the low, sexy rasp of his voice; and what it felt like between my thighs when his eyes were on me. I wish I could pick up the phone and call him.

Real question: Can it still be classified as a fling if you find yourself wanting to spill your deepest, secret truth to the guy?

Doesn't matter. I don't have the luxury of finding out what it would feel like to truly open up to Sam. To anyone. I'm on my own. And on a deadline. What else is new?

There's always a writers' room on Wednesday mornings, so I know that by tomorrow, I'll have to have done *something* to show the other writers on staff, but I'd rather hug a cactus naked than open the email Jude sent at 11:48 last night, subject line **Comprehensive Script Notes**. Pray tell, what wisdom did the genius impart via Outlook Express? I think back to his condescending suggestion yesterday that I "experiment," loosen up, think of the rewrites as a *fling*—and I get offended all over again. On top of everything, Jude doesn't even think I'm a fucking pro. Sure, he liked my writing in the season finale last year, but he also thinks my resentment at being asked to do these rewrites is a liability. That it will show in the final script.

What's he doing right now, anyway? There's an app on my phone that would let me pull up the monitors from here, to see what the cameras are filming. But the thing I want to see, against all reason, won't be on those monitors. It's behind the camera, in the seat that was supposed to be mine.

WHEN I STEP onto the soundstage, they are filming the scene where a zombie chews on her brother's brains. Three cameras are positioned around an actor named Heather as she grabs fistfuls of what I know is actually sausage mixed with unflavored gelatin and raises them to the special dentures the zombies use for feast scenes on the show. There are three men I've never seen before—one of them ponytailed, one with a shaved head, and one wearing a beanie. Who are they? Jude is in a suit again, this time a gray and white houndstooth, a white oxford shirt, and a green corduroy tie. He's on his knees beside Heather, elbow-deep in the sausage-gelatin combo. Okay, so he's hands-on. I would have been doing the same. I can't hear what he's saying, but it makes Heather laugh. People think Jude's so impressive, so exotic, but he's really just a dude talking to an actor. What does he have that I don't?

The whole scene makes me jealous to the point of nausea, and right as I'm about to turn away, to go right back to my

THE SPIRIT OF LOVE                                          145

trailer, Jude looks up and sees me. He waves. It's a big and friendly wave, the kind you give a beloved pal you haven't seen in months. And because his hands are still covered in sausage and gelatin, it goes everywhere, including my Gustav Klimt exhibit T-shirt. It's a good thing I got demoted so at least I'm not wearing my director power outfit today. Zombie brains stain.

"Shit, sorry everyone," Jude apologizes as the camera grips race to clean off the equipment. Ivy hands Jude a towel. But before he cleans his own hands, he jogs it over to me, so I can wipe the brains off my shirt.

"Fenny, hey." Jude's tone sounds more intimate than it had yesterday. Does he think we bonded at the cactus garden because he flattered me? I *was* flattered, but somehow that made things worse between us instead of better. "Nice shirt. Sorry about the brains." He points at my shirt, his eyes running over the graphic of six bare-breasted beauties on my chest. "You caught the Klimt show at the Getty?"

I nod, but before I can offer any of the interesting details about how I'd gone to the elegant opening reception Masha hosted at the Getty's outdoor restaurant, Jude adds:

"It was sloppily curated, but the art still holds up."

Strangely, Masha had said as much, using more generous phrasing, about her stressful experience hosting the exhibition. But I'm not giving Jude the satisfaction of validating his opinion, which no one asked for.

"I see your genius extends to the Vienna Secession movement. Why wouldn't it?" I point at the three men I don't know. "Who are those guys?"

"That's my team. They work with me on everything. Matt, my DP; Mark, my sound engineer; and Kevin, my editor."

"What about Jonah, the *show's* DP? Dave, the *show's* sound engineer? And Alyssa, the *show's* editor?" I ask, concerned about the people I've been working with for years. How deep is this JDS takeover going to go?

"They're still involved," Jude says. "We're just supplementing. I'm used to working with them." He's staring at my neck. "Why are you wearing an adder stone around your neck?"

The question derails me, makes me forget what we were talking about. It makes me feel protective of Sam and our time together. Of the moment he slipped this chain over my head and dreamed up another world.

Jude reaches forward, like he's going to touch it. I quickly tuck the stone inside my shirt. It's not for him.

Jude adjusts his glasses and clears his throat.

"So what do you think?" he finally says.

"Of what?"

"Of the first take? Were you watching it on the monitor?"

"Um, yeah. Everything looks . . . fine."

Jude tilts his head. "You don't trust me."

"I don't know you," I correct.

"Yeah, but you don't think I can do this." He nods. "Interesting."

"*Anyone* can do this. It's not exactly brain surgery." I'm in no rush to massage Jude's giant ego, but I don't know why *these* words came out. A) The show literally features brain surgery in almost every episode. B) Look how pathetic I am. Selling out

THE SPIRIT OF LOVE                                    147

the show I love, just to take a dig at Jude? C) It's not even true that anyone can do this. The powers that be have determined that I, specifically, cannot.

A flood of emotion fills the back of my throat. I cannot cry. Not here. Not in front of him.

"Sorry," he says, holding my gaze.

"For what?" My eyes are stinging. If there's a way to get out of this conversation with my dignity intact, I need to find it, stat.

"I just . . ." Jude says, studying my eyes, "get a sense that maybe you're going through something? Not about work. Something personal. And I'm not helping."

"That last part is true."

"Noted. But I'm here, if you want to talk." His eyes dart to the floor and he tugs on his beard. "That sounded weird. Why would you talk to me, of all people? Like you said, you don't know me—"

"No, it's a nice offer. I probably won't. But. Thanks anyway."

"Jude, we need your thoughts," Ivy's voice interrupts our conversation, feeling like an intruder. I realize that I didn't want to be interrupted just yet, not until I understand why Jude would make that kind of offer, like we're friends or something.

But Ivy's here. They need him, and nobody needs me.

Jude looks at me. "I should probably . . ." He points toward the action, toward the show he's making today.

I just nod at Jude.

"I'll let you get back to it," I say.

He turns toward the set, toward the action. Then he turns back to me. "Hey." He leans in so his shoulder brushes mine, which makes my body go very still. We're touching, but I don't move to pull away. "Going to the cactus garden today?" His voice is lower, almost a whisper.

I meet his eyes. They hold a hesitant smile. I can't tell what's happening in this moment, but it's not what I was expecting. "No . . ."

"Then, you're free?" His smile broadens. To the point where, once again, he reminds me of Sam.

I look away. It's too much. "I didn't say that."

"I need a favor. Can you meet me at the Universal Costume Department at eight o'clock tonight?"

# Chapter Thirteen

THAT EVENING, JUDE WAITS FOR ME OUTSIDE A WARE-house named for legendary Hollywood costume designer Edith Head. It's a warm night, the sunset golden in the sky behind the building, and he's taken off his suit jacket. It's the first time I can see the shape of his shoulders, the lean muscles of his chest. With the top button of his oxford shirt undone and his sleeves rolled up, exposing strong forearms, Jude's whole enchilada is giving me the kind of buzz I get when I meet a Tinder guy for drinks and he looks the same as he did in his photos online, yet also somehow better.

Jude holds two badges on lanyards, and I wait as he leans forward and slips one over my head. His fingers brush my collarbone, then the chain Sam's stone hangs from. I meet his eyes, surprised by how intensely he holds my gaze.

Chemistry: It's never a one-way street. But what's in it for *Jude*? I've not exactly been warm to him since we first met, and I have no plans to change that. Maybe he's the kind of closed-off weirdo who's into it when women are mean to him? It's clear enough that on my end, any chemistry with Jude—however bizarre and undesired—has everything to do with Sam. It makes a kind of sense that I keep conflating Sam and Jude, using Jude's eyes and his hands and those lips, which are *right there*, very close, as a way to wean myself off the intensity of my fling with Sam.

Lorena said it might mean there's something "not quite right" about my time with Sam, but I've had no time to ponder that conundrum this week. And what does that really matter anyway if I never see Sam again? For now, I'm content to let the memory stay golden, to call on Sam's sexy, teasing smile when I need a boost. Like every second for the past two days.

"Ever been here before?" Jude asks, holding open the door. "They close at five, but they opened it especially for me."

Inside, it smells like mothballs, leather, and Chanel. We flash our badges at reception and round a corner, and I have to suppress my audible awe at the vast treasure stretching out before me. I'm not telling Jude I've always wanted to see this place, that I deep-dived it on YouTube when I first moved to LA. This giant vortex of a warehouse stores every item of clothing and accessories that anyone in almost any film or TV show has ever worn or would ever possibly want to wear. It's room after room of double-racked costumes, from eighteenth-century ballgowns, to postapocalyptic armor, from the golden age jewelry to the world's largest selection of MC Hammer pants. I fucking love Hammer pants.

"So what are we looking for?" I ask, running my hand along a rack of beaded *Boogie Nights*–style vests. I follow Jude because he seems to know where he's going, down the seventies aisle and around the corner into the Wild West. I touch a pink taffeta

THE SPIRIT OF LOVE                                            151

gown that looks like it could suit a very badass saloon owner. "Is there a zombie aisle?"

Jude turns back to face me, confused. "Oh, no. We're not here for the show. Not directly anyway."

I narrow my eyes, suddenly guarded, sensing a trap. "Then what am I doing here?"

Jude flicks absently through a rack of colorful men's peasant blouses, the kind Westley wore in *The Princess Bride*, thereby cementing them as an evergreen stud clothing article. I picture Jude in the pale-green blouse at his fingertips. Actually, I picture him changing into it, unbuttoning his oxford shirt all the way to his navel, letting it drop to the floor.

I wonder: Could my erotic conflation condition make Jude's chest look like Sam's, too? Because I might be into something like that.

No. I'm not seeing Jude shirtless tonight. Or ever. The less of him I see, the better.

"I like it here," he says. "When I was a kid, my mom worked a bunch of different jobs. One of them was at our town's only costume shop. She took extra shifts the month of Halloween, and when I was in sixth grade, I got suspended from school for a week—"

"Because?"

"I might have skateboarded off the school's roof, narrowly avoiding my former kindergarten teacher's head. Stuck the landing though."

I give Jude an appraising look. The polished brogues, the permasuit. "I don't see it."

152                                          LAUREN KATE

He laughs. "You think I'm making this up to impress you?"

"Maybe try giving me a night *off* from you and see how impressed I am."

"How's tomorrow night?" he asks, meeting my eyes in this way that almost feels like he's asking me out. But he's not.

"You mean, *not* to hang out with you?"

He nods, but it feels flirty. To the point where I'm getting a little hot.

"I'd love that," I say, and I think it sounds like I'm flirting back. I take a breath, try to find my way out of this flustering moment. "So you were a wild child?"

"I used to be. And I thought my mom was going to be furious that I couldn't go to school the one week she made the most money. She was strict, you know, single mom, no patience for my shit. But that week, she let me spend every day in the shop with her. When it was slow, we'd talk. She'd ask me tough questions. Stuff I never wanted to talk about. But she made me answer her, dressed up in one ridiculous costume after the next. Something shifted. I started opening up. Neither of us could keep a straight face, even talked about my dad leaving, when I was dressed like Ace Ventura."

"I'm sorry," I say, "about your dad, and that I'm picturing how ridiculous you would look as Ace Ventura."

"When I moved here ten years ago," he says, "I started working on *Brujo* with my friend Matt."

I nod, putting it together that Matt is his DP, the ponytailed guy he brought on set with him today.

"That film came out of this nightmare I used to have as a kid. Matt and I were friends from high school, and he was al-

THE SPIRIT OF LOVE                    153

ways encouraging me to make something out of the idea. I didn't know where to start. The brujo in my dream was invisible, so when Matt told me about this place, I thought I might begin to see what he'd look like, what he'd wear."

"That's how you started working on your film?"

"Groping in the dark my whole way through," he says. "But this place"—he looks up at the racks of clothing triple-stacked to the high ceiling—"it became more than that for me. It reminded me of that week with my mom. I started coming here more often, when I was depressed."

"Are you depressed?" I ask.

He tosses his head. "I mean, yeah, on and off, but earlier today, I thought that you might have been feeling low . . ." He trails off, looks around again, and I understand. He brought me here to try to cheer me up.

It's strange and ironic and somewhat embarrassing. And at its heart, I think it also might be kind.

"I'm fine," I tell him. "I'm moving through some feelings of—"

"Hold on." Jude's hand stop-signs me. He takes my shoulders gently in his hands. His hands that feel like Sam's on my skin. And he moves me down the aisle, a few feet to the left, until I'm standing before a mirror. He grabs a stiff, broadbrimmed turquoise velvet hat with a giant feather plume and plops it on my head. It's huge, sinking over my eyes so I can barely see my reflection.

"Say it with the hat on," Jude instructs.

I straighten my spine, spread my arms, and enunciate like I'm on stage. "I'm moving through some feelings of indecision and inadequacy due to—" It's as far as I can get before I catch a glimpse of myself in the mirror and burst out laughing.

Jude's already laughing, face in the clothing rack and shoulders shaking.

"Your turn, asshole," I say, whipping off the hat. I grab another from the rack, this one a navy satin turban printed with golden stars and a heavy crystal ball wedged in the center front. I tug it down on Jude's head, but it's a little small, pinching his forehead, making his ears stick out. With his glasses askew, he looks absurd.

He softly shoulder-bumps me out of the way so he can stand before the mirror.

"So what's your problem, *genie-us*?" I ask.

He looks at himself. Shakes his head at his reflection. "I think my dog hates me."

I crack up.

"I'm serious," he says, but he's laughing, too. "It's so awful. I've bought every toy for him, tried every trainer, but he treats me with such contempt."

"What's your dog's name?"

"Walter Matthau."

"Because he's a grumpy old man?"

He shakes his head.

I think a moment. "Because you're turning over *A New Leaf* by getting a dog?"

"You got it! I've never met anyone who knows that movie."

"You aren't so mysterious," I say. "A little Wes Anderson, a little Japanese horror, and an industry that hasn't seen any film pre–*Home Alone*."

# THE SPIRIT OF LOVE                                        155

"Oh, is that my entire aesthetic?" he asks, his eyebrows shooting up inside the turban, which cracks me up again.

"I can't look at you in that," I wheeze. "Take it off."

He frisbees the turban at me, and we both catch our breath.

Finally, he says, his voice serious again. "You're so far from inadequate, Fenny. You're very talented."

I nod. It doesn't feel like he's paying me lip service. I know he likes my writing. But he doesn't know what he took from me, and I don't want to tell him. "I just want . . . more, you know?"

He studies me in the mirror. "Keep wanting it."

"Sorry about your dog," I say. "Maybe he doesn't get to see you enough. Forget the trainers and the toys. You probably need to make some time to bond. Do some stuff he likes to do?"

"Sniff ass and chew up my shoes? I guess I could try that."

"Try it," I say. "Hey, before we go, as payment for dragging me here, I'm going to need you to try this on." From the nearest rack, I lift a gold-brocaded men's Renaissance doublet with matching pleated shorts and a shimmery golden cape.

"Fine," Jude says. "But you'll need to wear this." Without looking, he grabs an item off the rack nearest to him. It's a gothic feathered black turtleneck shawl with sleeves long enough to drag the floor. He raises an eyebrow at the sight of what he's selected and then grabs a snakeskin midi skirt to pair it with.

"Deal," I tell him, and we swap clothes.

In the absence of dressing rooms, we retreat to different aisles. I can hear Jude on the other side of a rack of clothes. I listen closely to the soft swish of his shirt dropping to the floor.

I hear the metallic rush as the zipper of his pants goes down. I hold my breath as I picture him stepping out of them, wearing nothing but simple black briefs. My chest flushes with heat as I whip off my own shirt and unzip my jeans. Oh, God, did Jude hear that? Is he picturing me in my paisley thong? How did this silly, tender outing suddenly start to feel hot?

The sooner I get un-naked, the better. The shawl is impossibly itchy, feather tips poking out everywhere, and very hard to get over my head. But the skirt I love. It's slinky and cool, slightly rough to the touch. It hugs my curves and has a long slit up the left leg. I turn to the mirror and catch my breath. If I were the kind of person who could leave the house like this, I'd probably get a ton of compliments.

"I don't know if we should do this," Jude calls from the next aisle, which tells me he must look like a total fool.

"Oh, we're definitely doing this," I call back. "Ready or not."

We meet at the end of the aisle, and I start laughing so hard I almost don't notice Jude's not. I finally catch how he's staring at me, like he's hungry. His eyes run all over my body, sending electric sparks across my skin.

"Wow," he whispers.

"Ditto," I say, relishing his absurd gold barrel-shaped shorts and the doubloon that gives him Henry-VIII-at-the-disco vibes. And also relishing the way he seems to be thirsting for me—for this outfit anyway.

"So do you want to take pictures for future blackmail purposes?" Jude asks, holding out his arms.

"I want to take you to Medieval Times."

"I want *you* to rent both of those pieces and wear them to the

# THE SPIRIT OF LOVE                    157

*Zombie Hospital* dinner at Amy Reisenbach's house on Friday," Jude says. "I meant them as a joke, but they're not."

I smooth my skirt and laugh. "There's no way I'm wearing this to the *Zombie Hospital* dinner." But it crosses my mind: If I was directing this season, maybe I'd have the confidence to show up in something this bold. As it is, I have just enough confidence to blend in with Amy Reisenbach's drapes.

He's looking at me closely, like he's trying to read my expression. "I know," he says, "I always hate those dinners. You're working, but you're supposed to act like you're on vacation."

"*You'll* be fine," I say. "You're everybody's darling. You just stand there and soak up the compliments."

"God, that sounds horrible." Jude shudders. At first, I assume he's joking, but the longer I look at him, the more convinced I am that he's being sincere. It makes me wonder why receiving praise for his work wouldn't sit right with him. Imposter syndrome? Is he a fraud? There's more to Jude than I can fathom yet, and I'm surprised to want to know more.

"Have you ever brought your mom here?" I ask. "She'd probably love it."

Jude shakes his head. "She lives in Dallas now. We haven't talked in a while."

"Why not?"

"We don't really see eye to eye anymore," he says. "She's religious. Heaven's a big part of her worldview."

"I take it it's not a big part of yours?" I ask.

"Definitely not."

"*Definitely*? Really? Who gets to know that sort of thing for sure?" I say, surprised. Although I shouldn't be. Jude did make a whole movie about a character who believes in the darkest version of nothing. I wonder if that's when Jude and his mom fell out of touch, when his movie came out and she hated it.

"I'm not unique," he says. "Lots of people don't believe there's anything after this. Lots of people take comfort in exploring that darkness. Don't you ever, Fenny?"

"I'm no stranger to darkness, but I still choose to believe—"

"In what?" He interrupts me so cuttingly that I don't want to say it out loud. Not to him. Not anymore.

But I know what I believe inside. I've known it since I was ten years old and woke up in a hospital bed after seeing the beauty beyond this world. It gave me faith that we're here for a reason. To love each other, to be kind, to connect. That if we live accordingly, no matter what our public lives amount to, it's worth it on a soul level.

And then *I* feel like the fraud, because even though I *know* all this, I still find myself wanting the public validation of landing the role of director. I still find myself blaming Jude because I'm not getting what my ego thinks it needs.

"Sometimes," Jude says, filling in the space I didn't, "it just feels good to wonder: What's the fucking point?"

"I mean, just taking a stab in the dark here," I say, irritation creeping into my voice, "perhaps love and kindness are the point?"

"*Love and kindness?*" he repeats, squinting like I've suggested contracting head lice is the point.

"It does seem to be what we're here to do. It's not exactly a novel idea."

"No, in fact, it's a very tired idea."

# THE SPIRIT OF LOVE                                    159

I narrow my eyes. "Love is a tired idea?"

"In movies and TV, yes," Jude says. "That's all I mean. There's no potential for surprise. I was just talking to Buster about this today."

"Buster?" I ask.

"Yeah, we're exploring new ideas for his character to confront in the first episode."

I stiffen. "Because I'm responsible for rewriting that episode, it seems like you should be talking to me. All you've told me to do so far with the scripts is 'have a fling.'"

"I sent you fifty pages of script notes last night."

Right. Shit. "Which I am working my way through," I stammer, caught.

"And I'm talking to you now," he says. "I'm saying there's no salvation for Buster's character. No love or meaning."

"This is all wrong," I say, beginning to panic. I didn't want to get into the details of the show with him tonight. But there's so much he doesn't understand about *Zombie Hospital* that the subject is nearly impossible to avoid. "If there's one character who needs salvation on this show it's Buster's. Eleven million viewers *need* that kid to believe in something—"

He shrugs like we're debating whether to take the escalator or the stairs. "Unless they don't."

"People believe in love, Jude."

He studies my face. "People like you?"

He makes it sound like a bad thing. I feel stung and embarrassed, and so I sting back. "Is *this* why people think you're talented?" I demand, feathered hands on hips. "Because you believe in nightmares while everyone else believes in dreams?"

"I really don't know why people think I'm talented," Jude says, looking away.

"You're not a genius. You're a shell."

"Didn't take you long to crack the code," he says evenly, holding my gaze.

I want to give him a piece of my mind. About how, in the rare moments when *Zombie Hospital* has a chance to make our audience feel something, I want to make them feel connected, not alone. But if I told Jude any of that, then he'd know what he stole from me, and that's a secret I'm not willing to give him.

This shawl feels like it's choking me. I tug at the neck, trying to find the snaps. What am I doing playing dress-up with the enemy?

"I have to get out of this thing," I gasp. "I have to get out of here."

# Chapter Fourteen

MY GREEN-AND-YELLOW-STRIPED CANOE SWAYS GENtly in the water. It's tied to a wooden post on the small dock in front of my house, where I left it eighteen months ago, the first and last time I boarded it. On Friday, just after six o'clock, I climb inside it, use a paddle to push off, and begin to row down Linnie Canal. The sound of the paddle drawing up from the water is soothing as I glide past my narrow three-story bungalow, then the unique and colorful bric-a-brac bungalows that make up my block. Wind ripples the water, tousles my hair. A paddling row of ducklings travel with me as I glide around the corner, then under the bridge with the wire canopy where the children of Venice leave little paper notes with wishes written on them.

Neighbors wave at me, as if this is our nightly ritual. It should be. My hands feel sure of what they need to do, and my eyes can focus on the jacarandas and the bougainvillea and the palms swaying in the warm, end-of-summer breeze. My thoughts go to the last time I was in a canoe, with Sam on Catalina. I try to imagine showing him my neighborhood canals. He would like it here, I think. But the problem is . . . I can't quite call up his face in my mind. He's fading already, the way dreams do. I touch the stone at my neck, trying to bring the memory of him closer. I hold it up to my eye and let myself believe the sky takes on an otherworldly sheen as I look through the hole. I let myself believe the stone is humming with magic no one else can see. I let myself believe Sam's right here.

But he's not, and when I let go of the stone, I feel like I've lost him for good. Into the place I'd been holding open for him, all my ordinary worries rush back: the work I have to do tonight, *after* the dinner party I don't want to go to. Packing for the *Zombie Hospital* travel shoot in Joshua Tree early Sunday morning, which promises to suck. The fact that in the last three days, Jude and I have been together in the same space on set for at least eighteen hours of shoots and meetings and conference calls and huddles, but we've been avoiding one-on-one ever since I insulted him in the costume warehouse. I owe him an apology. Another reason to dread tonight's dinner.

I row faster, harder, turning this hobby into more of a competitive sport and catching odd looks from some of my super-chill neighbors. They don't understand. They must have less-shitty lives than I do, or else better cannabis. The worst part is, when I round the next bend, I have to park this ship and go inside and wash my hair and put on a party dress. And pretend I'm okay. Because it's the end of the first week of shooting on season seven and, like clockwork, time for the network's annual *Zombie Hospital* dinner party at the home of the president of CBS.

"GET OUT HERE now, bitch!" Aurora commands, pulling me by the arm out onto the oceanfront patio of Amy Reisenbach's Malibu mansion.

THE SPIRIT OF LOVE                                            163

"What's wrong?" I ask as Aurora weaves me around a tux-edoed server, from whose tray I accept a glowing red zombitini. Jude could be here any minute, and I need to steel myself with triple sec.

"I need you to see this view," Aurora says, spinning me *away* from the view to face her phone's camera in selfie mode. "Now serve," she commands, adjusting her black naked dress and striking her full-lipped smirk. She checks the photo. "Cute! What even is that in the background?"

"That's Catalina. It's the largest of the Channel Islands." I turn to see the real thing, whose coastline some forty miles to the south of Malibu is bathed in pink-hued sunset light.

"Random."

"Not really. I was just there last week."

My voice must hold some intrigue because Aurora leans close, looks at me, and then looks at the island. "Is it dope?"

"I had fun," I say. I hear the wistfulness in my voice as, in my mind, I see Sam on the porch of his cabin, binoculars to his eyes. He's birdwatching, but what if he could look through those lenses and see all the way across the water, to me, right now, missing him?

But because it's pointless and a little cuckoo to wonder that, I turn back to Aurora.

"Idea," she says, pointing a long, silver, spear-shaped finger-nail at Catalina. "What if I chartered a yacht to go play out there with some friends for my birthday? Is there a club scene?"

I wince at being asked to give away what I'd like to keep secret from her. She has the power to ruin the entire island in one fell yacht party. "There is a big ballroom you can rent called the Casino. The vibe is kind of Roaring Twenties Hollywood—"

164                                                      LAUREN KATE

"I love old-fashioned shit like that. Last month, I went to a 2015-themed foam party in Mallorca. Everyone had selfie sticks. I was so jealous of the host, I almost went down on him." She gazes at the island, foam bubbles popping in her eyes. "This could top that. How do we get to the Casino?"

"Most people go by ferry. Catalina has two terminals, two very different experiences." I feel the need to clarify, "Avalon is the main town, where the Casino and most of the tourist attractions are. But Two Harbors, that's the part of the island you can see from here—that's where I was last week. It's rustic and remote."

"You really know your shit, Fenny. You're like my cute little LA emissary." Aurora takes a sip from my drink. "Wait, I'm having an amazing idea—"

"Who's having amazing ideas out here without me?" Rich says, stepping out onto the patio wearing this season's douchebag couture: white jeans and a white shearling aviator jacket. He and Aurora take a beat to air-kiss and compliment each other's ridiculous outfits, then turn to me and fall silent, even though I'm wearing one of my very best looks, a flowy silk minidress printed with thick black and blue stripes. *Should* I have rented the feathered turtleneck shawl and snakeskin midi? Whatever.

The sight of Rich is always my cue to leave a room.

"Where are you going, ho?" Aurora says, turning to Rich to explain. "She was just about to help me start planning my birthday yacht adventure. You in, Rich?" Aurora takes another sip of my drink and then tries to return it to me. I wave her off.

"I'll grab another," I say, "I see the guy with the tray—"

"Come right back!" Aurora sings. "I'm not done with you!"

# THE SPIRIT OF LOVE                                          165

Stepping back inside the party, I grab a fresh drink. The idea of planning anything with Aurora is terrifying enough, but a trip back to Catalina? The decision I'd have to make about whether to see Sam? The thought alone causes me to accidentally guzzle my entire drink.

When I set the glass on a table, I have to steady myself on a dining chair as the triple sec rejiggers my cells. I need to stay away from that patio, that view, and probably alcohol for the rest of the night, or I'll end up drunk and crying in Amy Reisenbach's bathroom again.

The bigger issue is: Am I going to apologize to Jude tonight? Is there a way we can both just forget what I said and go on the travel shoot Sunday as if it never happened? No, the guilt will eat away at me. I've got to find a moment alone with him tonight, swallow my pride, and get it over with.

I notice President Amy herself stationed by the front door. I don't know her well enough to strike up a conversation, but I'd love to somehow make a good impression. I need to be at the front of her mind when she thinks of *Zombie Hospital*'s rising talent. Jude's not here yet to double my self-consciousness, so now's the time. I meander toward the door and decide that the next person who walks in will become my charming conversation partner and my gateway to Amy's attention.

Of course, a moment later, in walks JDS, bearing a bottle of champagne. He's dressed in a sleeker suit than usual, this one navy and pinstriped with a solid black oxford shirt that doesn't seem like it would match, but it does. Did he trim that beard? It looks . . . softer. Like if you touched it with your hand, you would also then want to touch it with your cheek and kind of nuzzle it?

He takes off his glasses and cleans them on a cloth, but before he puts them back on, he looks forward and catches me staring. The accidental eye contact sends a shockwave through my body that is definitely not attraction. It's a message shockwave, saying *Now you're going to apologize to this man* in front of *Amy Reisenbach? Bad idea. Go get your shit together.*

I stumble back into Miguel Bernadeau, who is regaling Amy's husband with the specs of his new electric truck.

"Sorry, Miguel," I say.

"Fenny, did you talk to JDS for me?" he whispers.

"Uh—"

"Jude, darling!" I hear Amy coo from the door. "Give me some sugar, you absolute rock star genius."

But Jude is looking past her, still staring right at me. "Fenny—"

Nope.

I duck around a corner and into the nearest escape—which turns out to be through the swinging doors that lead to Amy Reisenbach's restaurant-grade kitchen.

"I was hoping you'd come see me," a voice calls from behind a sage-scented cloud of steam.

"Summer, thank God," I say and give the chef a long, tight hug.

It's a little embarrassing to realize that I've been ducking into this kitchen—usually to escape Rich—for each of the past five years I've made the invite list for Amy Reisenbach's *Zombie Hospital* party. Luckily, Amy's tastemaker taste extends beyond TV, so whenever I have to hide out in her kitchen, I get to do it

THE SPIRIT OF LOVE 167

in the company of Summer, the Reisenbachs' personal chef and one of the coolest women I know.

I tend to see Summer only in person at this party once a year, but we have a pretty regular text conversation going. I message her whenever a new spice blend drops at Trader Joe's; she hits me up when she comes across a good podcast on near-death experiences. Tonight, she's jamming to Feist on low volume and snacking on sweet corn Turtle Chips.

"What's good, sister?" she says, coming toward me with a spoon. "Taste this zucchini Parm?"

I open my mouth and let her spoon in. I chew and moan. "You are an alchemist, and that is gold."

Summer smiles as if she'd been aiming for nothing less. "Courtesy of J&J Farms in the San Joaquin Valley. I'm glad to see you, but I wasn't expecting you in the back of house tonight. Don't directors get swarmed at these things?"

I think of Jude out there. I think of Amy's open arms. "*Directors* do."

"Uh-oh," Summer says, reading my tone.

Everyone who meets Summer or tastes her cooking wants to hire her, if they have the means to. She worked as a private chef for Rich for exactly one juice cleanse, after which she told him point-blank she couldn't take repeat clients she didn't respect. Summer and I have a wordless understanding when it comes to a lot of the guests at this party, which saves us both the valuable energy it takes to complain.

"You wanna snip some herbs and dance it out?" she asks.

I nod as she hands me a big bunch of chives, a pair of tiny

scissors, and a glass bowl. For a couple Feist songs, we prep and breathe and dance in Amy's fortress of a kitchen.

"Should we talk about something other than work?" Summer asks. "How your sex life?"

"Worse than my work life."

"Stop."

"I had a fling. Which I thought was great at the time, but which now casts my real life in this very dismal light."

Summer smears labneh on a plate and then drizzles chili oil over the top. "Maybe you need another helping of the fling."

"I can't. Doesn't that defy the definition of *fling*? Plus, he lives in a very inconvenient location for a booty call."

"Honey, that's why you make him come to you."

I close my eyes. "I think, more likely, I'll never see him again."

"Oh," she says, "you *like* him—"

The kitchen door swings open. My eyes snap open in horror at the sight of Jude ducking inside.

"Fenny?"

"Jude!"

Under her breath, Summer mutters, "Holy shit, is this *him*?"

Thank God Amy Reisenbach's kitchen is the size of a soundstage and Jude's too far away to hear. Why would she think that?

"Absolutely not," I mutter back.

"Whatever you say," Summer says between her teeth, "but there's major energy between you two."

"Like Tonya Harding and Nancy Kerrigan," I mutter. Turning to Jude, I call, "Wrong turn, Jude. The bathroom's one door

# THE SPIRIT OF LOVE                                      169

down." I know my voice sounds brusque, but this was supposed to be my sanctuary *from* him.

"Sorry," he says, looking around, confused by his surroundings. "I didn't know where this door led. I was trying to grab a second alone with you. Instead, I'm interrupting—"

"All good," Summer says, giving him a friendly nod. "I'm Summer. This is where the cool kids hang out at these parties. My artichokes oxidize at a faster rate in high-stress atmospheres, so you wanna be cool, Jude?"

"Thank you for the invitation," he says. "Yes, I do."

"Great. Then you can stay," Summer says. "Here's some scissors. Fenny, show him how to snip the herbs."

Jude comes to stand next to me. I breathe in his cologne, which I've never smelled before, a musky, spicy fig. He seems even taller when we're side by side in the kitchen, and I try not to stare at how well tailored his suit is. Really hugging all the right places. It's by far my favorite one he's worn this week. Second place goes maybe to what he was wearing Tuesday night, that slim-fit white oxford and the pants I heard him unzip.

Not that I give the slightest damn about this man or his bespoke attire.

Scissors. Herbs. Focus.

"So what do I . . ." He holds a sprig of dill. I move the blades of his scissors nearer to the end of the herbs.

"Snip," I say, and he does.

"You've done this before."

"It's not directing a show about brain surgery. You just want a very fine cut. You almost can't be too fine."

Does it sound like I just called *him* fine? Is that why both of us are blushing?

"You owe me an apology," he says, taking me aback.

"I'm aware."

"You said I'd be fine at this dinner, when in fact, I am in one of the lower circles of hell."

I look at him, confused. "Really? Which one?"

"Fraud," he says. "I believe that's number eight."

"You feel like a fraud here?"

"I did, until I found you in here. This is better."

He wasn't actually fishing for the apology I was planning on giving him. For being cruel in the costume warehouse the other night. No, Jude is truly struggling to handle the attention he's getting at this dinner. Is it possible that he doesn't want the acclaim, that he just wants to do the work? I don't quite understand that because I want it all. If I was in Jude's place, I would have glowingly soaked up a compliment and a hug from Amy Reisenbach. I would have written and delivered a grateful, witty toast to really luxuriate in tonight's moment. I've been hiding in this kitchen for years because what I get at these dinners is, at best, ignored. I'm curious and a little impressed that Jude doesn't seem to need or want that validation.

"You snip a mean herb," he says. "But how come you're in here when the rest of the party's out there?"

The kitchen door swings open again, and in blows Amy Reisenbach, holding a pad of paper with handwritten notes. She beams at Jude. "There you are! My guest of honor. Everyone's waiting for you."

I think I hear Jude groan as she takes him by the bicep and

THE SPIRIT OF LOVE                                        171

flips through the notes in her hands. "Fenny." She looks up at me. "I didn't realize you were in here. That's not good."

"I'm sorry?" I say.

"We'll have to add a chair."

Through a cloud of steam as she drains her pasta, Summer blows me a kiss. I have no choice but to follow Amy and Jude's linked arms out into the giant open dining room facing the ocean. At least the sun has set enough so I can't see Two Harbors anymore. Just a thirty-person seated dinner table, with only two empty chairs left.

"Jude, right here, next to me," Amy says. She turns to a member of the catering staff. "Could we squeeze in one more place setting?" She gestures at the far end of the table, the nether regions where some men from the finance department are talking about golf.

"Right here," Jude says, moving his own placemat to the left and gesturing for me to sit down. "I'll take the extra chair."

"No really—" I say.

"I insist." Jude smiles.

"What a man," Amy beams and then clinks her fork against her champagne flute.

I sit down next to Jude, who is given an extra chair squeezed in so tightly next to mine that there's no way to sit without our arms touching.

"Cool kids have to stick together, right?" he says.

"Listen up!" Amy clinks her fork again. "I promise this year I won't go on and on," she says, like she says every year before going on and on. "I know we all want to dig into Chef Summer's phenomenal first course. But as we embark on this, our seventh!

Season! Of our flagship! Series! I want to thank you all for your exquisite work, *and* I want to give a big welcome to our drop-dead brilliant new director, the incomparable JDS. We are so lucky to have him, a once-in-a-generation talent and a true fan of the show—"

I look at Jude, who has his eyes closed and his face tipped down as if to avoid being seen, and I hope for his sake—not even my own anymore—that Amy wraps up her JDS worship hour soon. The man can't handle it.

"Cheers, everyone! To zombies!" Amy says, so at least it's time to drink.

"To zombies!" the rest of the party calls out.

"And to writers," Jude says quietly, turning to me, clinking my glass. We lock eyes, and we take sips. If I don't do this now, I fear I'll never do it.

"Look, I'm sorry about Tuesday," I say as a waiter sets down salads in front of us, a temporary ceasefire made of endive and hazelnuts and Summer's anchovy vinaigrette.

"Tuesday?" Jude says. He takes a bite, and his eyes pop as he chews. Everyone does this when they first taste Summer's food.

I can't bring myself to eat yet. I push a hazelnut around on my plate. "When we were in the costume department? Our argument about the show and, I guess, existence? That thing I said about your nightmares wasn't cool."

He turns his whole body toward me, like we're not at a party, like we're entirely alone. And what I thought was going to feel contentious feels different. Apologizing to Jude feels unexpectedly safe.

"I didn't mind," Jude says, his voice warmer than I've heard

# THE SPIRIT OF LOVE                                      173

it before. So he almost sounds like Sam. "I heard what you were saying, and I think you're probably right. You were defending your point of view and the show you care about. You're more in tune with *Zombie Hospital* than anyone else."

"Oh, fuck off," I say, and my words are sharp but my tone is just as warm as Jude's. I think I'm testing him, trying to discern whether he's patronizing me. I don't think so, but my guard refuses to go all the way down just yet.

"No, really." Jude moves his chair a little closer, like he's about to tell me a secret. "People say you're the heart and soul of the show—"

"See, now you're doing the thing you hate to me." I take a bite of salad, sending telepathic chef's kisses Summer's way.

"But with you," Jude says, "at least it's true. I heard Aurora saying as much to Rich when I came in tonight."

I wave him off and take another bite of salad. "She just wants me to plan her stupid birthday party."

Jude tilts his head. "No, she was describing a scene you helped her figure out. How you sat down with her, rewrote the lines until they were in her voice, until—I think she said—until delivering them made her feel, for the first time, like an actor."

What he's describing with Aurora did happen. It was when we were trying to crack how she'd play one of her earliest scenes as an undercover zombie priestess. But the rounds of telephone it took this compliment to reach me is suspicious.

A server whisks away our salad plates, replacing them a moment later with the transcendent zucchini Parm I'd tasted in the kitchen earlier.

"The actors respect you," Jude continues. "The writers like

writing with you. The producers trust your knowledge of the series more than anyone else. You *are* the series bible. You're at the top of your game, and I'm out of my depth." He takes a bite of the zucchini Parm and shakes his head in disbelief. "Is there crack in this food or what?"

"I know. Summer is an alien from outer space in the kitchen."

"I see why the two of you are friends," he says.

"Thanks, Jude." His compliment is thoughtful, unusual.

He keeps going, "If you want to stick with Buster's climax scene as you wrote it, I defer to you."

"Really? I'm—what about Rich?"

"That insufferable worm? He doesn't get it. And I'll have your back."

"I don't know what to say." I want to say thanks for having my back and also to express relief that he's not bought a ticket on the Rich train, but part of me also wants to say that this is still not quite enough. That he still took something from me. Something he now seems to understand I deserved.

"Say it took me long enough," Jude says. "Say that I shouldn't have been imposing my personal beliefs on the show that already knows quite well what it's doing."

"Those really are your personal beliefs?" I ask. "What you were saying in the costume department? All that, 'What's the point? What is reality? What is there to believe in?'"

I give these questions my best zombie voice, and Jude laughs as the server sets down Summer's steak and forbidden rice.

"You make it all sound embarrassingly uncurious," he says. "But from experience, yes, that is essentially what I believe."

# THE SPIRIT OF LOVE                     175

"Okay, but all of us can *choose* to believe in something," I say, "and before you wave me off, I'm not talking about religion."

"Believe me," he says, "I'd prefer to believe in God . . . in *anything*—"

"What's holding you back?"

He looks at me but doesn't answer. I wish he would.

"I have it on pretty good authority that there is Something out there," I say. "Something beyond even Malibu . . ."

"You mean Santa Barbara," Jude jokes, but when I don't laugh, he asks, "What exactly do you believe in, Fenny?"

I put a hand to my chest, to my heart. "My sister. I believe in her. And my nephews. Even my brother-in-law when he's not being a dork. I know what you mean about how sometimes life serves us brutal emotional devastation, but when I go over to the east side, to hang out with my family, I choose to believe that my time with them is worth something. Maybe everything. It does all of us good if I can believe that."

Jude's quiet, thinking.

"How's it going with your dog?" I ask.

He takes a big sip of wine. "I walk into a room, he walks out of it."

I bite back a laugh. "Ouch. And you've tried bonding over destroying a pair of your shoes together?"

"I offered him tug-of-war with some very expensive Bruno Maglis yesterday. He didn't bite."

"Maybe you need to up your game."

"As in?"

"Grand gesture, dude."

"What are you thinking? I feel it's too soon to propose."

"How about a guys' trip? A grumpy old men trip! Go somewhere together and just figure out how to love each other."

We both take bites of steak, and Jude looks at me as if this is a good idea, but by the time he's chewed and swallowed and drank some more wine, his face looks drawn again.

"Love each other?"

"Don't knock it 'til you've tried it," I say, but I hear the waver in my voice. Just because I believe in love doesn't guarantee personal success in the act. In fact, recently for me, the opposite seems to be true.

"Aha," Jude says, picking up on my energy. "Perhaps you're not so sure?"

"I'm sure that if you love a dog, it loves you back, okay?" I quip, not wanting to get into my vulnerable love life right now.

"Right, I'll schedule 'grumpy old men do Vegas' as soon as I get a day off," Jude says. "TV is a grueling schedule. I don't know how you've done it for so long."

"You get used to it."

"With films, you go hard for months at a time, maybe a year, but then you're done. You get time off to recalibrate. But a successful TV show never stops."

"Life sucks and then you die?" I prompt.

"I knew there was a nihilist in there somewhere." He smiles. And I can't help liking his smile.

"Do you ever get away, Fenny? 'Grumpy young ladies' trip?"

"Not often enough," I say.

"Where would you go if you could go anywhere tomorrow?"

Because the emotional door was already ajar, I can't help

# THE SPIRIT OF LOVE

thinking of Catalina, of Sam and his cabin and his bed. I think of my schedule for the next several months and how I'll be spending more time with the people in this room—with Jude— than I will with my dearest friends, my family, and certainly with Sam. And how, for years, that was a choice I happily made in order to make strides toward the career I want.

But what about this week, when it all backfired?

What am I doing, next to this man who I like looking at and standing near and sometimes even talking to, but who wrecked my career simply by being good at his? In film school, my professors would say, "Art isn't a zero-sum game. There's room for all of you at the top."

But from where I'm sitting, it looks more like a savage session of musical chairs.

Maybe Jude's attitude is contagious, because as I stare out Amy's windows at the island I know is out there but can't see, I find myself wondering, *What's the point?*

# Chapter Fifteen

JOSHUA TREE NATIONAL PARK IS TWELVE HUNDRED square miles of quiet desert beauty located two hours east of Los Angeles. Ascending its giant craggy boulders, peering out at its mysterious expanses, is just about the closest an earthling can get to feeling like they're on the moon—if the moon served small-batch roasted coffee and date-palm milkshakes to boho-chic influencers. Joshua Tree, and the weirdo little towns east and west of it on Route 62, are where Angelinos head for a mystical weekend getaway, to see technicolored sunsets and soak up starlight—or to shoot that film sequence that needs a little post-apocalyptic zhuzh. This week, it's our backdrop for the action scenes in *Zombie Hospital* episode 7.01.

I scouted this location earlier in the spring with Jonah, our director of photography. And every step of the way, I anticipated directing today's travel shoot. Now, I'm climbing out of the dust-lacquered production van, knowing I'm on the call sheet but wondering what I'm really here to do. The lead writer of a *Zombie Hospital* episode is always on set for the shoot so that any changes to the script can be done in a consistent voice. This isn't an industry standard—I know lots of directors on other shows who don't like writers hovering after the baton is passed to them. But it's *Zombie Hospital* tradition to collaborate, and it's

# THE SPIRIT OF LOVE

something I've always appreciated. Until now. It's going to be a lot of time on set without a trailer to hide in. I'm worried I'll feel like I'm sitting in the back row of a wedding ceremony, watching my first love marry someone else.

And that someone else is Jude. He confessed to me on Friday that he's out of his depth with some aspects of the show. That on the script, he'd defer to me. Which should have been enough of a peace offering for me to let out my breath on this travel shoot. The trouble is, I keep thinking about what he'd said, about how personal experience has taught him not to believe in anything.

What happened to him, and why do I care so much? Why do I feel threatened that Jude might not believe in the things I know to be true? Aren't I just here to do my job?

I take in the scene being set in the desert: Parked cinematically between two thick and ancient Joshua trees is the Chrysler New Yorker Aurora's character is supposed to drive like a bat out of hell on her way to deliver a lifesaving treatment to Buster's character after a zombie attack.

If all goes well, which it never does, we should wrap by six and come back tomorrow morning for a few spots of pickup before we return to LA. It's twenty hours of work for a minute and a half of usable footage, but hey, that's Hollywood.

I see the production assistants gathered around the car, taking orders from Jonah. I see the trailer where Aurora is likely inside with hair and makeup. I see the tent shading the camera monitors and the director's chair parked behind them. My heart starts to pinch, but I look away, toward Ivy, approaching the van, holding what I call her "clipboard of catastrophes."

If I was directing today's shoot, that clipboard would strike fear in my heart. It holds records of everything that's going wrong—the car won't start, the stunt woman's drunk, the local sheriff has canceled our permission to shoot. Today, the blame for anything Ivy can't fix will fall on Jude's shoulders.

"What's the disaster du jour?" I ask, peering past the rim of her clipboard.

"Not much," Ivy says. "Just a zombie who got his beard trimmed too short for continuity."

"You adding cotton balls to fill it out?"

"You know it." She nods at my roller bag, which I'm unloading from the van's trunk. "You're crashing at 29 Palms tonight, right? I'm about to make a run to the inn to drop our bags. Dinner with everyone at the restaurant at eight, okay?"

"With everyone?" I cast a glance toward the director's tent.

"Yep. Rich's coming in. He wants us all to be there."

Another dinner with Rich and Jude. I should have brought my own clipboard to note my own catastrophes. I hand Ivy my bag and troop past several squat sage-green Joshua trees, eager to drown my futility in tea at craft services.

I've got my Earl Gray just the way I like it and am about to take my first sweet milky sip when my phone rings. Edie.

"Did you make it to JT?" Her words come out in a rush. "No flat tires? You're watching out for scorpions? How was dinner Friday?"

"Wow, how much coffee have you had today?"

"You know the desert makes me nervous," she says. "Ever since my hero-dose mushroom trip. Please, no drugs while you're there. They hit different in the desert."

# THE SPIRIT OF LOVE                    181

"In fact, I am far too sober," I tell her. "No scorpions in sight. I've only been on set for sixty seconds, but somehow nothing's gone wrong yet. And dinner was . . . surprising."

"What does that mean? You didn't end up crying in the president's bathroom again?"

"That wouldn't be surprising." I drop my voice to a whisper. "I was seated next to JDS."

"Uh-oh. And?"

"And it turns out he might not be as horrible as we thought he was," I say.

"*We?*" I hear her snicker through the phone. "I don't mind being proven wrong. Unless it involves my mother-in-law. So does this mean you're calling off the warpath?"

"TBD."

I break off because Jude is walking past me. He looks over and waves. For some reason, his face lights up, and I remember what it was like to talk to him at dinner, how there were moments when it felt like we were the only two people in that candlelit dining room. When our conversation became so engrossing, it was like the rest of the party disappeared.

"He doesn't know he stole your job, Fenny," my sister says.

I close my eyes and nod. "But I do."

And a small part of me needs to see the ripple effect of this injustice before I abandon my warpath.

"Just putting it out there that I like this warpath less than a hero dose with a scorpion chaser," Edie says.

"Yeah, but you're not here. Give the kids a kiss for me!"

I hang up to find Jude walking toward me.

He looks different in the desert. A little bit unbuttoned,

untucked, in his blazer and T-shirt, eyes shaded by a baseball cap. It's ninety-five degrees out here, too hot to wear anything more formal than cutoffs and a tank top, so I didn't even bother with my hair. His eyes run over my legs, which makes me wish I'd put a little more effort into getting ready this morning.

"Did you put on sunscreen?" he asks.

"Yes, Mom."

"Sorry, you just look like you burn easily. And the sun out here is . . ." He notices me side-eying him. "Okay, Mom is shutting up. I'm glad you're here. Can I show you something? Get your thoughts?"

Jude walks me toward the Chrysler, explaining how he intends to shoot the master shot of Aurora speeding up to the edge of the cliff. He describes the medium shot of her face through the windshield and then shows me the marker for her close-up where she'll get out and say her lines. It's not how I would have shot it, but I can see it working. There's more than one way to skin a zombie.

"Can we talk about Aurora's dialogue?" he asks. "She's got the line about having the amygdala on ice." He pauses and gazes up into shockingly blue sky. "I wonder if there's something missing."

"There was more," I say. "Once. We cut it. Rich wanted fewer words, more nipples."

Jude rolls his eyes. "The scene is complicated by the fact that Aurora's not delivering the amygdala directly to Buster—"

"Right." I nod. "She's handing it over to Miguel, who might be the love of her life—"

"Or at least the next season."

# THE SPIRIT OF LOVE                                    183

"That's what I was going to say." I laugh.

"I'm wondering," Jude says, "that is, if you even remember . . . how did you originally write Aurora's lines?"

I close my eyes and call it up. I never forget my first drafts. "It was 'I'm wearing an amygdala on my head, and my heart on my sleeve.'"

"That's the line," Jude says, amazed. "Aurora!" he calls as the actor steps out of her trailer, looking glamorously dust-battered and disheveled. "Come get your new line." Now Jude turns back to me. "Will you hang out in the tent with me?"

"I . . . yes."

For the next ninety minutes, I watch as Aurora drives the Chrysler to the cliff's edge eighteen times before Jonah and the sound guys are satisfied they've got all the angles they need for the take. Then it's time to reset the cameras so Aurora can actually get out of the car and say her lines.

I sit in the second director's chair that Jude had Ivy bring under the tent. He calls "Action!" and both of us watch. Aurora's committed, serving the right balance of camp and emotion. It's an excellent first take. Now she'll likely have to do it again at least a dozen more times so Jude will have choices in the editing room.

"Cut!" Jude calls. He bounds out of his chair, out of the tent, and up to Aurora. They're out of earshot, and I wonder what I would say to Aurora if it were me? Before I can decide, Jude comes back.

He sits beside me, puts on his headset, and says quietly, "Moment of truth."

Aurora takes a second pass. And it's brilliant. An actual tear slides down her cheek as she hands Miguel the frozen piece of brain. Then falls in for an unscripted kiss.

I glance at Jude and find him studying me.

"What do you think?" he asks, a rare glint of vulnerability in his eyes.

"Wow," I hear crew members murmur. Then I realize I'm among them. A "Wow" came out of my mouth, too. And I think it made Jude blush. Or is that just the furnace-like desert sun?

When Jude calls cut, we all applaud Aurora. This is usually a stoic set, but not today. Sometimes, even seven years in, we are collectively moved by our show.

"That's it. We got it." Jude says. "Nailed it, Aurora. And you." He turns to me. "Thank you, Fenny."

"That's it?" I say. "You've only done two takes. What if—"

"That was the take," Jude says with certainty. "I'll build the rest of the scene around it."

His confidence feels exciting—and a little reckless. I'd have shot ten more takes and still gone with this one in the end, but is it really as easy as Jude's making it sound? To know when you've got it and to stop there?

AFTER LUNCH, THE grips are finishing setting up the second set for today. The post-lunch lull is real, so sometimes actors overcompensate with caffeine. It looks as if Jude made this mistake himself. He's pacing nervously, and I think I hear him bickering with some members of the crew. As I get closer to the

# THE SPIRIT OF LOVE

185

scene, I can feel it. His energy is so different from his cool, calm confidence this morning.

In the scene they're prepping for, Buster is supposed to be living his best zombie life, tearing up the desert for his first taste of flesh. He has not yet chosen to come back as a human boy.

"Buster, I need you to take four steps toward me," Jude says.

"If we do that," a grip calls out, "I can't get the mountains in the shot."

"Doesn't matter," Jude says dismissively. "I can cheat that in editing."

The grip looks incredulous. "Then why did we all travel two hours to the burning desert so you could CGI the background?"

"Fine," Jude says. "But if Buster's standing there, I want to install the net."

The crew groans. The net is like the one you see at a circus, under a trapeze artist, stationed at the edge of anything an actor might fall off.

"Buster's got to feel free to devolve into darkness here," Jude explains. "He can't do that if he's about to fall off a cliff."

"The net will take us sixty minutes to build out," Jonah says, "at which point the sun will be completely different, so we'll have to redo all the lighting." He clocks Jude's expression. "Not that we can't do it—"

"I don't care if it takes us all night," Jonah says sharply. "I'd rather avoid a dead kid. Who is nervous enough as it is." He points at Buster, and everyone turns to look.

"I'm going to fall off the cliff?" Buster whines.

"No one's falling off a cliff," I interject, telling Buster, "We've practiced this, remember? You and me, back in LA, a couple weeks ago?"

The kid nods, but he doesn't look convinced.

What is Jude's problem? Buster wasn't nervous until Jude put the idea in his head.

Tempted as I am to kick back and enjoy the upcoming meltdown, I take in the full scene. Sound guys muttering and shaking their heads. Jonah still arguing with Jude. Buster clearly about to blast off on a rocket of nerves any moment.

My phone buzzes, and I assume it's going to be Masha and Olivia, sending pics from the plane Olivia should be jumping out of any minute, wearing a bachelorette veil. Instead, it's a message from Summer, Amy Reisenbach's chef.

It's a picture she must have taken at the dinner Friday night. It's Jude and me. We're seated at the table, sardines-close. We're turned toward each other, talking animatedly. My hands are expressive, and my eyes are sparkling. Jude's grinning, too. He looks more relaxed and comfortable than I can remember ever seeing him. In the picture, we look like old friends.

I look up at him now, looking far less comfortable. I don't know what got into him, but if Jude fucks up today, do I get my job back sooner? Or does it simply diminish the show I care about?

And suddenly, I know what to do.

"Buster," I say. "What do you think about letting Jude in on our secret?"

"Do we have to?" Buster says with a note of relieved surrender, the way my nephews sound when they're exhausted and are finally made to go to bed.

# THE SPIRIT OF LOVE

Buster, Jude, and I gather under the tent.

"What's this about, Fenny?" Jude sounds impatient.

I hold up a finger, take out my phone, and open the Calm app. But of course, I don't have service out here. I wrap one hand around my adder stone, and I decide I *do* have other worlds at my fingertips. Jude doesn't have to believe they're real to let them work their magic.

"Everybody close your eyes," I say.

And they do. I guide Buster and Jude through a five-minute meditation, set on a nature-filled island of my imagination, cribbed partly from my trip to Two Harbors with Sam. I give them the hummingbird, the baby eagles in their nest. I populate the world with a herd of stunning deer. I give them snorkeling across untouched coral reefs. I give them all the stars in the late-summer sky. I peak my eyes open toward the end and find Jude looking at me. His expression is cryptic, but then, before I can wonder about it, he smiles.

He mouths, *Thank you.*

The grimace on Buster's face has smoothed. It's time to wrap the meditation, to release everyone back to the scene at the cliff's edge.

"I don't need the net, Jude," Buster says as we walk back to the shoot. "I've blocked the scene with Fenny a bunch of times before."

"You have?" Jude asks, shooting me a quizzical look.

"I'm grounded. I'm ready to go," Buster says.

"Great," he says, eyes still on me. "Me, too."

## Chapter Sixteen

PRODUCTION DINNERS ARE A MIXED BAG. AT BEST, they can be a release valve at the end of an exhausting shoot, a way to blow off steam with the production assistants over company-expensed dumplings and inside jokes. But tonight, with Rich staying over, and with Jude's traveling team of set bros already pregaming loudly in the room next door to mine, I am feeling a strong urge to bail.

Even though Jude hasn't turned out to be as bad a director, or person, as I feared he would be, I don't think I'm quite enlightened enough to sit around another table praising his work today.

I shower and watch the sunset from my west-facing room— always the best fifteen minutes of any trip to the desert. Then I duck past the windows of the 29 Palms Inn restaurant, through which I see Ivy currently dictating place settings to two local teenage servers. I catch a cab back to town and slip into the Joshua Tree Saloon for a burger, beer, and some Old West–style solitude.

The walls of the saloon are made of clapboard and hung with desert relics, bull skulls, saddles, and rusted road signs from a hundred years ago. There's a rock band setting up on a tiny stage in the corner and a stretch of open barstools opposite the pool table. The last of the day's sunlight struggles through the smoked

THE SPIRIT OF LOVE                                          189

glass windows as I sidle up to the bar and peel a laminated menu
off its sticky top.

The bartender, a pretty Latina woman with a silver septum
piercing, smiles my way. "What's your poison?"

"A burger, medium rare, and a Sierra Nevada."

I open Instagram, and the first thing that pops up is a video
Olivia posted of herself and Jake screaming at each other as the
two of them leap out of a plane, holding hands. The caption
reads, "One week until we take this fight into forever. Can't wait
to marry you, Glasswell."

I can't believe they'll be married in a week. I can't believe a
week ago I thought about bringing Sam to the wedding as my
date.

What would Sam look like holding my hand as the two of us
jumped out of a plane? What would he look like in a tux, on a
dance floor, with me in his arms? All things I'll never know. I
don't mind going to Olivia's wedding solo. I'm used to that by
now. Even back when I was dating Eric, he made it clear that my
friends were my business, that he'd be glad to hook up after I
was done spending time with them.

"This beer comes courtesy of that gentleman," the bartender
says, gesturing to the side of the saloon.

"Oh, no, please," I say, "tell whoever it is I'll be paying for
my own hangover tonight." I don't even need to look at the el-
derly desert lizard who likely bought my drink to know this is
my answer. But then, on impulse, my gaze follows the bartender's nod, and who else would it lead to?

Jude de Silva.

He's sitting at the other end of the bar in his blazer, looking completely out of place. Why is he here? Why isn't he at the production dinner, being worshipped by all?

He points at his drink—a Sierra Nevada as well. He points again.

He's trying to tell me something. I lift my own drink off the coaster, where he's scrawled a note in pen.

*Acknowledging the obvious: We're both here.*

There's an arrow prompting me to flip over the coaster.

*Would you rather: A) lean into our introverted instincts and pretend we've never met, or B) celebrate you saving today's scene with another round?*

My chest tightens with trapped frustration as I tell myself Jude is the director of my show, so I can't behave like a completely antisocial Neanderthal. But one assumes Jude also came here to be alone, so what if he wants me to pick option A?

I reach into my bag for a pen and scrawl under his question:

*Dealer's choice.*

Just when the bartender—who seems to think this coaster-passing is cuter than it is—delivers my response to Jude, a horde of twenty-odd bikers flood the bar, crowding in around me as they bark out Budweiser orders.

I look toward Jude, who glances at the empty stool to his left. He raises an eyebrow and smiles. Surrendering to the cos-

# THE SPIRIT OF LOVE

mos he doesn't believe in, I rise from my stool, offer it to the hair-sprayed, leather-clad biker chick waiting behind me, and signal to the bartender that I'm moving seats.

"I was hoping it would go that way," she says.

I slide in next to Sam. "Those bikers were right on cue."

"Well worth the fifty bucks I paid them."

"I thought you'd be at the production dinner. Kevin and Matt were pregaming strong on the deck next to my room."

"I can see why you're here," he says with a wince. "Today was exhausting. Exhilarating but exhausting. I needed some space to come down."

Jude's comment makes me jealous. I want that exhilarating, exhausted feeling. I was supposed to have it on this trip. I was supposed to be the one needing to come down right now.

"Oh," he says, picking up on the shift in my mood. "I didn't mean I needed space from you."

"Two burgers," the server says, setting down our identical plates.

We reach for the ketchup at the same time but then both pull back to let the other take it. Finally, we both take a bite and chew in contented, if awkward, silence.

"I have an amazing burger recipe," Jude says. "I pack crumbled blue cheese and these homemade pickled jalapeños in this little secret lair inside the patty. Throw it on the grill . . ." He studies my expression. "What? Is this boring? Do you not like to cook? I thought because you were in the kitchen the other night, you were maybe into—"

"I cook," I say. "I don't know why, but I assumed you didn't. I kinda took you for a toast-burner."

"Recovered toast-burner," he says. "These days, my kitchen is the place where I can use my hands and let everything go."

"Apparently I only cook when I'm angry," I say. "My brother-in-law called me on that the other day."

"So . . . have you been cooking much since I came on *Zombie Hospital*?"

"I've packed my sister's deep-freeze full," I joke.

Something cold and wet nudges my ankle and makes me jump. I spin around and look down into the adorable brown face of some kind of shepherd mix puppy crouched under a barstool. "Woah, there's a dog in here!"

"Oh, shoot," Jude says, jumping up. "Where are my manners? Fenny, this is Walter Matthau. Walter Matthau, Fenny."

I put out a hand to Walter Matthau, who places his paw in my palm. He has soulful eyes but a puppy's wagging tail. I give his head a scratch and he nuzzles into my touch, the way my old dog, Milo, used to do.

"I can see why he hates you," I tease. "You take him to bars. You forget he's there. You don't introduce him to your colleagues."

"That was terrible," Jude agrees. "It's no excuse, but you—I—when I saw you here, I got distracted."

"Has he been with you all day?"

"I had a dog walker with him this afternoon while I was on set, but I'm trying to take your advice." He gestures around the bar, then at the dog giving him quite the side-eye. "This is the closest I could come to a guys' trip for now."

"That's great, Jude," I say, and mean it.

"Unless he runs off with you." Jude nods at his dog, who has

THE SPIRIT OF LOVE                                       193

all but crawled on top of me. I give him one more good belly rub and then rise to sit back next to Jude.

"I miss my dog," I say. "Milo died last year. Brindle boxer. Very wise and dignified."

"I'm sorry," he says. "I heard all dogs go to heaven."

"Which you don't believe in," I say with a smile. "Don't patronize me just because my dog died. Anyway, I think Milo was reincarnated as, like, a really beautiful spider, spinning webs on a giant cactus at the Huntington Gardens."

Jude looks at me as if he's trying to figure out whether I'm serious, but then he seems to get that that's not really the point. He smiles and so do I.

"Thanks for today, on set," he says, biting into a fry.

"Yeah, what happened there? Is it okay to ask? The morning went so smoothly. Is it Buster you have a hard time working with?"

"No, Buster's great. It was all me. This is embarrassing, but I get vertigo. Not great around steep drops. I was on my way to freaking out, but you saved me, Fenny. You saved the scene."

"It was nothing—"

"It was not. Why do you downplay your strengths?"

I blink, surprised. "I know my strengths. I don't downplay them. When I say it was nothing, I mean it changes nothing. I'll still be rewriting scripts later tonight and into infinity."

"You should be directing," he says, just as I've taken a sip of my beer.

I have to fight hard to not do the spit-take gag.

"I'm serious," Jude goes on. "You've got all the instincts. The actors revere you. You know everything, see everything, grasp everything. Buster said you'd already helped him block the scenes. You were made for this! You're *Zombie Hospital*'s unicorn. And unicorns need to direct. What?"

"Gee. It's a great idea, Jude," I deadpan, meeting his eyes. "Why didn't I ever think of that?"

There's a pregnant pause as I watch understanding flow into his brown eyes. They soften, turning down a bit at the corners.

"Oh," he says, still looking at me.

The energy between us is so fraught that I can't speak for fear of crying. I think Jude sees me, underneath the layers of protective sarcasm. I think he sees what I wanted, what he took from me, what it means.

"Fenny," he says, and his voice is different. "They told me there was an unexpected opening."

"It was unexpected to me, too," I say quietly.

"Rich told me—what an *ass*—he said something about the director they had lined up being institutionalized."

"Maybe he was gazing into the future." I take a drink. "But for now, she's very much still here."

"That's why you hate me."

"I don't hate you," I confess. "Not anymore. Not that much."

"That first day, when we met . . ." He trails off, studying me. "I couldn't figure out what I'd done wrong. I was like, *Do I remind her of some ex-boyfriend?*"

I almost spit out my beer again. I should really pause on the drinking until we've concluded this portion of the conversation.

"I'm sorry," he says, cringing. "That was—wow—embarrassingly presumptuous of me." Jude's cheeks have turned a surprising shade of rosy.

# THE SPIRIT OF LOVE

"How so?"

His voice has gone higher, clearer. "I did not mean to imply that I think I look like someone you would date or should date—"

"It's okay," I say. "It's simpler than all that. I just wanted your job."

"Because it was supposed to be your job. You should have it."

"Someday."

He puts both hands on the bar. "What if I walk—"

"Don't do that. Why would you do that?"

"Because this is your dream. It was never mine. I just got lucky. Well, first I got very unlucky, but somehow, I turned a bad thing that happened to me into the inspiration for a movie. And people liked it. And it landed me in a position where I got to pick my next project. *Zombie Hospital* was a whim—"

"Don't. Don't say that." I stare down into my beer.

"I'm only here because I loved something *you* wrote," he says. "Fenny, I'm so sorry. I'm going to make this right."

"If you walk, Jude, people will hate me. Everyone's so excited you're here. I would be an enormous letdown."

"Impossible," he says. "But maybe . . . we can find a way to work together."

He's smiling like we've made a great decision, but I feel nervous.

"I like it when you smile, Fenny," he says.

"You do?" I look at him and feel something pulse between us. It unnerves me—and I like it.

"I don't want to be the reason you're not smiling. Ever. I've got an idea to bring it back tonight. Will you indulge me for a little longer?"

"I'M VERY EXCITED about this plan," Jude says in the parking lot after we've paid our bills. I was about to hail a cab back to the hotel when he pointed down a darkened trail. "Take a walk with me and Walter Matthau?"

"Now? There? Really?" I can see nothing, but I know it's the direction of the national park, which is closed at night, unless you have camping permits.

"It's really stunning," he says, glancing over his shoulder. "We're camping out there actually."

"You're not staying at 29 Palms?"

"Do you know how many injuries and deaths occur each year due to hotel negligence?"

I stare at him, trying to fit this into my ever-expanding knowledge of the enigma that is JDS. "You don't trust *anyone*, do you?"

"You say that like it's an insult, but I have no problem admitting that when I can avoid putting my life in the hands of strangers, I avoid it."

"What about mountain lions? Do you know how many campers were mauled by mountain lions in Joshua Tree last year? Okay to put yourself in their paws?" I tease.

"Since 1986," Jude says, "there have been four fatal mountain lion attacks in all of California. No attacks, fatal or nonfatal, have been reported in Joshua Tree."

"Yeah, well, that's because the people were too dead to report them."

Walter Matthau whines.

# THE SPIRIT OF LOVE                    197

"When your jokes embarrass a dog," Jude says, "maybe it's time to rethink your approach."

"What happened the last time you stayed in a hotel?" I ask.

"A chandelier fell on me in the night." He points to a scar above his eyebrow, which I lean in to run my finger over.

"No way."

"Eight stitches."

My eyes fall on the longer scar that runs down the side of his jaw. It's very faint. Mostly hidden by his beard. I'd never noticed it, but then I've never stood this close to Jude de Silva. I point at it. "Is that from the chandelier, too?"

"No. Not that one." He turns and waves me forward. Together we start down the dark trail. "Do you know about night vision?"

"I know it takes eighteen minutes to kick in," I say, quoting Sam, remembering how he'd held me in his arms as he rattled off this stat.

"Very good," Jude turns to me. He sounds surprised, but in the dark, I can't see him yet. It hasn't been long enough. "So until eighteen minutes pass, I'm going to point out the dicey parts of this trail. Right there, small rock. Right there, subtle incline. Watch your step."

He takes my hand. His touch startles me. Warm, gentle. When I try to compare it to Sam's, I find I can't remember Sam's touch as clearly as I should. As clearly as I want to. And maybe that's for the best.

"Is this okay? I'd hate myself if you tripped when I could have prevented it."

"It's fine," I say. "I'm fine."

The three of us walk in silence for a while, Jude only interrupting the hooting of desert owls to tell me where and how not to trip. Finally we arrive at his tent, pitched next to a broad, flat rock.

I wish I'd thought to camp like this. It's a simple but cozy setup. Not much different from the one I had at Parson's Landing.

"I don't have any firewood," he confesses.

"Better to see the stars."

Jude hands me a blanket to spread out over the rock. We both climb up and then lie back. We look up at the stunning, spinning galaxy. Jude lets out a sigh that makes me wonder if he's feeling as grateful for this view as I am. I know reverence is not his style, but how could anyone not feel awe in the face of this?

"Stars," he finally says, breaking our comfortable silence.

"So many."

"No, I mean *stars*," he repeats. "You told me the other day that we can choose something to believe in. Maybe I choose stars."

"They're a great thing to choose."

"I can only see a couple from my condo," he says. "But maybe that's the point. Maybe if we believe in something, we have to be able to take it on faith that it exists. Maybe we can't have proof all the time."

"I like that very much."

"Don't. Move." Jude whispers.

I try not to move, but I turn my head to see what's going on. He points, very subtly, down his chest, where Walter Matthau has just snuggled up and laid his head on Jude's belly.

# THE SPIRIT OF LOVE                    199

"You did it," I whisper, grinning. "You bonded."

"I think we all bonded," Jude whispers back.

"Yeah. We did."

"Fenny," he asks. "Are we cool now? You and me? Are we okay?"

I can tell from his tone that he knows the answer, even before I do. Somehow, during the past week of bickering in cactus gardens, working crazy hours, trying on absurd costumes for no reason, eating Summer's salad as the sun set over Malibu, passing coaster notes in dive bars, and opening up to each other in unexpected ways, Jude and I have connected.

"We're cool," I say. "I think we might even be . . . friends."

"That's lucky for you, because now you can try my friends-only blue cheese jalapeño burger."

"Maybe I'll make you my famous pancakes with passion fruit syrup in return, like friends do."

"I hope I never taste your cooking."

I laugh. "What?"

"You told me you cook when you're mad. I don't want to make you mad. Not again."

I roll onto my side to face Jude. My night vision activates, and he looks beautiful under the stars, his expression relaxed and open. I'm petting Walter Matthau, but my hand is so close to Jude's body. One small move, and we'd almost be spooning.

"Anger is healthy," I say with a playful smile. "Besides, if history is any guide, I'd probably get over it eventually."

# Chapter Seventeen

"IS THIS IT?" OUR PRODUCTION DRIVER, MACY, ASKS, putting the van in park in front of my sister's house on Monday night.

"This is it. Thank you, Macy!" I call as I carefully climb over our sleeping DP and then Buster, who is deep into a Minecraft game on his iPad. When I finally make it out from the van's fifth row back corner seat and grab my backpack from the back, Jude has the passenger window rolled down and is studying Edie's front yard.

I'd been surprised when Jude and Walter Matthau caught a ride back to LA with the production van, which Rich calls the "Book Mobile." I know from having once negotiated my own director's contract that the show would have paid for Jude's private black car service back to his condo downtown. I'm even more surprised now, when Jude opens the front door and climbs out.

"Is this your house?" he asks, looking up at Edie's yellow-door two-story craftsman that sits at the top of a long staircase lined with all varieties of my sister's plant-babies—passion fruit and tomato vines, citrus trees, and raised beds bursting with rosemary and dill. Before having kids, Edie had triple the number of edible projects going, but the current state of her front

THE SPIRIT OF LOVE                                    201

yard feels pleasantly indicative of the current state of her life: a little chaotic, a little neglected, and weedy yet bursting with life.

"I don't know why," Jude says, "but I pegged you for a devout west-sider."

"I am," I say, surprised that Jude has taken the time to consider which neighborhoods suit me. "I live in Venice. This is my sister's place. We're having dinner."

"Oh. With your nephews, right?"

"Right." I glance at Macy, at the van packed with cast and crew members, who surely want to get dropped off at their homes, too. I'm not sure what Jude is doing, starting this conversation here and now, but he's looking at me like he wants me to say more. "Frank and Teddy, those are the twin toddlers. And my little baby nephew is Jarvis."

"So . . . who's cooking?" he asks in a leading tone. "I hope someone other than you?"

"Rude, Jude!" Macy calls, but I laugh.

"My brother-in-law is grilling, probably something with under point-five percent fat ratio, so it's bound to take a while to chew. But"— I drop my voice because Buster's headphones may not be fully noise-canceling—"I brought the pièce de résistance." Stealthily, I give Jude a peek inside my backpack, where I commandeered a sack of peanut M&M's from craft services and plan to gift them to my nephews for dessert.

"You bribe toddlers to love you?" Jude teases. "Is that what the cool aunts are doing these days?"

"Oh, shut up. They can't even deal with how much they love me. It has nothing to do with M&M's."

He smiles. "Need help with your bags? That's a big staircase."

"Bruh," I say, giving him a squint. "I'll see you in, like, less than eight hours." We have a sunrise shoot tomorrow morning, all the more reason I'm confused that Jude is now out of the van, having this chat. If I was the one holding up the van, I can imagine a lot of honks and some *What the fuck, Fenny?*s from the back rows. But everyone waits patiently for Jude to figure out what he's after with this conversation.

"Or," he says, "I could just walk you up. There's something I wanted to ask you." He turns back to the van. "Macy, thanks. I'll get out here. Come on, Walter Matthau," he says to the dog, passed out in the front passenger footwell.

"You sure?" Macy asks. "Bye, Walter Matthau!"

"Yeah," Jude says, grabbing his things from the back of the van. "We'll catch a dog-Uber home."

We wave as the van chugs away and then Jude and Walter Matthau follow me up Edie's steps. Walter Matthau gives my sister's lawn several hundred sniff tests, disappears, and eventually comes bounding out of a rosemary bush, tail wagging and smelling like focaccia.

Jude is quiet, climbing the stairs with his camping gear.

"You okay?" I ask. "You seem nervous."

"I am. I didn't plan this out very well. What I was going to say to you."

"No script?" I meant to sound teasing, but my voice is strained. I realize it's because I'm bracing myself for bad news. He's going to say he changed his mind about Buster's climax scene, and about finding a way to "work together."

Or worse. Jude could fire me.

# THE SPIRIT OF LOVE 203

We reach the top of the stairs and I turn to face him, readying myself to withstand the blow.

"I was wondering," Jude starts to say just as Edie's front door opens and Walter Matthau sprints inside my sister's house.

"Auntie Fenny got us a puppy!!!!" Frank shrieks at the top of his lungs. I peer inside to see the dog pummeling my nephew with kisses like Frank is his long-lost alpha.

"This is Walter Matthau," I tell Frank, then Teddy, who comes running out to pummel the dog with kisses of his own. "He's on loan only for a short visit!" I turn to Jude. "Well, now you have to stay for dinner. Or at least, Walter Matthau does. Sorry."

Edie appears in the doorway, wearing a towel and a shower cap, Jarvis in her arms. She hugs me tightly. Jarvis coos. "Thank God you survived that awful place."

Over my shoulder she must have clocked Jude because her body language shifts and she tugs up her towel, as if that's all that's needed to make herself presentable. "Who's this?"

"Um, Edie, Jarv, this is . . . Jude de Silva."

"No shit!" Edie says, then clamps a hand over her mouth. "Sorry, I haven't slept in several years."

"Jude, this is my sister, Edie. And Jarvis."

"Hey, Edie, Jarvis," Jude says warmly, shaking my sister's hand, then Jarvis's. "Great house. Great kids."

"Did you tell him to say that?" Edie asks me, suspicious. I give Jude a wink because he winged it and did good.

"They're staying for dinner!" Teddy shouts from inside, laughing with Frank as they discover Walter Matthau's tickle spot behind his ears.

"Come in," Edie beckons us. "I'll just throw something on real quick. I can shower when I'm dead."

We step inside her living room, with its views of the backyard, where my brother-in-law seems to be cursing at the grill.

"He doesn't know shit about propane," Edie says under her breath. She turns to Jude. "That's Todd. Can you help him? He needs help. A lot of help."

Jude glances at me, then at Walter Matthau, who seems to have a new lease on life. The dog is playing tug-of-war with Teddy, Frank, and a couch pillow.

"Is this okay?" Jude asks me.

"Totally. Good luck with Todd," I say.

Alone-ish, Edie grips my wrist and tugs me into her bedroom. I bounce Jarvis while she changes.

"What's going on?" She point in the general direction of the backyard, of Jude.

"I *don't* know."

"I told you crazy shit happens in the desert."

"One minute, the production van was dropping me off . . ."

"The next, he's out there talking to Todd about . . ." Edie leans in close to the window. "Brazilian soccer teams?"

I shrug.

Edie laughs. "Todd is pretending he knows a single damned think about soccer. Jude does though."

I look at my sister and then put my own ear close to the window, like a freak.

Through the glass, I hear Jude saying, "My dad's side of the family lives in Brazil."

# THE SPIRIT OF LOVE                                              205

"Did you know he was half-Brazilian?" Edie asks, and I shake my head.

Because someone's got to say it, I do: "Let's hope it's from the waist down."

I peek through the blinds to glimpse Jude talking to Todd. They seem to have gotten the grill going at least. Smoke plumes around them as they stand, drinking beers, avoiding eye contact, and taking turns poking at the meat.

"Because we're sisters," I tell Edie, "I can say weird shit to you and only you, so take this with a grain of salt, but . . . I feel like I brought over a boyfriend I didn't know I had."

Edie, now dressed in a clean sweatshirt and jeans, peeks through the blinds next to me.

"No," she says. "I already like him way better than any boyfriend you've ever had."

"You barely know him."

"But I know you, and you seem happy. You seem comfortable."

"That has nothing to do with him," I say, but I'm surprised to realize that I *am* happy. I am comfortable. I still want my shot at directing, but the anger I felt all last week has dissipated. I'm in a good mood, and I'm not mad at the fact that Jude is staying for dinner. I had fun with him last night, and I was feeling a little let down that we sat so far away from each other in the van and couldn't talk on the ride back.

"So what's the deal with you two?" Edie says, leading me out of the bedroom and toward the kitchen, where she opens a bottle of wine.

"Nothing!" I say, combing my fingers through Jarvis's new blond ringlets. "We're colleagues."

"And?"

"And I don't know if it was last night, or if it happened more gradually during the course of the week, but it's now undeniable: We're friends."

Edie looks like I just doused her birthday candles with a bucket of sewer water. "That's it?"

"That's it."

She shakes her head, sips her wine, and stares at the men outside. "You need to take that up a peg because he looks like he gives excellent head."

"Edie!" I peek around the doorway to see if one of her older children might be near enough to be traumatized, but they're both on the couch, making a Walter Matthau sandwich.

"It's the beard," Edie says. "Kind of a fantasy of mine. That, and a man who can talk dirty in Portuguese? Get out of here with that."

"It does sound rather hot," I say, reluctantly looking at Jude and unable now not to imagine such a bedroom scene. I shake my head and cast the thought out the window.

"Signed, sealed, delivered, I'm yours," Edie says. "Help me bring the cheese and crackers outside before the men spontaneously combust from having to speak to someone they don't already know."

The lead-up to dinner is a whirlwind. Frank and Teddy spill three glasses of water and break two dishes while helping set the table. Walter Matthau gets terrified by the neighbor's outdoor cat and cowers at my feet. Todd lights half the burgers on fire

THE SPIRIT OF LOVE                                207

while Edie tries and fails to put on a Spotify playlist that doesn't devolve into StoryBots.

When we're finally seated, just before sunset, when the sky is pink and dotted with silvery clouds, and Edie and Todd are consumed with serving and assisting the boys, who are now eighty percent ketchup and all want their food cut up in different shapes at different temperatures on different plates, I lean into Jude.

"This is probably a lot." I point at his plate, which looks like it was badly glued back together after a recent smashing. "Sorry."

"It's terrific," he says sincerely. "Everything is." He points at Walter Matthau, who has his chin resting on Teddy's lap and is occasionally gifted with charred bites of bison burger. "I think maybe, all this time, he's just been lonely."

"Maybe," I say. We both know we're talking about more than just the dog. My eyes linger on Jude's beard, and I can't get Edie's words out of my head. I feel a little breathless when he says:

"And now, tonight, he isn't lonely anymore. He's really happy to be here."

After dinner, while Edie and Todd take the kids upstairs to get ready for bed, Jude gets up to clear the plates. "Anyone want to do dishes with me?"

"I do," I say, following him into the kitchen.

He scrubs, and I dry and put things away. I pour us each another glass of wine. And it's nice, with the din of my family upstairs and us in here, quiet and slightly cramped and feeling new at this friendship thing.

"Have you and Edie always been this close?" Jude asks.

I could just say yes, but of course there's more to the story, and I can't believe I want Jude to know it. Because I don't talk about this with anyone. Only ever Edie. And Sam, I try not to think. But earlier tonight, after dinner, when he spoke about Walter Matthau, I'd felt Jude opening up to me in a way that I want to reciprocate. And if I'm opening myself up, this is what I hold inside.

"So, funny story," I start to say, keeping it casual. "When I was ten, I kind of . . . died for a minute—"

Jude drops the plate in his hands. My reflexes kick in, and I catch it just before it shatters.

"You good?" I ask.

"Sorry," he says awkwardly. "I just, wow. That's very interesting. And not what I thought you were going to say. What happened?"

"Pneumonia first, then I spiked a fever. They took me to the hospital. And I . . ."

I look at him, feeling the bright warm rush of his full attention on me. He seems interested, like he doesn't think I'm crazy yet, but can he handle this? Jude, who doesn't believe in anything, will he believe me when I tell him? If he laughs, or dismisses me, then at least I'll know.

"I left my body for a little while," I say, holding his soft brown gaze. "I saw how much more there is."

"How much more is there?" Jude asks, transfixed.

If I closed my eyes I could call it all right back. But I don't want to look away. My eyes are caught on his.

"It's everything you've heard," I whisper, and it feels like we're closer than we were a moment ago, although I don't think either of us has moved. "It's far beyond words."

THE SPIRIT OF LOVE                    209

"Wow," he breathes.

I nod. "And I almost, you know, *went* there."

"But?" Jude whispers.

My eyes sting. I want to say this part without my voice cracking. Because it isn't sad, and I don't want to be misunderstood. "But I saw Edie. On this side. And I came back."

"Fenny." He's looking at me in amazement, like I just did something impressive. Maybe I did. It certainly feels important that I shared this with Jude. But what do I really want him to know? Not just an explanation for why I'm close with my sister. I want him to know how my experience then shaped who I am now.

"I guess what I'm trying to say," I tell him, "is that, in that moment, I knew exactly what I was supposed to do. I felt so clear, seeing Edie, choosing to come back. You could say I've been chasing that feeling ever since."

"The feeling of certainty? Purpose?" Jude asks.

"Yes."

He nods. "And you'll have it when you direct. I get it now. Fuck that jerk who stole your job."

"It's not your fault," I say, meaning it. "There's a way in which I let it happen. I've put in all this work on *Zombie Hospital*, but sometimes I fear I've yet to make myself stand out."

"You stand out to me. Thanks for telling me that story. Is it weird to say I feel honored?"

"Thanks for listening, for not laughing. That moment changed my life. And I'll always feel grateful to Edie. It keeps us tight."

Jude hands me a platter to dry, and I'm surprised by how

quickly we're moving through the dishes. He gets easier and easier to talk to.

"I'm an only child," he says. "I don't often imagine what siblings might have been like. My parents split when I was really young. But this house, your family, it does make me wonder . . ."

"What?"

"I don't know. What I'm missing. What Walter Matthau's missing."

"Probably a lot of tummy aches for Walter Matthau," I joke. "But yeah, I know what you mean." This conversation is so nice that I don't want to wreck it, but I won't sleep tonight if I don't ask: "You were going to ask me something, earlier. Something about the show, I think?"

"Oh. No. It wasn't about the show."

"It wasn't?"

"I was going to invite you to this thing I have to go to . . ." He trails off and peeks at me out of the corner of his eye, which makes me smile.

"What is it?"

He takes a breath. "Feel free to laugh in my face . . ."

"Oh, I always reserve that right."

He clears his throat. "By any chance, would you want to be my plus-one at a wedding next weekend? I don't know anyone else going, and—"

"Oh, I can't."

"Right. Of course. Big weird ask."

"No, I would have loved to. But I'm already *in* a wedding next weekend. One of my best friends. So unless, miraculously,

# THE SPIRIT OF LOVE

211

we're talking about the same wedding, in a city of four million people—"

"Jake Glasswell and O—"

"Olivia Dusk and Jake—" I break off and clamp a hand over my mouth. "You're the one who doesn't believe in cosmic coincidences. Explain this."

He laughs. "Maybe we entered a vortex in Joshua Tree."

"That and you were recently a guest on Jake's show," I say, remembering what Olivia had told me about Jude back when I first met and hated him. "He liked you."

"Every once in a while, that happens," he says, running his eyes over my face.

"So let's go together," I say brightly.

"You don't already have a date? I have this image in my mind of you being disgustingly happy with some cheerful beefcake."

"Maybe I was, once . . ." I confess. "Unfortunately, that relationship was unsustainable."

"Too good to be true?" Jude asks.

"Too far away."

"Alas."

"Alas." I smile at Jude. "It's all right, because I think I just got a pretty decent replacement date. You might have heard of him. Scorsese can't do an interview without raving about him."

"I will try my best to live up to that hype."

"Jude? One more thing?" I say, partly because I see Edie on her way into the kitchen and partly because I'm honestly curious. "Would you ask me to the wedding again, in Portuguese?"

Jude puts down the dish he's holding and turns to face me.

He looks surprised but also game, and his voice drops to a husky rumble as he speaks in the loveliest language I have ever heard.

"*Você seria meu acompanhante no casamento de Jake e Olivia no próximo fim de semana?*" he asks just as Edie comes in.

"Sim!" I answer.

"I don't know what's happening in here," Edie says, gazing around her newly cleaned kitchen, her eyes landing first on Jude and then on me. "But it sounds R-rated, and I approve."

# Chapter Eighteen

"THIS IS A TERRIBLE IDEA."

I'm standing next to Jude at the bottom of Olivia's staggeringly steep driveway an hour before her wedding. I look down at my green sequin vintage stilettos with their unfortunate five-inch heels. (The shoes were an impulse purchase once I forecasted the wedding photos in which my date was more than a foot taller than me.) I look up at the long stone path, which winds through topiary, several fountains, and probably a layer of clouds before ending at Olivia and Jake's Laurel Canyon hilltop home.

We're too early for the golf cart service that will be shuttling guests to the summit for the backyard ceremony. But we're too late to drive Jude's Rivian up and park in Olivia's garage with the rest of the wedding party. The pedestrian gate is open, but the *Jurassic Park*–like driveway gate is closed, and when we buzz the call button, it just rings and rings. Masha's not answering her phone, I'm already twenty minutes past my arrival time for photos, and I'll never make it up this cobblestone driveway in these goddamned shoes.

"Piggyback?" Jude offers. His tailored slate-gray velvet tux hugs his trim body. He looks electrifyingly attractive, and I'm really feeling his beard-and-glasses combo against his formal wear. But the man is not an ox. Sam, I might consider letting haul me up this mountain. After all, he's done it before. But Sam is far away today, and Jude's a different breed of date.

"Or we could steal that golf cart." Jude points toward the opened garage of the one-bedroom bungalow at the base of the driveway. Olivia used to live in this bungalow, before she started dating Jake. Now, she's converted the bungalow into a recording studio where she and Lorena produce their podcast. And, Jude is right, tucked inside the garage is an immaculately unmanned golf cart.

I eyeball the width of the open pedestrian gate leading up Olivia's driveway. I take another gander at the golf cart. I touch the adder stone at my neck. I hadn't planned to wear it to the wedding, but when I put on my bridesmaid dress, the combination looked too right to take off. No, Sam isn't my date to this wedding, or probably to anything else ever again. That fling has flung. But for a moment, holding the stone he gave me on the secret beach, it's like his spirit is with me. There's no way in hell Sam would let a little driveway stand between him and his dear friend's wedding.

I hobble toward the golf cart.

"What are you doing?" Jude asks.

"Finally, I get why everyone says you're a genius!"

"I was joking," Jude says behind me. "We cannot steal that golf cart."

"We cannot *not* steal it. That's what these things are for!"

"I thought they were for golf."

"And pedimergencies! Get in."

# THE SPIRIT OF LOVE                                    215

"Fenny—"

"The train is leaving, Jude." I pat the pleather bench beside me. "I know you want a seat."

"Have you ever driven one of these?" He sounds concerned as he slides in next to me.

"We'll be fine!" I throw the vehicle into reverse. "It's like riding a bike. I think."

"Watch out!" Jude cries, gripping the metal frame as we whiz out of the garage and onto the quiet residential street.

"Dude, we're going four miles an hour. It's cool." I make the hard right from the street onto Olivia's driveway. Two brown-haired girls around ten years old point to us and laugh. This is a rush, and I'm enjoying it.

Jude winces, holding his glasses to his face. "You should come with a warning label."

I glance over at him as we *barely* squeak through the pedestrian gate. "You're cute when you're nervous."

"You're very beautiful *when you keep your eyes on the road.*"

The compliment, couched as a panicked threat, does something unexpected to my chest. It makes my heart pulse stronger. It makes me sneak another glance in his direction to see if he meant what he just said. I thought his eyes would be glued to the road, but when I glance over, he's looking at me.

"Sorry," he says. "That slipped out."

"Hey!" A pair of young, tuxedoed valets run in tandem down the driveway toward us. "You're not supposed to drive that! Stop the cart!"

"And now we get arrested," Jude says, throwing up his hands.

"We got her warmed up for you!" I say to the valets, punching the pedal to swerve around them, laughing when they spin on their heels to chase us up the driveway. "That was fun. Should we circle back and do that again?"

I'm not usually like this, but Jude's cautious nature brings out my recklessness. My wild side runs on the optimism that everything will turn out mostly okay in the end because I've glimpsed the end and I *know* that this is true. Something about Jude makes me want to tempt fate, if only to prove to him that it's real. Didn't he used to have a wild side as a kid? I have this urge to wake it up.

We reach the top of the driveway without injury or death, and I can tell Jude is pleasantly surprised—or, at the very least, breathing again. I park the golf cart, climbing out with an exhilarated sigh.

"Run," Jude commands, glancing over his shoulder. "The valets. They're coming."

"Oh, shit. They look *mad*." Giggling, I grab his hand and we run into the safety of Olivia's house, closing ourselves in the half bathroom in the foyer and locking the door.

I collapse into Jude, laughing until I can't breathe. I should pull away and catch my breath, but he's got his hands resting lightly on my shoulders and I find that I can't move. I look up at him, grinning.

"What else can we steal today?"

"Flats," he tells me, out of breath. "I'm buying you flats from now on for every major holiday. You're getting Halloween flats and Election Day flats—"

"The perfect shoe for stealing more golf carts," I tease him, enjoying the way his eyes crinkle. There's that smile, so hard to

THE SPIRIT OF LOVE                                    217

earn that when I do, it feels like a triumph. Even though he'll never admit it, he's enjoying this, too.

The pain in my feet reignites now that I've been upright in these shoes for several minutes, and I wince, letting myself drop down onto the closed toilet seat.

"How fast can you get those flats delivered?" I ask. "I can't believe I have to stand in these for the ceremony."

"Would it help if I . . ." Jude trails off, lowering himself to his knees and lifting my left foot off the ground, onto his lap.

"Is this okay?" he asks as he slips off my shoe and sets it on the bathroom floor.

I nod.

Jude uses his thumb to apply firm pressure to the ball of my foot. He's looking at my bare foot—freshly pedicured this morning, my nails painted with a pale-yellow polish—as if it's a painting on a museum wall that requires careful study. I might be embarrassed by the intimacy of this moment if it didn't feel so good.

I moan in deep relief as Jude massages my throbbing feet until the impossible happens: The pain dissolves. He uses both hands now, which are wonderfully strong and make it hard for me to keep my eyes open.

"Where did you learn to do this so well?" I ask, a little breathless. "And why have you been hiding this incredible skill from me?"

"I've never done this before in my life," he says, his cheeks a little pink. "Just kind of winging it."

"Liar. You've been trained by a leader in the field. Can we stay just here all night?"

His eyes dip to my lips, so, purely on reflex, mine dip to his. I'm starting to really like the way his beard frames his lips. The texture of that scruff is so inviting—a little rough, like scratching an itch.

"Fenny?" There's a knock on the bathroom door. It's Masha. "Is that you?"

I snap my foot down, and Jude pops up to open the door, to Masha on the other side.

"Oh!" she says, her gaze moving all the way up to Jude's face. "Hi. Is this—"

"This is Jude. My friend. From work." While hauling myself off the toilet and hopping back into the shoe of death, I try to communicate a whole brunch's worth of download to Masha with my eyes. Life's been moving fast since Joshua Tree, and my friends and I haven't yet had a chance to catch up.

"Your . . . friend. Great."

"Sorry Fenny's so late for her bridesmaid duties," Jude leans forward to tell Masha. "It took me forever to convince her to steal a golf cart to get up here."

Masha points at Jude. "I like him. Can I steal *you* now, Fen, for the processional?"

"Of course." I glance at Jude. "You'll be okay?"

"I'll be fine, just shoe shopping for you on my phone. Size seven?"

"How did you know that?"

He wriggles those magic fingers at me, making me wonder how they'd feel elsewhere on a woman's body.

"I still owe you the other half of the massage," he whispers in my ear as I leave the bathroom with Masha, a little flustered and only half-relieved.

FAVORING MY RESTORED left foot like a flamingo, I take my place at the altar next to Masha, across from a beaming, green-tuxedoed Jake and an unusually teary Eli. This backyard, always beautiful, has been stunningly transformed for the wedding today. Everywhere I look are roses and rhododendrons in shades of pink, orange, and white. The pool has been covered in plexiglass to make way for the aisle running up the center of the yard. Beyond the altar, I can see the skyscrapers of downtown to my left, and to my right, it's clear enough today to see all the way to Catalina. But I'm finding that my favorite view is the one of Jude, sitting in the audience ten rows deep, smiling up at me. When our eyes lock, he flashes his phone, and I squint to see what looks like some sort of shoe purchase. It makes me laugh, and then wonder—how long would Jude and I have stayed locked in that bathroom if Masha hadn't knocked? What else would have happened in that tiny little room? A flush warms my neck at the thought.

But nothing happened. We're just friends. Who work together. One of whom speaks fluent Portuguese; may or may not give excellent, bearded head; and has offered to work with me on directing the show we both love.

When the music changes to the opening chords of "I Will Always Love You," the wedding guests all rise. And there stands my wonderful friend Olivia at the back of the crowd. She has both boobs inside her magnificent purple dress. She's arm in arm with Lorena. Mother and daughter cry openly as they walk down the aisle, which makes me start to cry, which makes me look toward Jude. Does he think it's pedestrian to cry at weddings? Worse, does he think that it's pointless? I know how directors' minds work. Everything is inspiration. Is he sitting there now, studying every detail of this wedding until his mind lands on the bleak twist that might turn this whole scene into a Palme d'Or–winning horror classic?

Was it a mistake to write off Sam so soon? Because Sam would have no problem crying at a wedding. Sam would have kissed me in that bathroom out of victory and the simple joy of being alive.

Or Sam might not have come at all. Jude is the one who's here. I study him, this new friend of mine, as everyone sits back down. I can't tell what he's thinking. I wish I had day vision that kicked in after eighteen minutes and let me see Jude with the open clarity I'd seen him with under the Joshua Tree stars. He's sphinxlike now, like he is most of the time.

And then, suddenly, I can't see him at all. Because a pretty, waiflike woman wearing an enormous, veiled, Kate Middletonian hat featuring a large, lace-wrapped hummingbird's nest, sits down directly in front of Jude. Her hat blocks his view of the ceremony entirely. It also blocks my view of him.

Meanwhile, at the altar, Yogi Dan, the same officiant who married Masha and Eli, is making a speech about soulmates. I'm holding back laughter at Jude, who keeps trying and failing to peek out from behind this woman's hat. He leans left; she leans

# THE SPIRIT OF LOVE

left. He edges right; she drifts right in front of him. Finally, he reaches up and subtly parts the hummingbird's nest from the lace so he has the narrowest crevice of a view—not of the bride and groom, I realize, but of me.

He winks. I smile.

"You may kiss the bride," the yogi says, and as much as I want to see Jake and Olivia kiss, I've only just gotten my view back of Jude and I find I can't look away.

LATER, I'M STANDING with Masha at the edge of the plexiglass-covered pool. Both of us are barefoot, but she has the excuse of being pregnant. I'm sipping champagne and she's got a mocktail, and we cheer as Olivia dips Jake in a choreographed ballroom version of "Don't Stop Believin'."

A hand comes around my waist.

The last time someone held me like this was Sam, the night we'd watched the sunset on the secret beach. His touch made me feel naked—and something about this touch ignites a similar yearning in me. When I turn toward the feeling, it's Jude. He's tugging me gently against him.

"Oh, are we dancing?" I ask, wrapping my arms around his neck and beginning to sway.

"I'm dancing you away from that plexiglass death trap," he says. "You never saw my film *My Schizophrenic Grandma*?"

I shake my head. "Did she meet her demise at a Laurel Canyon wedding?"

"A frozen lake, actually, but to prep for that sequence, I

watched a lot of YouTube shorts where these kinds of dance floors crack. They can take out entire bridal parties."

"Your algorithm must be a very stressful place." I gesture down to the grass beneath our feet. "Look. Solid ground. Can we just dance now? Or do you need to rescue the bride and groom, too?"

I glance over my shoulder to where Olivia and Jake are both about to throw out their backs in time to the chorus of "Once in a Lifetime."

"I'd honestly love to evacuate them, along with every grandparent out there," he says. "But you're the only one I know well enough to indulge my darkest fears."

"I'm honored. And grateful my life has been spared."

"I have to spare your life. Without you, I'd be screwed at work."

"Relax your hips," I tell him. "Just like that. Hold mine a little closer." I smile as Jude follows my direction and we ease into the music. Into each other's bodies. I feel more comfortable being this close to Jude than I expected to. We fit together the way two people on a dance floor are supposed to. I look up at him. Does he feel this, too?

No, I guess not. His brow is furrowed as he looks across the reception.

"What is it?" I ask. "Other threats I need to be aware of? Are the valets coming back for us? Do you see a reviewer who dared to give you three stars?"

"I'm just trying to figure out the color palette here. Why is Olivia wearing a purple dress?"

"It's rum raisin," I explain. "An homage to one of Liv and

THE SPIRIT OF LOVE                                    223

Jake's earliest fights. Their wedding theme is a greatest hits of their arguments. They hated each other for like ten years."

"Enemies to lovers, eh?" Jude says. My eyes widen in surprise. "What? I've seen a couple rom-coms in my day." He dips me. "You might be surprised to learn that I was tapped to direct a second-chance rom-com."

"Who in the world would tap *you* to direct a rom-com?" I hear myself and grimace. "Sorry. That was harsh. I would pay to see a rom-com directed by Jude de Silva. And yet, you turned down this offer?"

Jude tosses his head. "I'm still looking for a great friends-to-lovers script. Somehow I find those more believable."

I lean in closer so Jude can't see my cheeks get hot.

"Do you want all this one day?" Jude asks me as the DJ plays U2's "Sweetest Thing." "Big purple dress? Yogi officiant? Shoving cake in some lucky guy's piehole?"

"I don't know," I say. "Not in and of itself. I've never met someone who inspired me to picture myself in purple tulle."

"Not even your phenomenal long-distance lover?"

I'm pretty sure I never told him Sam was a phenomenal lover.

"We did have chemistry," I say.

Jude stiffens in my arms. "I'm failing to see the problem."

I sigh. "Me, too."

"You still have feelings for him?"

"It's confusing. This all happened very recently."

Jude nods. "So why isn't he here with you tonight? Why me?"

"Jude?" The waify woman with the hummingbird hat suddenly flings her arms around Jude's neck and sways. "Hiiiiiiii!"

224 LAUREN KATE

Hummingbird's grip on Jude is so tight, and has landed right on top of mine, so it makes it impossible for me to pull away.

Now we're a threesome dancing to U2.

"I didn't see you during the ceremony!" she sings.

"Maybe because he was lost in your hat," I mutter, finally extricating myself.

I study Jude's visitor. In her sequined dress and minimalist makeup, she's one of those sculpted, highlighted LA types who could be either twenty-three or forty-three.

"It's Tania," she says, pressing a hand to the keyhole of exposed cleavage in her dress. "Do you remember?"

"Of course," Jude says slowly, his eyes moving toward me as I take a step back. "We shared that—"

"Unforgettable connection." She winks at him. Now she glances for a fraction of a second at me. "Listen, I don't want to interrupt—"

Jude gestures at me. "Oh. No. We were just—"

"I saw you from across the room," Tania says, "and I *had* to come tell you"—here she drops her voice and giggles—"I did the *thing*. Remember? What we talked about? What you said I was *made for*?" She swats him playfully across the chest. "You changed my life, JDS!"

"Surely not." He laughs, embarrassed.

Tania looks at me. "He is so humble."

"Is that the word?" I say.

I can't help noticing the interest with which Jude is looking at this woman. And why wouldn't he? She's sexy, vibrant, and, yes, makes bizarre hat choices, but who cares when she's got keyholes full of cleavage and is so clearly into Jude? He's looking

THE SPIRIT OF LOVE 225

at her the way I might look at a new near-death experience pub-lication, as if, finally, *this* one might be *the* one to unlock all the mysteries of the universe.

I don't know why I'm jealous. Is it because Jude has very clearly hooked up with this Tania person? Jealousy toward Tania would make no sense. Jude and I are just friends, and just barely at that. It's been, what, six days since I stopped hating him? And forty seconds ago, I was extolling my incredible chemistry with Sam. I have no claim on Jude. I've barely even thought about him that way. At least not for a full, extended fantasy or any-thing.

And now my mind is going to all the stupid places . . .

What would Lorena say if she wasn't tangoing on dangerous plexiglass with her elegant date right now? Would she say that I'm not jealous of the sexual tension between Tania and Jude? That actually, I'm jealous because I want Sam to look at me the way Jude and Tania are looking at each other?

"I'll let you get back to dancing," Tania tells us both, taking Jude briefly by the lapels. "But you have my number. *Call me.* Make. That. Move."

And then she's gone, but Jude doesn't put his arms back around me, and I don't put my arms back around him. A waiter passes and we both grab more champagne and chug it down.

"She seems nice," I finally say.

"Yeah," he says. "Um. What were we talking about before?"

"The periodic table, I think."

"Right," Jude says, bringing me back into his swaying arms. "Chemistry." His voice is a low rumble against my neck. "You were telling me about your last relationship."

"It's nothing."

"It doesn't sound like nothing," he says. My chest warms, and the feeling spreads to my cheeks until suddenly the dance floor feels very hot and very small. And I wonder, if I tipped my face toward Jude's right now, what kind of chemistry would we have? I look up at him and—yes, his eyes give me the answer I was hoping for. He's wondering about it, too. Does he feel the same pull I'm feeling? Does he suspect that if we kissed right now, we might never stop?

He takes one hand off my waist, but just when I think he's going to touch my cheek, draw me toward him, he rubs his beard and clears his throat. Something cools between us, and I break a little inside.

"Does this guy know how you feel?" Jude asks. "If he doesn't, you should tell him."

"I . . ." I'd forgotten we were talking about Sam. I don't want to talk about Sam right now. I want—

But Jude's not even looking at me anymore. His eyes are across the party, on Tania.

Speaking of people who should tell other people how they feel. I should get out of his way and let him at this woman. We're friends. I want happiness and beauty and sex for my friends. And Tania is very clearly putting forward all those options for Jude.

Then why does it twist my heart to imagine her getting one of Jude's foot massages? Why is it so hard to say what I know I should say next?

"You're right," I force myself to say at last, hearing Tania's sultry rasp in my head. "Maybe we should both go ahead and make that move."

# Chapter Nineteen

ON THE WALK TO RICH'S OFFICE THURSDAY MORNING, my knees are shaking in the leather cargo power pants I decided to reprise for good luck. Jude's stride is confident, and his eyes are bright and excited, but I've gotten to know him well enough this month to perceive that he's as exhausted as I am. Jude and I both arrived on set disgustingly early, huddling in my trailer to give today's script a final read. He's as impeccably dressed as ever in an olive green suit and tie, but his beard's a little scragglier than usual, and the crease between his eyebrows is a little more pronounced. We both need a good night's sleep. Luckily, the whole show has tomorrow off. After today's eleven-hour shoot, *Zombie Hospital* gets a well-deserved long weekend.

For the past three days, the two of us have been finding every opportunity to steal away and tinker with the script. We've dissected every line of dialogue and talked camera angles and special effects. We discovered our shared obsession with the 1943 underground classic film *I Walked with a Zombie* while dining on smoked salmon handrolls delivered late-night from Katsuya.

I've worked in many writers' rooms, but nothing's ever felt this good, this easy, or this fun. Collaborating with Jude is joyful, challenging, and wacky all at once. When we disagree, it's built on mutual admiration for each other's strengths. And when we agree, I feel that elusive collaborative spark I've always dreamed of sharing with someone else on set.

Now all that's left to do today is to take our plan to Rich, to see if what Jude and I built is strong enough to withstand a deluge of doubts from *Zombie Hospital*'s management, cast, and crew.

"Are we sure about this?" I ask Jude right before we pull open the door to Rich's waiting room. "Are *you* sure?"

"Fen," Jude says warmly, using the nickname for the first time but making it sound like he's used it forever. When he puts a hand on my shoulder, it makes me want to close my eyes and lean all the way into him. "You were ready last month. You're ready now. The only difference is that I've got your back."

"You say that like it's nothing, but it's a big deal. I want you to know that I'm grateful." I put my hands on his lapels, resisting the urge to pull him closer. Ever since the wedding last weekend, dancing with Jude, there's something in me that wants to stay close to him.

"This is only the beginning of the cool shit you're going to direct," he says lowly in my ear.

"Thank you, Jude."

"Least I can do," he says, and pulls open the door. "Now, come on in. Let's make steam come out of Rich's hair plugs."

"Fenster," Rich says, not looking up from his phone when Jude and I walk in. "I've got five—eh, four—minutes for you before my eight o'clock. Hey, did you happen to see my Postmates guy out there? I'm dying for my chia pudding—"

"Rich," Jude says.

THE SPIRIT OF LOVE                                          229

"Oh, hey, man!" Rich jumps up, all smiles now that he's not the only dick in the room. "Didn't know you were joining, bruh."

"Just came to drop off revised sides for today," Jude says, "and to let you know I'm turning the camera over to Fenny for the climax sequence."

Rich tilts his head to the side and squints like he's misheard. "It's the *climax* sequence."

"It is." Jude nods. "It's Fenny's climax. She wrote it. She conceived it. All her inspiration. She'll shoot it best."

Rich looks at Jude, then at me. "Did I miss the punch line? What's the joke?"

"No joke, Rich," I say. "This is my scene, built of my sweat and tears. I've been working with Buster on it for months. You know, I know—everyone here knows—I can do it. I *should* do it."

"So . . . what?" Rich says, pointing at us. "Are you two fucking?"

"Rich!" Jenny, his assistant, cries out in disgust from her cubicle. "Not okay!"

"What?" Rich shrugs. "I'm not allowed to ask the obvious anymore?"

Of course Rich's tiny mind would drop down to its comfort zone: depravity. I realize he's sitting there right now trying to picture what I did to get a man like Jude to stand up for a woman like me.

"You know what, Rich?" I say, raising my voice, almost trembling with frustration. "When Hollywood started, there were just as many female directors as male directors. It was only when movies started making huge profits that guys like you came sniffing around and pushed out the female artists, telling

230                                              LAUREN KATE

them they had no idea how to do what they'd already been doing. Which was what made Hollywood successful in the first
place!"

I want to slap Rich so hard his hair comes back. But then I
look at Jude, calm, strong, and serious. And on my team. I
exhale.

"The episode is Fenny's," Jude says, as unfazed by Rich as I
am boiling inside. "It always has been. She's going to shoot the
rest."

Rich folds his hands over his desk, his power move. I know
it well. He levels his blue colored-contacts gaze at me. "We appreciate all your effort, Fenster. The hours you've put in on
this—"

"This is happening, Rich," I say. "I'm directing the scene
today."

"And I'm sharing credit and compensation with her," Jude
says.

Rich laughs indifferently. "That would be an HR situation—"

"Then I'm sure you'll work it out with HR," I say.

"And if I say no?" Rich says.

"Then I quit," Jude says.

"Can I just say, I feel uncomfortable?" Rich says, putting
both hands in the air like we've pulled a weapon on him. "You
two coming in like this. It's very aggressive." He shouts out the
door, "Jenny, where's my goddamned chia pudding?!"

Jude closes the door to Rich's office, then walks back and
puts both hands on Rich's desk. "You and Amy weren't trans-
parent when you hired me. I never would have come on if I

THE SPIRIT OF LOVE 231

knew you were displacing one of the show's veteran writers and most promising, rising directors."

"She's a kid. She can wait her turn, like everyone else—"

"I've been in this business almost exactly as long as Jude has," I say. Why is it that men's careers seem to age in dog years compared to women's?

"And she's got more than enough skill and experience required for the position," Jude says.

Rich's face tenses. "You want to share credit and compensation? With her? Dude, are you high?"

"For once in your life, man, do the right thing," Jude mutters. "Get us the revised agreements by the end of the day," Jude says. "Or I'm out."

Rich's mouth is agape. Now would be a great time to chuck some chia pudding at him, but Jude is gesturing me out the door of the office and I realize there's no reason to stay.

"After you," he says.

"YOU WERE INCREDIBLE in there," I tell Jude as soon as we've closed the door of my trailer. Then I hug him in a victory dance.

"You were incredible," he says. "We were incredible. This is going to be incredible."

My mind is a geyser. I can't keep up with the torrent of thoughts and emotions shooting up from within me. After all this time, when I'd finally given up, I'm getting what's mine. It couldn't have gone better in there. I think of Rich's expression.

Jude's steely conviction. And very soon, of me shooting *my* scene.

"I feel like having a party," I say, flopping onto one trailer couch as Jude flops onto the one across from me.

"Let's have a party!"

"I want to shout this from the *Zombie Hospital* rooftop. I want to call every person in my phone and scream."

"The guy?" Jude asks, looking over at me.

"What guy?"

"Chemistry guy?"

"Who's chemistry guy?"

Oh. He's bringing up Sam? Right now? Why?

I laugh, playing off the awkwardness. "I wouldn't go that far. He's actually not in my contacts anyway."

"That's a little suspicious," Jude says, sitting up to face me. Something in his voice is confrontational.

"What's suspicious?" I turn toward him and prop myself up on an elbow.

"Miss 'We're Here to Love Each Other' is afraid to make good on the claim?"

"Who said anything about being afraid?" I snap. "I'm simply realistic. And that relationship wasn't real."

Jude tosses his head, as if he has the inside scoop on everything that happened with Sam. As if I'm the one missing a piece of crucial information. "Chemistry is real."

"I know chemistry is real, Jude. But it's not everything. And you don't know what you're talking about. You don't know my life, my experiences."

"I know what you've told me. I've listened."

THE SPIRIT OF LOVE                                    233

"I don't understand why you're bringing up some guy I met on a vacation. I don't understand why it has anything to do with our work today, or with you in general."

"Because hanging around with you, Fenny, I start to believe you." He sounds angry, like I've done something to betray him. "You talk a big game about knowing what we're here on Earth to do, but you can't even do it yourself? If you learned so much when you saw the other side, why don't you live by it?"

I flinch, hurt. "I wasn't talking any 'big game,' Jude. I trusted you with that story because I thought you wouldn't judge me."

"I'm not judging you." He blinks. "I just see through you. And I think you're just as lost as the rest of us."

"*He didn't want me!*" I practically shout. "Is that what you need to hear me say? That he rejected me?"

"Bullshit."

"Jude—"

"Any man who has the chance to be with you would seize it. Would never let it go. You're making excuses."

We stare at each other for a moment. I'm out of breath and raging, and also—did he just say if he had the chance to be with me, he would never let me go?

"Maybe I am," I admit. "I've never said love isn't scary. That kindness always comes easy. When I try to connect with other people, more often than not, I fail. I'm not claiming expertise, but I still believe. I believe it's worth it to try. You can call that bullshit. But I know you, Jude. I know you want the same things I want, the same things everyone wants. You just cover it up better, because not getting it hurts so much that you don't know how to handle it."

"I don't feel that way."

I stare at him, say nothing.

"You're putting words in my mouth," he says.

But he *had* felt that way. I saw it with my own eyes, how much connection matters to him, with Walter Matthau, with Buster. Even just meeting Edie and the boys, I could tell. And I heard the pain in his voice when he talked about his mother. We'd connected, hadn't we?

But it feels too personal, on too big of a day, to bring up those things right now. So instead, I change lanes to the subject of work. Like we do. Because that way, we can keep fighting, but we'll have our storytelling shields up. We can pretend all this isn't so close to the bone.

"If you think my point of view is so embarrassing," I demand, "why back me today? Why cheerlead my directing a scene that celebrates the infinite meanings of life and everything that awaits us after this?"

Jude narrows his eyes. "Better you than me."

"Wow," I choke out a laugh. "That's it?"

He stands up to leave and turns his back to me, and when he speaks again, his voice has gone cold. "You've never needed my approval, Fenny. You just needed me to get out of the way."

NINE HOURS LATER, I still haven't spoken to Jude. The last time I saw him, he was making a speech before the cast and crew, transferring the power today to me. His words were complimentary but sounded hollow, and he barely looked at me. He

# THE SPIRIT OF LOVE

disappeared from set as soon as he was done, leaving me alone on my first day of directing.

It's what I wanted, but I didn't want it like this.

To their credit, the actors and the crew accepted the news without fanfare, as if it was a perfectly natural event in the life of this show. But it doesn't feel like I thought it would. My nerves are frayed, my spirits low. I wanted Jude here with me today. Or at least, I wanted the Jude who doesn't think so lowly of me.

But it isn't all bad. Thanks to the rest of my colleagues, and their swift, focused work today, we've laid down three complicated shots already, and the stage is set for take one of Buster's final scene. Moments from now, he'll stand at the edge of the Hospital Roof stage and say with tortured, glossy eyes:

*Sometimes you have to die to find out what you're living for.*

Then, with the help of special effects, Buster will leap off the building, into a hurricane, and through a burning hospital window, landing in a room just in time to stop his non-zombie grandmother from flatlining from a broken heart. After the scene is edited, the episode will end with an emotional embrace between our resurrected Buster, his non-zombie grandparents, and his non-zombie dog, Bologna.

The post-lunch report from Buster's meditation guru is that he's feeling calm and confident—a mood I'm trying to share.

"Places," I call out to the team.

The body double is dismissed, and our star kid, my talented friend Buster Zamora, takes his place. He looks my way and gives a thumbs-up.

I nod at Jonah, and a moment later he calls out, "Quiet on the set!"

236    LAUREN KATE

Our assistant director Ripley calls, "Rolling camera one!"

Let's do this.

"Action!" A thrill runs through me as I say the word, as Buster faces the abyss of the hospital roof. He delivers his line with conviction, maybe more than at any time we've practiced it before. This is it. It's happening. My training, my talent, and my life experiences are all melding together, allowing me to stand here now and complete this moment, this essential scene that means so much to me.

I'm *not* here because Jude de Silva got out of the way. I'm here because I should be here, because I want to be here, because I deserve to be here.

I sense movement in my periphery and look over to see Jude, who has come to stand right next to me. His presence cheers me instantly. It feels supportive, even if we haven't yet made up, and I suddenly feel like we'll be able to. I'm so relieved, so buoyed, tears well in my eyes.

I should be looking at Buster, at the scene, but I can't help meeting Jude's gaze, his tentative *Are we okay?* smile. And suddenly, here comes the clarity I hadn't noticed I'd been missing: We're okay. We will be. I reach over and squeeze his hand.

In the dark soundstage, his phone lights up. We both look at the screen.

The word *Tania* flashes in the dark room.

My heart sinks, and the sureness I felt only a moment ago? It vaporizes as Jude steps outside to take the call.

# Chapter Twenty

I TAKE IT ALL OUT ON THE WATER, DRIVING MY OAR into the canal like I'm training for the women's eight. The jacarandas are in bloom on either side of the banks, dropping purple petals on the water as I pass and filling the air with a sweet, buzzy smell. Seagulls caw in the pink sky, dancing under wisps of golden clouds, and the late-summer air is still warm enough that I'm comfortable in a T-shirt, jeans, and Birkenstocks. It would be a lovely evening for a canoe ride, if one were in the mood to enjoy it.

I round the corner at the Grand Canal, kicking up a wake and gaining speed as I pass under the "A Wish for Others" Bridge. I *wish* I wasn't so miserable. I *wish* Tania would teleport permanently to Tunisia, or at least that she had less-spectacular cleavage. I *wish* I knew how to push through my disillusionment and locate the triumph I wanted to feel today.

I *directed*. My dream since I was a kid, training my camera and my eye, is finally a milestone past-tense crossed. A real event that can't unhappen.

And objectively speaking, I did well. In the eleventh hour of shooting today, with the help of cast and crew, we got *the* take from Buster. I think. I hope. We'll check in editing—fingers crossed. But maybe today I secured the cathartic missing piece to our season-opening climax sequence.

Why didn't it fill me up? Why do I still feel the same hole that I so frequently feel? Adrift. Unworthy. Unsure.

I thought if the team at *Zombie Hospital* could see me succeeding today, it would mean something to me. I thought I'd feel a concrete sense of my value. I thought reaching this goal would be the career equivalent of the clarity I felt when I chose Edie in the hospital. But something still feels muddy. Something still feels missing.

And I don't know if I'll ever find it.

I lower my oar, letting the boat glide on its own as I rip into the six-pack of Grapefruit Sculpin I grabbed from the Canal Market on my way home from work. I crack open a can and take a long, hoppy swig, willing the alcohol to loosen some of my angst. What was so important about that phone call that Jude had to step out of the soundstage? Why didn't he come back for the rest of the shoot?

One way of looking at recent *Zombie Hospital* events is that Jude did far more for me than he needed to. He fought for me to direct and helped me claim an opportunity I would not have had otherwise for who knows how long.

"That's not nothing." I tell the white heron who has paused above me on the railing of the wishing bridge. But it's also not enough. Because I was beginning to take it for granted that Jude and I were a team, that he would have wanted to share today with me.

I tell myself I don't need his approval. Until three weeks ago in Rich's office, I didn't even know he existed!

THE SPIRIT OF LOVE                                      239

Then why did I still want him there, meeting my eyes, giving me his serious, closed-mouth smile, half hidden in his beard? Why have I come to rely so much on that smile?

If Jude had been there at the end of our shoot today, I would have mouthed *I'm sorry* from the across the set. And he would have done that thing where he tips his head to the left and kind of grimaces, and he would have mouthed *Me, too.* Or we would have written it down on a coaster, or stared it out under the stars. There are many ways our rift might have been patched, but all of them required him sticking around today. Which he didn't. And now, I fear the chasm between us will widen all weekend long. I fear that, with every passing minute for the next three days, I'm going to get both angrier at Jude and less confident in myself.

Why is he under my skin this much?

The beer slips from my hand. *What the hell are Jude and Walter Matthau doing crossing the wishing bridge over* my *canal?*

As I stare at the apparitions, my canoe veers into the sandbar on the right bank of the canal and I plough into one of my neighbor's boats, making a fairly loud metallic crashing din. My beer has spilled all over my Birkenstocks. Jude stops, and I crouch in the canoe so he can't see me, but I strain my neck to look at him.

He's hasn't changed out of the suit he was wearing this morning, and he's carrying a large white paper bag. I watch as he takes out his phone, as if double-checking something, and then looks up at the gold numbers of my address nailed to my front door. He strokes his beard. Walter Matthau sits. Jude's shoulders rise and fall. Then he turns around and the two of them start walking back the way they came.

Over the bridge.

Right above me.

I drop my head a moment too late. Our eyes lock for half a second, and I see Jude freeze in the middle of the bridge.

"Fenny?"

"Shit," I mutter, snatching my beer can from the belly of the canoe and pretending to sip it, pretending I'm not wearing its contents. "Changed your mind?" I ask, pointing in the direction of my front door.

"You saw that?" He sighs. "That's embarrassing."

I lift a shoulder and gesture at the state of my canoe. "Not as bad as running into your neighbor's swan-shaped paddleboat at the sight of the last person you were expecting to see tonight."

Concern takes over Jude's expression. "Really? I made you crash? Let me help!"

He bounds over the ramp of the bridge and hurries across the path leading down to the water. At the sight of me, Walter Matthau barks excitedly, pawing the mud on the riverbank. When Jude gets closer, I make out the lettering on the paper bag in his hands.

Monsieur Marcel, my favorite French grocery store in the Original Farmers Market.

"What's all that?" I ask.

"This is . . ." He glances down, at the bag, and at his dog, pausing before he answers. "Six types of tinned fish. Two baguettes. And one apologetic homme."

I cover my laugh with my hand.

Jude cringes. "Awful, I know. I wrote those lines while I was

THE SPIRIT OF LOVE                                    241

working up the nerve to ring your doorbell. You can see now why I gave up and had to turn around."

"It's the delivery that needs work," I tease. "But let's just go with it. Maybe it will lead somewhere interesting. Take it from the top," I coach, gesturing for him to retry.

"You mean the—"

"Say the line again, like you've perfected it. Like you've workshopped it with Scorsese and made him cry. Say it like it's undeniable."

Jude nods. He takes a moment and then holds the shopping bag above his head like John Cusack in *Say Anything*.

"Are you going to cue me in?"

"Hey, Jude. What's all that?" I repeat.

When Jude speaks again, his voice is alive with a youthful bravado I've never heard from him before. "This, Fenny Fein, is six types of tinned fish, two baguettes, and one apologetic homme!"

"Wow, *so* much better."

"Yeah, but what happens next?" he asks. "I've never been the writer."

I think a moment. "I think my line would go something like this: 'So all you need is the sad femme in a canoe with two thirds of a six-pack of beer to go with it?'"

Jude's expression falls. "You're sad?"

"I've been happier. It's okay."

"Can we talk?"

I nod toward the seat across from me in the canoe. I pat my thighs to call the dog. "Come on, Walter Matthau. Get in."

242                                          LAUREN KATE

"APOLOGY ACCEPTED," I say with my mouth full ten minutes later. I'm finishing the most perfect bite of chewy baguette topped with Majorcan sardines in preserved lemon oil, which Jude prepared while I rowed to the south end of Linnie Canal.

"That's a huge relief," he says, handling the oar now while I eat. "I was going to need multiple takes to get anywhere near what the food can do in one. Food is better than, like, Marlon Brando."

"Maybe that's why he gained so much weight. Can't beat 'em, join 'em."

Jude laughs and we chew, a little shyly, and it feels almost like we're back to the way we were this morning, before the things we'd said in my trailer, back when we'd been a team. At our feet, Walter Matthau is curled up, his chin propped on the gunwale of the canoe, watching a squirrel run up a palm tree. I'm glad that he and Jude seem more connected. I wish I could say the same thing for Jude and me.

"Fenny?"

I look at Jude, his brown eyes sincere and worried. There's something tender about his anxiety tonight, something open and vulnerable.

"Yeah?"

"Even though I know I'm going to fuck it up," he says. "I still want to apologize."

I meet his eyes and nod to let him know I'm listening.

"Maybe it seemed like I flipped a switch this morning," he says, looking at the water.

# THE SPIRIT OF LOVE

"I'm sure it was weird, having me step in to direct scenes you'd already prepped," I tell him, honestly.

"Yes and no," he says. "But there's more to it than that." He pauses. "Do you remember Tania, from the wedding?"

I watch his hands moving the oar because it feels too hard to look at him.

"Big hat?" I say. "Breasts like beach balls?"

"That's her."

"Never seen her."

"She called me this afternoon."

"Cool. Yeah. I noticed you took some sort of phone ringing thing . . ."

What's wrong with me? One mention of this woman and I become as inarticulate as tinned fish.

Jude looks up at the sky for a moment, where the moon is new and near invisible. "Getting back in touch with her has been good for me."

"I'm sure," I say, meaning it. "You two had that amazing connection."

"You're probably wondering what she has to do with anything," Jude says.

That and why the stirring in my gut feels like jealousy.

"When Tania and I spoke today," he continues, "she held me accountable for some things she says I've been denying myself."

"I see." Heat fills my head with dizzying anger. "Like the scenes you should have been directing today?"

"No. It isn't that." Jude shakes his head. He swallows, stares hard at the water, then looks up at me. "This is hard for me to say."

"Just say it," I encourage him. "I've told you a crazy thing or two before."

"I know. I'm kind of leaning on that." He takes a deep breath. "The thing is, I wasn't always like this." He gestures at himself, grimacing. "And I want to explain, but I don't talk about this much."

"Did you talk about it with Tania?" I can't help asking.

He nods. "And she and I both agree I need to tell you." He takes a deep breath. "So here goes. Ten years ago, I was in an accident. I fractured twenty-eight bones and spent six weeks in the ICU."

"Oh my gosh. Jude!"

"I'm okay now," he says, waving off my concern. "But my recovery was long and painful. There were whole months when I didn't think I'd make it, when maybe I didn't want to make it."

"Jude."

"I don't like to think about that period of my life. Until a few weeks ago, I tried hard not to. But recently, I've been having these flashes."

"Of the accident?"

"No," Jude says. He stops rowing. I reach out and take his hand. He squeezes mine, and his strength reminds me of the foot massage he gave me at Olivia's wedding, but this is different— as if he's asking something of me instead of giving it. And so I try to receive a piece of what's making this so hard for him.

"I don't remember the accident at all," he says, running his thumb over mine. "It's my recovery I've been having flashes of. The pain. Waking up in the hospital. There was this fog around me. And a jagged void inside."

# THE SPIRIT OF LOVE 245

"That sounds terrible."

"I tried to put it behind me. Once I was well enough, I changed everything about my life. Rebuilt myself, from scratch. I thought . . . all I had to do was be careful, so nothing like what happened to me before would ever happen again."

I put my other hand around his, wanting to reach him, but not sure how. "You built something great, Jude. Your body is healed now. You're strong and talented, and everyone wants to work with you. You're having a brilliant career. If that's what came out of the accident, maybe it's okay."

He shakes his head, looking very sad. "There's more I want to do," he says, "but I still feel like I'm broken. I'm sorry about what I said in your trailer today. If I made you doubt yourself behind the camera, even for an instant, I'm not sure I'll forgive myself."

"That's just another Thursday, Jude. You didn't do it. I doubt myself without any help all the time."

"You shouldn't."

"Okay," I laugh darkly. "I'll just stop then. Look, I know what it feels like to be guided by crystal-clear intuition. But I can't seem to get there anymore. I doubt the clothes I wear, the things I say. I've doubted every date, every relationship I've been in for years. I break up with people because I'm never *sure*. I thought, with my work on *Zombie Hospital*, I was finally on this path toward what I wanted. But then you showed up. And . . . what if nothing is clear? What if I'll never be as sure again as I was when I was ten years old and not even in my body? What if I lost something essential on reentry? What if my intuition is busted?"

Jude smiles sadly and scratches Walter Matthau's ears. "I assure you, Fenny, it's not."

"When you're on set," I tell him, "you seem to know exactly what you want. I did okay today, but I also realized I'll never be a great director until I know what I want."

"For what it's worth, behind the camera is the *only* place I know what I want," Jude says. "Everywhere else, I'm lost. I think you're underestimating yourself. I think you know a lot more than you give yourself credit for."

I squeeze his hand. "I didn't know about your accident."

"Because I never talk about it."

"Maybe you should," I say.

"I only told you tonight because you seemed so brave the night you told me what happened to you. I've spent years trying to pretend my accident didn't happen. That I didn't lose something irretrievable that day. But I realized recently that I did. Lose something. And that I want it back."

Our knees are touching now, and there's a pulsing energy between us, drawing us closer. I don't want it to stop.

"And what is it you want?" I say, my voice soft.

He stares at me. We're still holding hands when Jude's other hand slides forward so that he's gently holding my knee. He leans in. I must lean in, too, because suddenly his face is close to mine.

Just right there.

My breath is in my throat, my heart is beating quickly, and Jude's face is tipped to one side. I watch his lips and, oh my God, Jude de Silva is going to kiss me.

I gasp.

# THE SPIRIT OF LOVE

The sound makes him rear back, a startled look in his eyes. His features twist into extreme discomfort, and his cheeks flush bright red.

"I'm sorry!" we both say at the same time, which makes me laugh, and I look at his eyes, in the hopes he's ready to laugh, too.

Our eyes lock, and there's a moment when it feels like maybe we can save things. But then Walter Matthau lurches to his feet.

We teeter.

Every muscle in my body tenses, trying futilely to find some purchase, but there's no stopping what's begun. Inertia takes over, and the three of us tip into the freezing, brackish water, landing this disastrous take with a humiliating splash.

And . . . scene.

# *Chapter Twenty-One*

AS I HEAD DOWNSTAIRS IN MY DRY PAJAMAS, I FIND Jude and a towel-dried Walter Matthau at my front door. His back is to me, and he's wearing the sweats I lent him after the three of us staggered like swamp things out of the Venice canal. I clock Jude's wrung-out, balled-up suit in one hand, then the note scrawled on my *Zombie Hospital* notepad in the center of my kitchen counter. It doesn't take Veronica Mars to make sense of these clues. We scurriers recognize our own kind.

Still, it feels like someone is folding my heart into origami.

"You're leaving?"

Jude spins around, his eyes moving up the stairs to me. He looks destroyed, and the sight of his expression sends me down the last few stairs to reach him.

"I'm sorry," he says, nodding toward the note. "I tried to explain. I should go—"

"Please don't go. Not yet."

I notice he's lit the gas fire in my living room, something I've not been able to figure out in a year and a half of living here. It makes my small, open-floor-plan first-story kitchen and living room feel wonderfully cozy, romantic. It makes it feel as if something pleasant is about to happen here—if it weren't for

# THE SPIRIT OF LOVE                                    249

the two massively uncomfortable people and the shivering dog populating the scene.

There's something exciting about the way these casual clothes look on him. Not just because they show off his sculpted shoulders, but because comfort wear puts me in the mind of curling up on the couch, in front of the fire, which I would love to do with him right now.

I gesture at my butter-yellow sofa. "Can you stay? Can we talk?"

"You don't owe me any explanation," Jude says. "You did us both a favor, stopping what I was about to do. I'm just . . ." He rubs his face. "Not entirely myself right now."

Discomfort rises off Jude like steam. I know that the kindest thing would be to let him slip away from the source of his discomfort—me. But I don't want him to go.

"I'll make pancakes," I offer, moving into the kitchen and opening my fridge. I take out eggs and buttermilk. "I'm not even raging mad, and I'm offering to cook. I think you've helped me reach enlightenment."

Jude cracks the smallest smile, and I feel like someone's spread a weighted blanket over all my worries. When he pulls up a barstool and sits down, I celebrate with a low-key fist pump under the counter.

"What'd your note say?" I ask, as Jude quickly crumples the paper.

"Bad first draft. Nowhere near ready for a table read."

"Question for you: Does the thought of quinoa in your pancakes make you want to run screaming?"

"It makes me want to run screaming toward the pancakes."

I grin and dump some quinoa into the bowl of dry ingredients.

"Question for you," he says. "Where'd you get this sweatshirt?" He points at the clothes I've given him to wear. The gray sweatpants must be my brother-in-law's, left behind when they needed someplace to stay while they fumigated for termites.

But the sweatshirt—the only top I could find that would fit Jude's six-foot-four frame—is the one Sam loaned me in Two Harbors when I was the one who needed dry clothes.

"You like Taj Mahal?" Jude asks, looking down at the graphic of the singer's face on the front.

I hum a line from "Fishin' Blues," my favorite song off *The Real Thing* album, which I listened to a lot right after I met Sam. I suppose the music was a way to try to feel him with me, to try to know something more about him, even though I never got around to asking what the sweatshirt meant to him.

Jude surprises me by joining in my hum. The sound is rich and honey-smooth, and unexpected, coming from him.

"I saw him on this tour," he says, glancing at the sleeve where the cities are listed.

I put down my mixing bowl and cross the kitchen to see where he's pointing. "That's kind of wild, isn't it?" I say. "Which stop?"

"Salvador." He runs his index finger over the white print of the word.

I remember what I'd overheard him telling my brother-in-law at the barbecue. Half of Jude's family is from Brazil.

# THE SPIRIT OF LOVE                                    251

"I spent summers there as a kid," he explains. "At my grand-mother's house."

"Well, it fits you," I say. "You should keep it." I'm unable to resist putting my hands on Jude's shoulders. There's that spark between us again. The one we're trying to pretend we didn't just ignite on the canal.

I drop my hands. We're still standing very close. My eyes fall on the thin, pale scar running down Jude's cheek. The one I'd noticed in Joshua Tree. The one almost but not quite hidden by his beard.

"That's from the accident," I say softly.

"Yes."

I reach out and trace my fingers over Jude's scar. He says he can't remember the accident, and I've read in plenty of articles how common that is with near-death trauma. But I wish I could know what he went through.

He said in the canoe that he lost something after his accident. If I could only see it, could I help him get it back?

Is that what he was trying to ask me earlier, on the canal? For help?

Tucked under my pajamas, I feel the weight of the adder stone at my neck. What would happen if I looked through this stone at his scar? I know Jude doesn't believe in that stuff, but maybe I do? Maybe I could believe for us both.

We're inches apart, eyes locked on each other's lips. I draw my hand slowly down the side of his cheek, and I think I feel him tremble just a little at my touch. I run my fingers through his soft beard with one hand. Then with both hands.

"Fenny," he whispers, closing his eyes.

I answer by pressing my lips to his.

Jude kisses me back with heat and hunger, the kind that builds. The kind that needs to be sated. It's such a turn-on that when his hands circle my waist and his knees part so my body can slip closer, I'm ready to tear his sweatshirt in half. My hands are in his short, soft hair. My nails run up and down his neck. His lips trail my throat with soft kisses.

"Your neck makes me crazy," he murmurs.

I giggle, surprised. "My neck?"

"It's the first thing I noticed about you. Your smooth, elegant skin. Goes all the way down to your feet. Your perfect feet."

"My feet?" I whisper.

"Ever since the wedding, I've wanted my mouth on so many parts of you. God, Fenny. I can't believe this is happening," he gasps. "Is this okay with you?"

"I kissed you, remember?"

"I will never in my life forget it," he says, breathless. His hands move down my body, to my hips, my thighs, my ass. His tongue slips softly to meet mine.

It almost feels as if we've kissed before, as if we've practiced getting to know exactly what the other likes, exactly how much pressure of his mouth against my neck makes me moan like I just did.

What else could explain why we're so good at this?

This is not *un*like the chemistry I had with Sam, in that it's fiery fucking hot. But these kisses feel deeper, like there's even more to discover if we keep going. My desire for Sam came on

# THE SPIRIT OF LOVE                    253

sudden and strong, like a crack of thunder, but with Jude, it's like a well I want to drink from forever and never run out. I want to dive into his depths with my mouth and my hands and my soul.

"Come upstairs," I tell him.

He moans, which I take as a yes, but a second later Jude stops kissing me. He pulls away.

"Fenny," he says, like it hurts.

I close my eyes, because it does.

His forehead presses to mine, and he sighs. "I want to come upstairs with you. I so badly want to do everything with you."

"But?" I whisper.

"But I'm scared that if I don't stop kissing you right now, I may never stop. Like ever."

His hands hold mine.

"What's wrong with that?" I say, peeking my eyes open because—

No.

Jude is letting go of my hands. Standing up, pushing back his barstool, moving toward the door. He reaches for Walter Matthau's leash. He winces at the ingredients spread around my counter. And that makes me feel like someone punched me.

"Sorry about the pancakes," he says. "I guess I've set you back into rage-cooking tonight. But it's best if I go. We both have some things we need to figure out."

He picks up his dripping suit off my entry mat and opens my front door. I feel too paralyzed with shame to stop him.

"What do I have to figure out?" I say, annoyed.

Jude takes a deep breath and then steps outside, onto my

stoop. Turning to face me, he says, "You should figure out what's going on with you and that other guy."

It's not what I wanted him to say.

"What do you have to figure out?" I ask.

Tania.

Jude looks at me with his downturned brown eyes. He gives me a smile that feels like a frown. "I have to figure out what to do," he says, "about the fact that what just happened here felt way bigger than a kiss."

# Part Three

# Chapter Twenty-Two

"GET IN, WINNER," THE VOICE CALLS FROM BEHIND ME the next morning at the Port of Long Beach. "We're going to Catalina!"

"Olivia?!" I say, stunned to find my friend and her new husband waving from the bow of a silver yacht whose hull is painted with the words *The Midlife Crisis* in turquoise letters. The small yacht is docked one slip over from the public ferry I was about to board.

"Ahoy!" Olivia waves brightly from across the dock. She and Jake are both dressed in white pants, white polos, matching white captain's hats, and giant rhinestone-bedazzled sunglasses. No one's ever accused them of avoiding a couple's costume.

"What are you doing here?" I call, disentangling myself from the hiking sticks, sleeping mats, and carabinered cutlery jutting out from the giant backpacks my fellow ferry passengers are carrying. At last I break free from the crowd and jog toward my friends and their yacht.

When I texted Olivia and Masha a screenshot of my ferry ticket to Catalina for this morning, all I'd needed was your basic double exclamation mark reaction. Instead:

**Masha:** Hmm, impulsive . . .

**Olivia:** You haven't even told us how the shoot went!

**Olivia:** Are you out celebrating?

**Olivia:** With Jude?

**Olivia:** Wait—are you seeing Sam this weekend?

**Masha:** What brought this on, babe? You okay?

I hadn't thought I was seeking my ride-or-dies' approval to go see Sam. More that I was location-sharing in advance should anything weird happen to me this weekend. But my friends' underwhelming response had me setting my phone to Do Not Disturb for the rest of the night. It made me realize that when I'd first come back from Two Harbors, my friends asked about Sam all the time. But neither Mash nor Liv has so much as referenced him, even as the butt of a sex joke, since . . .

Since the night of Olivia's wedding. Since the night they both met Jude. Ever since then, they've been asking me about work. And Jude.

I didn't want to talk about Jude last night, not after he left me alone with a bowl of quinoa pancake batter. I didn't want to burden honeymoon-bound Olivia and pregnant-exhausted Masha with my dumbass bullshit. And I certainly hadn't wanted one of my friends to make me connect the emotional dots between my dumpster-fire evening with Jude and my impulse to see Sam. But Olivia must have intuited there was something wrong, and—true to her friend brand—she sprang into action. Decadent, yacht-shaped action.

"I thought you two were going to Big Sur this weekend," I call to them across the dock. The last I heard, Liv and Jake were

# THE SPIRIT OF LOVE

259

off on a three-day mini-moon at the Post Ranch Inn this weekend, meant to tide them over until Jake could take a couple weeks off from *The Jake Night Show* at Christmas for a proper honeymoon in Kyoto.

"Change of plans," Jake calls, holding their terrier, Gram Parsons, who is wearing a blue doggie life jacket.

"There was a mudslide on the PCH!" Olivia says. "Our hotel is closed until they can clear the road!"

"Oh no!" I say.

"We're not mad about it," Jake says, in his famously casual way. "We've always wanted to check out Two Harbors. So when Liv mentioned you were headed here this weekend, I figured out how to redirect our mini-moon. Because I am a genius."

"Yeah, he's a regular Ada Lovelace," Olivia says, wrapping an arm around Jake. "It was utterly my idea."

"Collectively, *we* thought maybe you could use a ride," Jake tells me with a smile.

"Aka moral support," Olivia says. "Aka lube. I've got warming varieties, cooling varieties, and I think strawberry, which I cannot actually in good faith recommend."

"Seriously?" I say, glancing back at the crowded terminal. "I mean, I know you never joke about lube."

"Because it's a godsend."

"But you really got this whole yacht to take me out to Two Harbors?"

Olivia winks.

No shade at the Catalina Express, but this news is an actual godsend. I've never needed a pep talk so much. I'm not even sure what I'm going to do when I get to the island. Because what

I can't stop thinking about isn't running into Sam's arms. It's kissing Jude in my kitchen last night. And what he said when he walked out my door.

That what happened between us felt way bigger than a kiss.

Am I going to Catalina because I want to see the man I had mind-bending sex with a month ago? Or am I following Jude's decidedly less fun advice to "figure out what's going on" with Sam?

"You remember Captain Dan from our wedding," Jake says as a white-bearded man steps out from the yacht's bridge. "You can thank him for the lift, actually. We're lucky he was able to secure *The Midlife Crisis* on short notice."

"What I want to know is when we're going to christen the ship," says the captain. "I know it's a short jaunt, but you don't fuck with the sea."

I'm used to seeing Dan in kirtan yoga attire, standing at an altar, but this salty incarnation suits him, too. He offers me a hand from the hull and pairs it with an enigmatic look. "*You're* on a journey."

"How many hats do you wear?" I say, accepting his firm grip, which practically catapults me onto the yacht.

"Anything ceremonial." He lowers his bejeweled sunglasses and offers me a wink. "Somebody get her some sunglasses. And meet me on the bow in five minutes!" Then he bows before disappearing back into the cockpit.

"We also brought along these two party animals," Olivia says, sliding bejeweled shades onto my face and nodding toward Masha and Eli, who stagger up from the companionway. They're

THE SPIRIT OF LOVE 261

holding hands, and their bedazzled sunglasses are tucked into the necklines of their white oxford shirts.

"It's acupressure, babe," Masha is explaining to Eli. "You have to put the band three fingers' width up your wrist, then press on the white button when you think you're going to puke— Fenny!" She looks up at me and grins, tugging Eli over so they can both give me a hug. "I'm so glad we didn't miss you! I was worried you might have taken the earlier ferry. Do you need anti-nausea bracelets? Motion-sickness patches? Ginger gummies?"

I shake my head. "Thanks, Mash. Liv already gave me her strawberry lube, so my trip's guaranteed to be smooth."

Masha closes her eyes, cradling a hand to her belly. "I think the baby inherited his daddy's constitution."

Eli steps close, kisses Masha's forehead, and gives the bands on her wrists a gentle squeeze.

Looking at my four friends, I feel tears prick my eyes. I thought I was looking at a lonely, soul-searching voyage at sea. This is quite the opposite. This is the kind of loving solidarity I could really use today.

"How did you know?" I ask, dabbing my eyes dry.

"That you'd need us?" Liv fills my hand with hers and squeezes. "I mean, we're all a little witchy here, right? Also, there's another world where I'm pretty sure you saved my life when I needed you most, so consider this my interdimensional thank-you."

Some friends might dismiss this as a joke or straight-up weird. But I know better. I know that in life's most essential mo-ments, there's always more connecting us to the people we love

262 LAUREN KATE

than we can consciously grasp. So I hug my friend, and when she hugs me back, I know she feels this, too.

From the cockpit come two blasts of a horn, followed by Captain Dan's voice crackling through the speakers on the deck.

"All right, sailors! Meet me on the deck!"

When we're all assembled, Captain Dan takes a bottle of champagne from Olivia. "Has anyone ever read *Gulliver's Travels*?" he asks, meeting my eyes. "Where a storm sends a boat and its passenger into another realm?"

"Dan," Jake says, "stay on topic."

"Sure," Dan says and holds the champagne aloft. He closes his eyes. "I hereby christen thee *The Midlife Crisis*. May you know love, laughter, and sex hereafter." He leans over the bow and smashes the shit out of the champagne bottle.

We all cheer, Jake goes to fetch another bottle, and moments later, we're pulling away from the marina, headed for the island of Santa Catalina—named for Saint Catherine of Alexandria, patron saint of philosophers and unmarried women and the protectress of sudden death.

I hold on to the railing, tuck my hair behind my ears in the wind, and watch the ferry recede in the distance. At no point today have I been sure I was making the right decision to come out here. Not when my alarm went off. Not when I packed my duffel bag with clothes I'd actually want to be seen in . . . and possibly out of. Not when I locked my bungalow, or drove to the south bay, or paid for parking for two nights in advance. I still don't know if I should be doing this. If Sam will even want to see me, or if seeing Sam is something I should want myself. But I know that Jude stopped kissing me last night—at least in

THE SPIRIT OF LOVE                                            263

part—because I have unfinished business on this island. And knowing my friends will be nearby gives me an extra and much-needed boost of strength to finish it, come what may.

Olivia links one arm through mine as Masha stands at my other side.

"Tell me you all didn't come because you expect my showing up at Sam's cabin to go horribly, horribly wrong?" I say to them.

"That is definitely not why we came," Masha says, patting my hand.

"You're never going to know until you try," Olivia says. "The way I see it, if the reunion with Sam is as amazing as the first time, then we're going to want to meet him. And . . . if it leaves something to be desired, there's always room for you on *The Midlife Crisis*. We can play late-night poker!"

"I do need to make it known that I will be in bed by ten p.m. both nights," Masha says, "but early-evening poker is very much on the table."

I try to imagine my reunion with Sam going well enough that I invite him to come meet my friends. It's hard to picture him on *The Midlife Crisis*, maybe because he hasn't even reached his quarter life? Or maybe because everything with Sam is hard to picture—all dreamlike and removed from reality—when I'm not right next to him. Which is why I'm going to get next to him again. I would like to get clear on whether there's still something between us. To do that, I'm definitely going to need to stop thinking about Jude.

Jude, whom it's actually easier to picture on this boat, playing poker with my crew, talking art with Masha and Eli, entertainment with Jake, and personal growth with Olivia. I sigh and push away the thoughts.

Jude will never be on this boat, never hang out with my friends, because kissing me last night made him want to flee.

The pop of a champagne cork comes as a welcome interruption to my shame spiral. Olivia, Masha, and I all turn around to find Eli holding five glass flutes and Jake filling them with varying strengths of bubbling drinks.

"I'll make the toast," I say when Jake hands me a glass. I lift it, looking each of my friends in the eyes. "To sailing together through whatever *The Midlife Crisis* brings." I pause. "And also, Jude and I kissed last night. Cheers!"

I down the contents of my glass before I have to look at my friend's faces. Olivia's and Masha's jaws have dropped, but Eli and Jake somehow are nodding.

"What, you knew?" Olivia demands of her husband, as if he's been keeping a money-laundering scheme a secret for a decade.

Jakes puts up his hands, gesturing innocence. "I didn't know it was a last-night thing, but I figured it was a sooner-or-later thing. They looked like they were about to jam at our wedding. Did they not, Dan?"

Dan honks the yacht's horn in the affirmative.

"You saw us?" I had no idea anyone was watching.

"Did I not tell you they were vibing?" Eli nudges Masha.

"You did, baby," Masha says, then looks at me. "He did."

"Remember that picture I took?" Eli reaches into his pocket and pulls out his phone. He scrolls to find the photo and flashes the screen at me, and I study the still of Jude and me mid–slow dance, mid-conversation, mid-smile. We're in the middle of all

THE SPIRIT OF LOVE                                    265

the things, and we look as natural as I felt last night when we were in the middle of that kiss.

It's just the edges, the surrounding moments, when Jude and I have friction.

The end of last night. Ugh.

It hurts my heart a little to see how good we look together in this picture. But as a newly initiated TV director, I know how much smoke and mirrors cameras can capture. Tricks of light. Frozen frames that capture just a moment and not their subjects' full complexities.

Even if this picture *looks* like what I want, it's not what Jude and I actually have.

"What am I doing?" I wonder aloud.

"You're in the middle of telling us about kissing Jude last night," Olivia prompts. "Set the stage. Who kissed who? Against what surface? How far did you go—"

"Is there any chance you're pregnant?" Masha asks.

"Ladies," Jake says. "Let Fenny tell it her way."

"Looking back," I say, "it may have been building for weeks."

"Ya think?" Eli says under his breath.

"Shut it," Masha says to him.

"We've been working so closely together, getting along so well. Having fun. Yesterday's shoot was . . ."

I look at my friends, windblown and hanging on the edge of the yacht's railing for me to complete that sentence.

"Not without its drama—"

"It *is Zombie Hospital*," Olivia says with a knowing laugh.

"I wish you could have seen it, Liv," I say.

"Me, too, babe."

"Buster nailed the climax scene. The whole cast and crew were in great spirits when we wrapped for the day. I used to think directing made a person so untouchable, so removed from the rest of the cast. Jude made me see it differently. The way he brought me in when he was directing inspired me to bring in as many people as possible yesterday when I was. The whole cast was tremendous, and if I had anything to do with it, I'm grateful. I never would even have had that chance if it wasn't for Jude. I mean, actually . . . I would have . . . if we'd never met, but . . . you know what I mean."

"You mean you're glad you met," Eli said.

"Jude went above and beyond, going to bat for you yesterday," Masha said. "And he knew, like we all knew, that you'd crush it."

"And then . . ." Olivia prompts.

I nod. "Well, we had an argument on set. That's not breaking news, but something about this one felt different. It rubbed me raw. And then he came over to apologize, and we went out on the canals in my canoe. We tried to kiss on the water, but instead the two of us and his dog went overboard."

"WHAT." Olivia starts laughing.

I tell my friends how we both surfaced under the canoe and started laughing, how we swam to shore and wrung out our embarrassed asses, then dashed to my place to dry off. And how we tried that kiss again.

I sigh. "Everything about it felt right."

I pause, realizing I've just hit on the truth. I close my eyes.

"But?" Masha prompts me after a minute.

## THE SPIRIT OF LOVE                                          267

"But he stopped. Because he said I needed to figure out what's going on with Sam."

"Wow," Jake says. "I knew I liked Jude."

"Which brings us to now," Olivia says. "*That's* why you're here?"

I nod.

"So what do you want to be going on with Sam?" Masha asks.

"I don't know. I'm completely confused."

"I think you'll know," Masha says. "I think by the end of this weekend, one way or another, you'll know."

"I'm terrified I won't."

Olivia puts an arm around me and gives my shoulder a squeeze. She points toward the island, now coming into view beneath a mist of fog.

There's magic here, for sure.

"The answer's inside you, Fenny," Olivia says. "You'll know it when it's time."

# Chapter Twenty-Three

THIS TIME, THE DEER DON'T FUCK WITH ME. I ROAM under high stratus clouds, along the northern rim of Catalina. Down winding, narrow paths hedged by tall pink-flowering bush mallows. To the cliff's edge overlooking Parson's Landing. And, finally, to the small, solitary wood cabin, and the man I hope to find inside.

It's a little after noon on Friday when I finally see Sam's cabin, still nestled at the edge of the island like something out of a fairy tale. I've lucked into my own transportation for this reunion visit—a periwinkle blue Blix electric folding bike, one of six available to borrow from the stowage cabin of *The Midlife Crisis*.

Captain Dan offered to drop anchor off Sam's secret beach, which I pointed out to my friends on our approach into Two Harbors. Olivia and Masha wanted to bring me to shore by dinghy; escort me up the short, steep trail to the cabin; and then, as Olivia put it, hide in the bushes until they'd made sure I got in okay. Until they made sure I still wanted to be there, after seeing Sam again.

I was less worried about whether I'd want to hang out with Sam once we reunited. I haven't forgotten how well we got along, how easy he is. Even if a relationship with him is unrealistic.

THE SPIRIT OF LOVE 269

What worried me more was the idea of knocking on Sam's door, uninvited, unannounced—with an emotionally invested, spying entourage in tow. Including one very pregnant spy who would likely have to pee.

The bike saved me the social pressure of a door-to-door *The Midlife Crisis* drop-off. If at any point my visit with Sam gets uncomfortable, I'll be just a six-mile, moderately inclined ride back to Two Harbors. To the Del Rey Yacht Club, where my friends are docked for the night, with a mini-fridge full of snacks and very good wine and an extra cabin with twin bunkbeds and their favorite fifth wheel's name on it.

Was it easier showing up to Sam's cabin the first time, when a cataclysmic storm had handled the decision-making for me? Yes. But is it time for me to take matters into my own adult hands? To determine not only what I want from this weekend, and how to make it happen, but also what I want from life—and what to tell Jude on Monday? Also yes. Hell yes.

My calves are tingling with exertion and my chest is a hornet's nest of nerves by the time I reach the edge of the path that leads to Sam's front porch. I press the brakes on the bike and look up at the blue curtains covering the window of the bedroom where I once laid with Sam. Smoke again curls from the chimney. His boots are kicked off in the same place at the same angle to the left of the same sunrise-colored rattan welcome mat.

*He's home*, I think with simultaneous glee and dread.

It's been one month, and yet it feels like a lifetime ago. Since I was last in this place, I've experienced one career freefall, one partial career rebound, one galivant through a costume warehouse, one best friend's wedding, one desert stargazing session, one tipped canoe, and one episode of *Zombie Hospital* filmed. What surprises me is not how much or little calendar time has passed since I was at Sam's cabin. What surprises me is how, in measuring my post-Sam era, I think in terms of milestones I've experienced with Jude.

I'm annoyed that Jude gave me these marching orders to figure out what's going on with Sam. I'm not here only because of Jude's words last night. I should—and do—want to know what's going on with Sam for myself. I want to know if what I experienced with Sam is worthy of the memory I've stored. Or if this weekend will show me that I painted those days and nights with shimmery, sentimental nostalgia—like music director James Horner did in the climax scene of *Titanic*, using violins like drugs to induce tears from the audience.

At this point, I just want to know.

If it's nothing, it's nothing. I can truly let this whole fling go. This place, this man, the echo of our connection in my bones.

If it's something . . . that's harder to say. Being back on Catalina reinforces that Sam's life is very much on this amazing island. My life is very much across forty miles of sea.

From the oceanfront eastern edge of the cabin's wraparound porch, motion catches my eye. It's an elbow.

Golden and gleaming with sweat, suggesting strength and flexibility beyond ordinary mortal capacities.

Lord, Sam's *elbow* is doing it for me.

I lean the bike against a manzanita bush hedging the cabin. I follow the path on my approach toward Sam, each body part revealing itself like the world's sweatiest, sexiest cabaret show. Elbow, bulging biceps, straining shoulder, flexing neck, and

THE SPIRIT OF LOVE                                      271

gorgeous, handsome face. A man at once strange and familiar, doing one-armed pull-ups, facing the sea.

He wears thin black joggers. Nothing else. His feet are bare, his shoulders orgasmic, the nape of his neck damp with a sheen of sweat. His muscles flex like the hills of Catalina as he raises his body up and then lowers it down. Up then down. I want to put my hands on his skin. I want him to see me, to turn around right now, say my name, and run his hands through his hair. And smile.

And I'll smile back.

But when Sam releases the bar and his feet drop to the porch, I panic and try to duck out of view, to race back to my bike before he sees—

"Hello?"

I bend my knees in busted agony, spinning slowly around to face Sam. I make a broad, awkward wave.

I dare to look Sam in his chocolate eyes. They widen now in something like stupefaction. I should have announced that I was here while his back was still to me. I should not have ogled him from behind for God knows how long, no matter how good his deltoids looked. I must now acknowledge the awkwardness of my attempt to flee when caught ogling, because with every passing second, I only look like more of a creeper.

"Fenny?" Sam uses both hands to rub his eyes, like he can't believe what he's seeing. "Is that really you?"

"Just an excellent body double," I say, waving clumsily with my other hand now because the demonic choreographer controlling my body isn't done laughing at me yet.

Sam bounds down the stairs toward me, stopping tantalizing inches away.

"Not possible," he says, crossing his arms over absolutely stunning pectoral muscles. "Your body can't be replicated."

Which is rich coming from this shirtless Adonis. I allow my eyes to trail down Sam's bare chest. It's the oddest time to wonder about Jude's bare chest, which I didn't get to see last night. I wonder if I ever will.

"Wow," Sam says. "It's good to see you."

"It is?" I blink, stunned, snapped back into the present moment by Sam's unabashed honesty. "Even with the weird attempt to flee just now?"

"I'll let that slide." He grins as his eyes run over my face, my hair, my body. It's warm outside, but goosebumps dot my skin. "What are you doing here?"

"I—well—"

*I came because a man I kissed last night suggested it—*

*I came to sort through my feelings for you and my feelings for someone else I might be falling for in a big way—*

*I came because, once upon a time, you and I shared something bone-deep and blissful in this cabin, on that beach. At least, I think we did. It's getting harder to remember clearly.*

*I came because I need your help figuring out my life. And I'm hoping you can mind-read, too, because I've never been as good as you at saying the true things out loud.*

"I'm sorry," Sam says. "Maybe that came out wrong. I meant to sound amazed and grateful. Not to put you on the spot."

He runs his hand through his hair in that way that he does. It reminds me of what his hair feels like, sun-warmed and silky.

The chemistry between us is real and very much alive. Two minutes together is long enough for me to know I want all of

THE SPIRIT OF LOVE 273

Sam back all at once. I want as many inches of his skin against mine as is physically possible. I want the heat of his breath in my ear. I want his strong hands on my hips, rooting me to him. I want his laughter echoing through canyons on a zip line. I want his cold-water gasp, and his softest kiss, and his burnt toast, and his whispered *Stay forever.*

And I wish we could skip the need for explanation because this weekend already feels too short, but Sam's looking at me as if there are things he needs to say.

"I didn't think I'd get another chance," he says.

"Isn't there always another chance?"

"That seems too good to be true," he says. "Do you know how many times I've relived that day we said goodbye?"

I shake my head, surprised. "How many?"

"I must have fantasized a hundred ways it could have gone differently, Fenny. I've just been so . . . stuck. What tears me up, ever since then, is that you might have left without knowing . . ."

He trails off, licks his bottom lip, and looks away.

"What?" I whisper, letting the tips of my fingers brush the tips of Sam's. A tingling spark trips up my hand, my arm, then all the way into my core. I meet his eyes and melt as his fingers gently drag up my arms. Soon he's holding me by the elbows, his hold firm, but his hands so soft.

"I didn't know how to find you." His voice is lower, a little raspy. I tip up my face and see him haloed by the sun.

"I'm here now."

"You're here now," he says, amazed. "How long can you stay?"

Logistics and Sam don't go together, so even though I've got a tight two and a half days left, I cast aside reality. "A while."

"I want to kiss you," he says.

"We could see if it still works?" I rise on my toes and press my lips to his, feeling the synergy between us swell with heat. Sam moans, or I moan. His hands on my back are such a vast, deep turn-on that I'd go to bed with Jude right now.

I stiffen, realizing my brain just trip-wired. *Sam.* Sam is the one I'm kissing. Sam is the one turning me on enough to make me want to take him to bed.

Jude is far away, asking me to get my act together. Telling me that kiss last night was more than a kiss.

Sam very gently pulls away from me. "You okay?" he murmurs against my neck. "You still here?"

"I'm here," I breathe.

He tips his head toward the door of his cabin. "Will you come inside? It'll make my decade."

I smile and tug him toward the door. This is going to get easy. Look how gorgeous he is. Look how happy he is to see me.

Inside, Sam's wondrous cabin smells familiar—hickory, cloves . . . and a hint of something savory cooking. It feels like time stands still here. Everything is just as it was when I left, down to the placement of the logs in the carved Blake-inspired fireplace and the geometric heirloom quilt folded over the back of the couch.

"I like what you've done to the place," I say.

"Really? Oh, you mean, because it's the same?"

"If it ain't broke . . ."

"It's so crazy that you're here—"

"Is that"—I sniff the air—"boeuf bourguignon on the

THE SPIRIT OF LOVE 275

stove?" My eyes widen, and I would laugh except my mouth is already watering.

"It ain't broke!" Sam says, heading to his custom bar. "Highball?"

"You remembered."

"Shoot, I'm out of honey," he says, rummaging through the bar.

"You were out of honey last time, too," I remind him. "It was still just right."

He hands me a drink, then clinks his glass to mine. "Cheers! Hey, I have incredible news for you."

"Really?" I'm surprised. "In addition to this cocktail?"

"After you left," Sam calls from across the room where he's facing his bookshelf. "I found your camera."

"My Panasonic AG-DVC30?" I practically shout as Sam puts my first, best video camera back in my hands. It's salt-stained and probably ruined, but I don't care. I close my eyes and let a tear squeeze out. I'm so glad I came back. I'm so glad he found it. He saved it for me. "Where did you . . . how did you . . ."

"I found it on the beach," he says. "I kept it over there with your viewfinder thing. My mementos."

I touch the adder stone. "I still wear this every day."

He smiles. "Camera still works, I think. It's kind of a miracle, right? I tested it out. Filmed some dumb stuff." His voice lowers a little. "I didn't think you'd come back, but that shows what I know!"

"Thank you," I say, hugging the camcorder to me. "You were born to Search and Rescue."

"Just let me delete what I filmed," Sam says and takes the camera. He furrows his brow and fiddles with the controls.

"You don't need to erase anything," I say, curious.

"I can't figure out how to anyway." He sighs and hands it back to me. "Don't judge."

"Oh, I'll judge," I say. "That's how I repay kindness."

Sam laughs. "So the stew won't be ready for a bit. . . . Do you want to go for a hike? Or we could swim—the water's still warm enough. Do you want to do the zip line again? If you're bored with all that, just tell me. I could also take you to a part of the island you've never seen before. We can have a totally new adventure—"

"Sam?"

"Yes?"

"I want all that. Soon. But first, I'm conducting an experiment. Can you help?"

"You're asking a man who signed an oath to assist anyone in need on this island."

"That's what I thought." I lift my dress over my head and toss it to the floor. I'm not wearing anything under it.

Sam gets down on his knees. "I can help," he says, pressing his mouth against me. "I've been certified in this."

AFTER THE SUN has set and we've disentangled our limbs briefly for a steaming bowl of stew, Sam and I lay in his bed as his fingers draw pictures of Catalina flora and fauna on the bare skin of my back.

THE SPIRIT OF LOVE                                    277

"So when do we get the results of your experiment?"

"They've just come in. It turns out, I wasn't imagining the bone bliss your body gives me."

"I could have told you that," he says and kisses the top of my head. "Let's get up early tomorrow morning. We can still go on a hike before sunrise and then we can come back here and I can survey your bones again for any absent bliss before breakfast. Also after breakfast. And maybe mid-hike, too."

"Good plan." I roll over to face him and smile. "And I have an idea for something fun we could do after breakfast."

"More sex?"

"What if we headed to town? Did you get your Jeep fixed yet?"

"That Jeep is totaled, Fenny."

"Did you get a new car?"

He sits up in bed a little straighter, drawing a few inches away. It isn't much, but it's noticeable. Have I said something that upset him?

"I'm still trying to work out the specifics of some things since the accident."

It's been a month and he still doesn't have a car. How has he been getting around?

"But you have a bike, right? I thought I saw one in your shed the last time I was here."

"Yeah, I have a bike."

"Great. I borrowed one for this weekend, too. If you want . . . I have some friends here from LA. We all came over together. They'll be hanging out at the Harbor Reef for brunch tomorrow. Around eleven?"

He raises an eyebrow, as if trying to figure out where I'm going with this.

"It could be cool if we . . ."

I trail off. I don't know why I'm having trouble telling him that I've already committed to meeting Olivia and Masha tomorrow. It was Masha's condition for letting me take the bike, as opposed to the drop-off committee. She said she needed proof of life in the dead zone of island cell reception. Which now seems silly, because of course I'm safe here with Sam, but I don't want to explain Masha's reasoning to him. Especially because he seems suddenly a little withdrawn.

"Sam?"

"I'm sorry. I can't."

"Can't . . . what?"

"Go to Two Harbors. I don't go there."

"The whole town? The only town in this entire vicinity? You don't *go* there?"

"Correct."

I laugh. "Why not?"

"I don't really want to get into it."

"Okay . . . well, we don't have to go into town. My friends are staying on a yacht. We could go to the yacht club and hang out with them there. Just for a little while. You look like you hate this idea. But I want you to meet them. I want them to meet you."

"Why?"

"Why would you ask why? Because I like you. It's not a strange request."

"I like you, too. I like this"—he gestures between us in the

# THE SPIRIT OF LOVE
279

bed—"very much. As far as I'm concerned, there's no need to muddy the waters with anything else."

I flinch, stunned by the harshness of his words. "I don't consider meeting my friends muddying any waters. They're part of my life."

"Look, I want to be the kind of guy who says yes to this, but I'm just not." Sam's tone hasn't changed. He says these words with such warmth that it doesn't feel like he's being an asshole. I feel like I'm missing some vital piece of information.

So I keep probing.

"I tried new things for you," I remind him. "I said yes to a *zip line* and spearfishing and sex on the beach, all of which are distinctly out of character for me, and all of which paid major dividends. What if you say yes to me? To this? You might surprise yourself."

"I'm sorry," he says and shakes his head.

"Really?" I say, feeling myself growing annoyed. "You won't even entertain the idea?"

"I know my limits."

"Maybe they're due to be stretched?"

"Some people change. I don't. I won't."

I scoff. "I'm not asking you to quit smoking or resume a relationship with an estranged relative. I'm asking for fifteen minutes of your time to say hi to some people I care about. People who care enough about me to be worried that I came all the way out here to spend a secluded weekend with a guy I barely know!"

"I didn't think we'd get to this point so quickly," he says with a sigh. "I was hoping for more time."

"Real question: Are you always this rigid with the women you date?"

He doesn't answer.

"Oh. It's just me."

"Fenny, it's not you. It's definitely not you. It's me."

"Ugh," I groan. "It's a known fact you can't use that phrase unironically after *Seinfeld*. But don't worry, I can give you a quick tutorial on the newfangled misogynistic phrases cool guys like you are using on the mainland."

"I'm actually telling the truth," Sam says.

It's too dark to take off on my bike back to the yacht club, so I roll over onto my side. "Good night, Sam. I hope you have a static, totally inflexible rest."

## Chapter Twenty-Four

I WAKE WITH AN EMPTY FEELING. WHEN MY EYES OPEN to the sight of Sam's small, blue-curtained loft window, I remember where I am. I remember what happened last night and how lonely it had felt to try to sleep after our argument. I remember the restful sound of his breathing as I lay tossing and turning, only able to drift off after assuring myself we'd work it all out in the morning. Now, I reach for him—

But he's not there.

"Sam?" I call, sitting up in the bed, drawing the sheets around me because it's cold in this cabin and I'm naked. There's a stillness in the air that tells me right away he isn't here. Not downstairs burning toast. Not out on the porch finessing his one-armed pull-up. He's somewhere else. I don't know where, but I know he's gone before I can prove it. And the hollow I feel in his quiet bedroom is heavy.

I get up to search for my clothes, and that's when I see the note Sam left on his pillow. I sink back onto the bed to pick it up. I've never seen his handwriting before. It's quick and blocky, confident, all caps but not aggressive. Very much the way he speaks.

282                                        LAUREN KATE

FENNY,

I'M SORRY ABOUT LAST NIGHT. I WISH I WAS BETTER
AT EXPLAINING.

WANTED TO GIVE YOU SOME SPACE THIS
MORNING. IF YOU'RE NOT STILL MAD WHEN I GET
BACK, WE CAN GO CLIFF-DIVING THIS AFTERNOON?

LOVE,
SAM

Each of the three times I read Sam's words, they make less and less sense. *If I'm not still mad?* Is the duration of my anger what the rest of our weekend rides on? Whether *I* get over *his* bullshit before he deigns to come home?

So we can go *cliff-diving?*

Moreover, is his simply phrased *wish* that he was *better* at explaining all he needs to let himself off the hook? And how magnanimous of him, by the way, to give me some space this morning! Where the hell does he get off, tacking on the word *love* at the end of such a useless excuse for communication?

There's nothing loving about this note. It's a goddamned middle finger. It's a gesture that holds me and my emotions at so great a distance, I might as well have stayed home in Venice this weekend. Wait a minute. Is this the kind of note a guy writes when he's started dating someone else since you last slept together but he's too scared to say so?

I hate the thought of this—of Sam giving someone other than me those bone-deep orgasms—but it's also the most rea-

# THE SPIRIT OF LOVE

sonable explanation. Why else would it be such a nonstarter for him to go into town with me today? He doesn't want anyone to see us together and report back to his new girlfriend.

I crumple the note in my fist, recalling how Jude crumpled the note he was going to leave for me not thirty-six hours ago. What had his note said? Something less infuriating is a safe bet. I never should have kissed Jude. Or perhaps, I *should* have kissed Jude but also already have figured out what was going on with Sam.

If only I'd known then what I know now. Sam's total disinterest in developing anything real with me.

I should have known better. The signs were all there the first time I left Two Harbors. Now I've tainted everything with Jude. Our working relationship. Our friendship. And whatever else that kiss might have become.

What might that kiss have turned us into?

And why didn't I tell Jude that it felt like more than a kiss to me, too?

I throw on my clothes and climb down the loft ladder. This empty cabin is making me claustrophobic. I go to the bathroom to brush my teeth. It still smells like hickory and cloves—Sam's very pheromone-friendly aftershave—and his razor still leans against the green bar of soap in the dish next to the sink. The cap of his floss is open. I click it closed, just like I did a month ago.

I look at myself in the mirror and shake my head.

"Cliff-diving," I mutter.

There's no way I'm diving off a cliff, probably ever, and definitely not until Sam and I have gotten a few things straight. Why do men default to giving women such a wide berth when we get pissed off? What is it about our anger that sends them scuttling into shadows like rats? At work for the past five years, Rich has whined to anyone who'll listen that I'm "still mad at him for some reason," but has he ever once tried to talk to me about it directly? Now Sam seems to think that *space* is the ideal solution to *my* moving past *our* conversation last night. It feels like it's all on me to get through this rough patch, and nothing more is required of him.

I stand in his kitchen, staring down his toaster, not hungry exactly, but hungry to prove something. To myself. Or to Sam's absence. I don't know. I take two slices of bread from the bag of whole wheat, the same brand Sam had the last time I was here. I slip them into the toaster and press Start.

I put both hands on the counter and find myself thinking about Jude. How each time I've been mad at him, he's followed up about it, in person, engaged, asking to spend time with me until we could work through whatever it was. It was like my rage had a magnetic effect on him, drawing him to me instead of repelling him. I'd thought him presumptuous at first, but now I know he was simply trying to get to the bottom of my anger at him. So that together, we could get to the other side.

And we did.

And it was good. For a minute.

Jude's confident enough in his own positions to be able to listen to mine.

That is, until I kissed him and fucked everything up. Jude knew I was mad when he left my house on Thursday, but he couldn't get out of there fast enough. And that's on me.

"There's nothing going on with Sam and me," I say out loud,

THE SPIRIT OF LOVE                                    285

definitively. I'm too late to tell this to Jude, but at least there's still time to tell it to myself.

My physical chemistry with Sam is every bit as ridiculous as I'd remembered it. But when it comes to the world beyond the orgasm, to the real, messy the heart of the matter, Sam would rather push that mess onto me. He doesn't care whether I deal with it, or choose to let it go, because the issue is mine, not ours.

And that makes me feel the loneliest of all.

An acrid smoke fills my nose and makes me cough. Of course I burnt the fucking toast. I pop it out of the toaster, blowing on a singed and smoking crust before dropping both pieces in the trash. I stare at the smoking embers in the trash can, feeling a freaky sense of déjà vu.

"I've got to get out of here."

I find a pen and paper and break the news to Sam as honestly as I can.

Sam,

I'm glad we met. I won't forget our time together. But what you want to give isn't enough for me, so this is goodbye.

—Fenny

I pack up my things. I take the camcorder and leave the viewfinder. I touch the adder stone at my neck. I consider keeping it, but it's too special. It belongs with Sam. I take it off and leave it on the kitchen counter next to my note.

I lace up my sneakers, pull on my sweatshirt, and dab

sunscreen on my face. I take one last look at Sam's stunning, mystical cabin, then I walk out the front door. I mount my bike and watch a pelican dive-bomb into the ocean, knowing what it wants and how to get it. I feel suddenly as desperate to get away from this place as I'd been desperate to arrive less than a day ago.

The sun is strong, the wind unfriendly, and the trail steep and narrow. On my left, it's edged with sheer drops into the ocean; on my right, it's seasoned with cacti and boulders the size of my bike that must have tumbled down from rockslides past. Every hundred yards or so, I huff past signs warning of the dangers of charging bison.

When Two Harbors finally comes into view below my path, my limbs are burning and my heart feels spent, but I'm relieved to have arrived. It wasn't a mistake to leave Sam's cabin. I can tell from the subtle loosening in my chest at the sight of this tiny town. I can miss him and still be clear that I could not have stayed at his cabin any longer than I did. I have one more night on Catalina. I'll find my friends. I'll get some food. I'll stare at the sun-dappled sea until I know what to do about Jude. However long that takes.

I'm approaching Isthmus Cove, Two Harbors's large east-facing harbor, which is home to the public ferry terminal, the public beach, and the rental offices for all the water sports. This harbor looks out toward the mainland, and on a clear day like today, you can see Marina del Rey across the water and all the way up the coastline to Malibu.

Two Harbors's other harbor is a few minutes' bike ride farther west, through the one-street town and minuscule residential neighborhood containing some forty houses. On the other side

# THE SPIRIT OF LOVE 287

of this half-mile-long isthmus sits the west-facing harbor. It looks out on thousands of miles of open ocean and contains the sleepy Del Rey Yacht Club, where my friends are anchored and will hopefully soon anchor me.

I take the last downslope of the trail even faster now that I can see the Harbor Reef. I want to be there on the bar's worn wood patio, parked under an umbrella, connecting to Wi-Fi and sipping the island's signature cocktail. The buffalo milk is a nutmeg-dusted frozen Kahlúa concoction, heavy on the whipped cream and good for drowning sorrows.

There's a ferry docked at the harbor and a crowd of adventure-seeking passengers unloading. Most come here to hike the Trans-Catalina Trail. I remember the last time I was here, how the sight of this ferry broke my heart a little because it meant saying goodbye to Sam. This morning, it's a welcome sight, a breath of civilization. I see families gathering their gear from the ferry's hold, friends helping each other cram one more thing into a backpack. I notice a couple huddled close together by the information booth. They're consulting a map, disagreeing about something as they plan out a future memory. I'm sure they have their own issues to contend with, but I can't help feeling jealous of the two of them and their map. It's so simple, but I want that—the mundane, everyday moments in between the high notes. With Sam, it was all about the high notes.

By the time I park my bike in the tiny town square, it's still only nine forty-five in the morning. Olivia, Masha, Eli, and Jake aren't planning to meet me here for over an hour. They're probably still in bed. I think about biking the few extra minutes west toward the yacht club. If any of them are up and on deck, I might wave them down and they could send over the dinghy to pick me up. But then I decide I could use the solo time to get my thoughts together first. Maybe I can grab some souvenirs for my nephews.

The Harbor Reef isn't open yet, but next door there's a small mini-mart where I can get some tea and island trinkets. The market is part bookstore, part pharmacy, part make-your-own ramen station, and part gourmet grocery store, where everything's three times as expensive as it should be and also expired. I find an iced chai in the refrigerated section and a couple garibaldi stuffies that say "Two Harbors" on the fins. I carry my items toward the front of the store to check out.

I'm heading up the checkout aisle when I see a tall, familiar man with his back to me. He's wearing a thin gray T-shirt, fitted black swim trunks, and a well-worn pair of New Balance sneakers. His broad-brimmed straw hat shields his head and neck, but I recognize his height, his hands, and the telltale bulge of his deltoid as he reaches for a squeeze bottle of honey on the shelf.

Sam. He's here. In town. Holding a bundle of firewood because we used the last of his stash last night. What do I do with this new information? Back at his cabin, I'd ended things—but he doesn't know that yet! He's at the market, shopping for the missing ingredient of the cocktail he knows I like. Which is sweet. And maybe there's more sweetness where that came from. Would he come to brunch and meet my friends? Would we talk through last night's argument? Would that make up for what he'd said in his note?

Is running into him here a sign that there's something worth salvaging between us? Do I want to salvage it? I can't tell.

THE SPIRIT OF LOVE 289

In my heart, I don't think there's a future for Sam and me.

But is there one more night together?

I can't deny that I'm touched to find him here. And so, without fully thinking through the implications, I approach him from behind. I rise on my toes and slip one hand over his eyes. I slip the other around his waist.

As soon as I've got my arms around him, I realize my mistake. This man is too thin to be Sam. The knowledge that I've just pounced on a stranger makes me rear back, pulling away my hands. Just as the stranger spins around in shock.

"SorryIthoughtyouweresomeoneelse!" I blurt out.

"Fenny?"

I look up and stare. The man standing before me, with the honey and the firewood and the skinny waist . . . is Jude.

And he's not happy to see me. He looks horrified.

Which makes two of us.

"What are you doing here?" we both demand at the same time.

"I'm sorry about that handsy moment," I say, taking another step back. "I swear, I thought you were . . ."

I stop talking because something is happening, something that makes it hard for me to tell whether I'm actually losing my mind. This is not the first time I've mistaken Jude for Sam. I appreciate Lorena, but she was talking out of her ass with that erotic conflation stuff. Something else is going on. Jude is thinner and older and bearded and scarred, but his eyes are Sam's eyes. I knew it that first day in Rich's office, but I convinced myself I was wrong. I wasn't. Staring into them now is a mindfuck I wouldn't know how to begin to express on film. Real life needs

290    LAUREN KATE

the ability to jump-cut to another scene, a moment in my future when I've had time to make sense of this insensible situation.

"I'm not stalking you," is the thing Jude decides to say, whipping off his hat so I can see more of his—Sam's—his—face.

His bizarre defense is so out of step with the whirlpool going on in my head that I begin to laugh.

"Honestly," he insists, and I laugh harder. "I did not know you would be here. What *are* you doing here? This is really the opposite of stalking—"

"Two minutes alone and you start stalking?" a female voice says from behind Jude.

He turns to reveal Tania, who slips a bottle of wine into his hands.

"I can't take you anywhere," she says, then looks at me. "Oh. Hello." She smiles, showing radiant white teeth. "You're Fenny, right?"

Jude clears his throat. "Fenny, you remember Tania?"

"Impossible to forget Tania!" I say peppily as my heart plummets. "Hi."

I make myself put my hand in hers. I can't be jealous. Can't be jealous. Can't be jealous. But I'm so jealous. And a little shocked that, two nights ago, Jude said that thing about our kiss being more than a kiss. It must not have been much more because he's already over it. He's spending the weekend with Tania. He needs wine and honey and firewood with Tania.

"I really can't believe I ran into you here," he says.

"I'm struggling with the odds myself."

"Would you like," Tania asks, "to have brunch with us? We're

# THE SPIRIT OF LOVE                                   291

staying just up the road at the Banning House. The view is to die for. Literally." She glances at Jude, then squeezes his elbow in what's clearly an inside joke.

"I'm sure Fenny's busy," Jude says before I can answer.

I nod. "I'm about to meet some friends."

"What about tomorrow?" Tania says. "Tomorrow might be even better for us, right, Jude?"

They're an *us*. An us I'll probably have to run into twelve more times before the weekend's over because that's how small this town is. I suddenly want to crawl into the top bunk bed in my cabin on *The Midlife Crisis* and embrace the full meaning of the ship's name.

I look at Jude. He's looking at me, distinctly uncomfortable, unfairly attractive. Our eyes are on each other's lips again, and I can't stop myself from thinking about what it was like to kiss him.

Tania must know by now how good he is at kissing. Does she know other things Jude's mouth can do?

I think of Sam. The note I left. I don't regret it. Not even now.

"You two enjoy your weekend. I think I'd just be in the way."

# Chapter Twenty-Five

ON THE TOP BUNK OF THE KIDS' CABIN ABOARD *THE Midlife Crisis*, I sit between Olivia's sleeping dog, Gram Parsons, and my two new stolen Garibaldi stuffies. I vow to go back later and pay for the souvenirs, but I couldn't stand in that market with Tania and Jude another minute longer. I was halfway to the yacht before I realized the fish were still clutched in my hands.

"We're going to get to the bottom of this, fellas," I say to the fish and the dog.

Before us is my laptop, my reclaimed camcorder, and my phone. The yacht is quiet. Captain Dan took my friends on a bike ride across Catalina's western rim—everyone except Masha, who is taking a nap in the cabin next door to mine.

Someday I'll have a life where I can join my friends on aerobic island larks, but not today. It's time to do what I should have done weeks ago. It's time to figure out what the fuck is going on.

Last night Sam said he tested out my camcorder, that he'd filmed some "dumb stuff" to see if it still worked. Maybe it will be just dumb enough to help me. I turn it on. When it powers up, I cry. It feels like a miracle. I scroll to find the most recent footage. And there he is.

# THE SPIRIT OF LOVE

Sitting on the couch he'd sat on the first night he brought me to the cabin. He placed the camera on the coffee table, probably propped on his copy of *The Tempest*.

Late-afternoon sun comes in through the window, gilding his skin. I can see him fully for what feels like the first time. Smiling into the camera, effortlessly at home in his skin. How at home, how uninhibited, how enviably free he is as he flicks his hair back from his beautiful eyes and smiles.

"Found your camera, Fenny. It washed up on the beach, looking for you. But all it found was me." There's a pause while Sam looks out the window, the one that faces the sea. There's longing in his expression, and when he speaks again, his voice is softer and there's longing in it, too. "Where do you go when you're not with me? What are you doing all the way over there right now?"

I watch this clip a second time, trying to find the connection between this man on the couch and the man I just ran into at the market. They're so different, and yet, there's something between them. Something connects them, something more than me.

I didn't ask for this mystery to fall into my lap; I was simply trying to live my life. In the past month I have cared about them both. I've been inspired by—changed by—them both. I've been driven slightly bananas by them both. And sure, if I could make the perfect-for-me man, I would take Sam's honeyed drawl when he predicted I'd be a great kisser, and I'd meld it with Jude's thoughtful contemplation of my *Zombie Hospital* motifs. I'd take Sam's zest for adventure, tearing through canyons on zip lines he built himself, and link it to Jude's focused generosity when he's guiding an actor through a demanding scene. I'd take Sam's brawn and Jude's depth, Sam's confident lips and Jude's sure dance steps. Sam's heart, Jude's mind, Sam's warmth, Jude's wit. Their laugher and their eyes and their hands.

I'd make one man.

And he'd be perfect.

But he wouldn't be real.

And even if I could, magically, make him real, he wouldn't want me. Not after the way I've acted with both of them.

I wish so many things could be different. I plug in the cable between the camera and my laptop and begin the slow process of transferring the files. While the devices work, I open YouTube and search "JDS."

There's footage of him on several red carpets. There's an interview with Scorsese for *Directors on Directors*. But every video I watch shows Jude being professional, polite, and more than a little bit guarded. Like he was when I first met him. Before we became friends. There's no comparing this walled-off version of Jude to the smiling version of Sam I know *or* the longing version of Sam he's showing in his video diary.

But then I remember a time when I saw Jude smile on camera. In the photograph Summer texted me from the *Zombie Hospital* dinner at Amy Reisenbach's house.

I reach for my phone and scroll through my texts, stopping at Summer's name. I open our conversation, then the photo. It's one of those "live" iPhone shots, so when I tap and hold, I can see half a second of Jude and me in motion. This is the angle, the tip of the head, the smile. I AirDrop it to my laptop and, without thinking, overlay it so the clip of Sam telling me he found my camera dissolves into the live photo of Jude telling me about his troubles bonding with Walter Matthau.

And when I watch the two men become one, I scream and slam my laptop closed.

"FENNY?" A GROGGY Masha pokes her head inside my open cabin door a few moments later. "Are you okay?"

"I need you to look at something and tell me my eyes are malfunctioning."

Masha looks at the ladder and then the tiny crevice of space between the top bunk and the ceiling. She looks down at her beautiful orb of a belly and rubs it.

"This is friendship, baby," she says to her bump and begins to climb. She sinks down next to me with a groan. "So what are we looking at? Scoot over, Gram Parsons."

"Remember when I told you and Olivia about the first time I met Jude? How I mistook him for Sam?" I take Masha's hand and press Play.

We watch it eighteen times. The whole time Masha is shaking her head.

"Holy doppelgänger," she finally whispers. "Did you read that article in *The New York Times*?"

"Yeah, but—"

"I know," she says. "You're right. This is more than that. Unless my eyes are malfunctioning, too. Which would make sight the final of my senses to fall prey to baby side effects." She rubs her eyes. "We need Olivia. She believes in crazy shit like this." Masha sighs and watches the footage one more time. "Okay, it's Occam's razor: The simplest solution is the best one. Jude and Sam are the same person."

"How is that simple?! What do I do with it?!"

"So at the Getty," Masha says, "when we're looking for counterfeits, we need multiple originals. Do you have any other footage we could look at for a side-by-side comparison?"

"There's plenty of Sam on this camcorder, but finding footage of Jude we can use is trickier. All the clips I've found of him online show him looking so stiff that there's no comparison to Sam."

"I've got it," Masha says, reaching for her own phone. "I have a shared photo stream with Eli. That picture of you two dancing at Liv and Jake's wedding."

She AirDrops it before I can respond. The Live Photo opens before I'm ready to see it, especially now that Jude's probably sitting fireside at the Banning House, licking honey off some body part of Tania's. But I can't look away from the looped image of the two of us, all dressed up, dancing in each other's arms, looking like we belong together. From Eli's angle, you can't see my expression, but I remember how it felt. The camera does pick up Jude's expression, and that look in his eyes . . .

It's longing.

I overlay it with the moment Sam started talking to the camera with the same expression, when he wondered what I was doing away from him.

Masha gasps as she watches me merge the two together, manipulating each one only slightly so they sync right up.

# THE SPIRIT OF LOVE

"It's like ten years passed"—she snaps her fingers—"like that."

"That's it," I breathe. I hadn't known how to put it into words, but Masha's right. Sam seems like Jude if I had met him ten years ago. Jude seems like Sam all grown up.

"What do I do about it?" I ask Masha.

"What I do when I don't know what to do," Masha says with her phone in her hand. She puts it on speaker. I hear it ringing. A moment later, someone picks up.

"You've got Lorena, but Lorena doesn't have you."

"Lorena," Masha says. "I've got Fenny here. We need your help."

"I'm listening."

I take the phone from Masha. "Remember when we spoke at Liv's dress fitting about erotic confluence?"

"You're ready for me to tell you it's a bunch of bologna?"

"Lorena," Masha says, "we're looking at some very unsettling footage Fenny put together, and we're pretty sure—even though this is impossible—that the two men are actually one man, spanning some sort of ten-year time warp."

Lorena is quiet, then lets out a low whistle.

"Okay, girls," she finally says. "This is beyond my level of expertise. I'm more Brené Brown than Marianne Williamson. But recently I met someone who might be able to help. I'm sending you her contact info now. Maybe you know her? She's a friend of a friend of Jake's."

Masha looks at me and shrugs.

"She works as a soul integration midwife, very highly reviewed," Lorena says. "Her name is Tania."

"Tania from the wedding?" I groan and palm my face. "She's on the island right now. *With* Jude. They're *together*."

"Are you sure?" Masha asks.

"We just had the most awkward run-in at the market. They're definitely here. Definitely together."

"It sounds to me, honey," Lorena says, "as if a bigger storm is brewing. My two cents: Find him."

"Which him?"

"The one you want. The one you were dancing with at the wedding."

"Jude."

"Find Jude. Tell him the truth—"

"That I think he's two men, caught in a ten-year loop?" I say.

"No, honey," Lorena says, straight up laughing at me. "Tell him how you feel. That's the only truth there is."

**"EW," I SAY** to Masha, tossing aside the phone after we've hung up with Lorena.

Masha gives me a look. "The thought of telling Jude how you feel is ew?"

"It's very uncomfortable. Telling Jude how I feel requires me *knowing* how I feel."

"That seems like a great place to start," Masha leads.

I shake my head. "I know things by reading books, studying films, spending years apprenticing, or"—I point to my laptop—"having physical evidence."

I close my eyes and remember the one time I knew some-

# THE SPIRIT OF LOVE                           299

thing impossible, intuitively, with total certainty. Edie, in the hospital, when I was ten years old.

I think about Jude. And I do know. I want more of him. All kinds of more. But . . .

"Haven't I mentioned," I say to Masha, "that he is here with Tania?"

"Why do you assume it's romantic between them?"

"Firewood. Honey. Wine. All signs point to kinky, sticky sex. And I'm back to ew."

"Fenny, what if we entertain the possibility that you might be wrong?"

"Speak English please."

"Tania isn't here with Jude to try to seduce him. And even if she were . . ." She points at the computer screen, where the video of me dancing with Jude plays on loop.

I stare at it, and I see what it looks like: two people who are really into each other, dancing. I stare at it and remember how good our connection that night had felt.

"I hate to break it to you," Masha says, "but . . . Jude is into you."

"Maybe he was that night," I say with a sigh, "but since Olivia's wedding, I managed to mess up everything."

Footsteps sound overhead on the deck. I hear Olivia's voice, then Jake's. They seem to be arguing over who makes better piña coladas, which sounds like it's going to result in something called a colada-off.

"Before I was pregnant," Masha tells me, her eyes still fixed on the computer screen, "I used to love when they argued about cocktails."

300                                    LAUREN KATE

"When mixologists war," I say, "everybody wins."

A moment later, there's a knock on the doorframe.

"Olivia?" Masha says.

"We're freaking out," I say, looking at my computer screen. "We need help from someone who believes in parallel universes—"

Masha smacks me, her eyes cutting toward the doorway.

"*Jude!*" I scream at the sight of him. He's standing, in the flesh, on *The Midlife Crisis*. I slam the laptop closed. "What are you doing here?"

Masha smacks me again. "We thought you were—"

"Someone else?" Jude asks, looking at me. "That keeps happening to me today."

"What are you doing here?" I repeat because I need to know.

"Sorry to barge in on you." He really does sound sorry. "I heard you were here, Fenny . . . Is it possible we could talk?"

"You know what?" Masha says. "It's been almost thirteen minutes since I peed, and I'm dying." She scoots toward the end of the bunk bed, then climbs carefully down the ladder. "I'll be back!" She slips out the cabin door, and Jude and I are alone.

Without Masha next to me, the setting becomes ridiculous. Jude is too tall to hunch in the doorway, but I can't see his eyes if he stands in the hall. There's zero room inside this cabin that is not the bunk bed, but he definitely won't fit up here with me. The lower bunk is even more cramped. Not to mention . . . bed-like.

"Maybe we should go somewhere else?" I offer—just as the boat starts to move. I hear a blast of horns from above deck and Captain Dan's voice calling out, "Anchors up!"

# THE SPIRIT OF LOVE                                      301

"Hey!" Jude calls up deck. "I haven't even asked her yet!"

"Now would be a great time," Captain Dan calls back.

"Asked me what?" I study Jude, who looks a little green. "Are you okay?" I point at the deck. "Do you need some air?"

Jude nods and takes the stairs two at a time. I look around the cabin and wonder what the hell transpired in the last five minutes. I climb down the bunk bed ladder and head up the stairs to the deck.

The first person I see is Tania. She's in the cockpit with a bare leg wrapped around Captain Dan's waist. Her painted red lips are tickling his earlobe, and he's loving everything she's serving, as evidenced by his roving hands. I stare at this, then look at Jude, who gives me a conspiratorial laugh.

I move toward him. "You're okay with that?"

"That Tania has a healthy sexual appetite?"

"That and—"

"That she's super down with PDA?" Jude shrugs. "I don't know if it's for me, but I think everyone should do what makes them happy."

"That's very open-minded of you."

"Even though I'm not sure I get it," Jude says, "it's pretty clear that Captain Dan adds something to her life."

"Right." I nod, ever more confused. "So what were you going to ask me?"

Jude looks over his shoulder at the isthmus we're pulling away from. "I was going to ask you if you'd take a boat ride with me to another part of the island. But it seems I am too late. If you want to jump ship, you could probably still make it to shore—"

"Why do you want to take me to another part of the island?"

Jude nods. "That's a fair question I was hoping you wouldn't ask."

"Why?"

"Because I'm still working out how to explain it myself."

Olivia appears before us, four cups of piña coladas on a tray. "A taste test." Out of the side of her mouth, she whispers, "Mine is on the left, so you know how to vote." She winks as Jude and I take one of each.

We sip.

"You're cheating!" Jake cries, appearing before us in a green swimsuit, whisking his glasses out of our hands. "Mine are meant to be served in coconuts. Using a glass is drinking with one tongue tied behind your back."

"Oh, give us all a break!" Olivia shouts at the sky.

Masha appears between the arguing newlyweds. "Lovers, I need you," she says, pulling them both away and giving me a *You're welcome* look. "Let's give these two a minute."

"A minute's all they need to judge the colada-off," Olivia argues.

As soon as they're gone, Jude pours both his drinks into the coconut, downs the whole thing, and says to me, "I think they pair especially well together."

I smile. "That's it exactly."

"And, having just shot-gunned a very large serving of rum, I think I'm ready now."

"For what?"

He points at the island. I hold my breath as Jude reaches for my hand and says, "To tell you the truth."

# Chapter Twenty-Six

AN HOUR LATER, JUDE AND I STAND AT THE EDGE OF A trail, staring down a hundred feet into a ravine where the upside-down letters are still visible in the brush:

**JEEP**

*The Midlife Crisis* brought us as far as the cove at Parson's Landing. Then we borrowed a Jet Ski from the yacht and I drove us to shore. We parked under the serpent head–shaped rock on the beach as gray clouds combed the sky. After that, for reasons Jude has yet to explain but that are making my chest feel like a breeding ground for butterflies, he led me up the path and stopped here.

The wind feels cold and strange, the sky overcast and close. The clouds have turned the sea from turquoise into a treacherous steely blue. It feels like anything might happen, and I need to be prepared.

Jude seems frozen by the side of the ravine. He steps close to the edge and puts out a hand, as if he's touching something unseen.

"Jude?"

He hasn't spoken in a long time. Not since we started up the trail together. But I can tell from the manic motion of his eyes, from the tension in his neck, that there's a lot going on in his head.

"What I'm about to tell you is going to sound . . ." He shakes his head, closes his eyes. "Completely crazy."

Well, he's taken the words right out of my mouth. But at least he's going to go first.

"I'll tell you mine if you tell me yours," I say.

"I don't want to," he admits. "This is so difficult for me. But I keep thinking, maybe the fact that you showed up—here, now—is a sign."

"What kind of sign?"

"That I can tell you my story. That maybe you'll still be here when I finish."

I turn to face him, trying to read the apprehension in his dark eyes. "I'm not going anywhere."

"Thank you." Jude exhales. "So far so good."

"It's raining," I say, turning up my palms to feel the first drops. "It wasn't supposed to rain."

"Or maybe it was." Jude shivers. We're both just wearing T-shirts. It was hot, the sky bright blue, ten minutes ago on the yacht. Now thunder rumbles in the distance.

I look around, wondering if we'll need to duck somewhere for shelter, and as I do, my eyes fall on the embers of a recent fire, which the light rain is causing to smoke.

"Is that . . ." I start to say, spotting the container of honey and the bottle of wine I'd seen in Jude's hands at the market.

"Yes," he says. "Tania and I came here earlier."

"Oh?"

"Right after we ran into you. We built that fire."

# THE SPIRIT OF LOVE

305

I swallow, gathering the courage to be an adult about this. "You and Tania are . . ."

Jude must see the unspoken end of my question in my eyes, because he starts laughing heartily. He shakes his head. "No. No! There's *nothing* going on romantically between Tania and me. I hired her for this weekend. And this is where it's going to start to sound strange."

"That's okay!" I'm so relieved that he's not here *with* Tania, that the wine and honey aren't remnants of some al fresco fun-bag fiesta. Jude can tell me anything right now and I'll go with it.

"I met Tania at this workshop led by Captain Dan," he says. "Not exactly my kind of thing generally, but Jake invited me after I was on his show, and I can't help liking that guy."

"He has that effect on the planet."

"Anyway, I met Tania while I was there. She was about to get her certification in something called—"

"Soul integration midwifery?" I say. "Olivia's mom mentioned it."

Jude laughs. "Yeah, I didn't foresee myself being in this demographic, but here we are."

He looks at the sky, at the soft but steady rain.

"Okay," he says. "Here goes. Do you remember what I told you about my accident?"

"Twenty-eight fractured bones, six weeks in the ICU? That's not the kind of thing I'm going to forget. Did your doctors consider writing in to *Guinness World Records*? It's probably you and Evel Knievel."

I'm joking because what else am I supposed to be doing? Staring down at those four letters in the ravine? Listening to

Jude, who looks like Sam, tell me this? Knowing in the pit of my stomach that everything that's been making absolutely no sense for weeks might be suddenly converging?

"It happened here," Jude says and nods toward the ravine.

"Here?" I say, like I don't already know.

Jude puts out his hand again, and this time I understand. He's feeling the past. He's feeling the trauma his conscious mind can't remember. The rain pricks my skin, which feels hot enough to sizzle.

"When?" I ask, just to be sure.

"Ten years ago," he says, and looks at me. "When I was working here as a Search and Rescue specialist for the Island Conservatory."

I nod, not because I understand how or why any of this is possible, but because I knew. Even though it doesn't make sense.

"Do you remember in the cactus garden at the Huntington," I say, "when I made that joke about wanting to be a Search and Rescue specialist on Catalina?"

"I was so confused by that," he says. "You were mocking me, but I didn't know how you knew—"

"I didn't know. Not really. Not then. But at that point, the truth was harder for me to admit."

"What was the truth?"

"That a month ago, I met a man who was training to become a Search and Rescue specialist for the Island Conservatory!"

He flinches. "Really?"

"*He* was my long-distance fling. *He's* the man you advised

## THE SPIRIT OF LOVE

307

me to figure things out with after we kissed. *He's* the reason you left my house that night."

"Part of the reason," Jude says. "So that's why you're here, on the island? To see him?"

I nod, looking down at my feet. "And it's over, in case you were wondering."

"I'm sorry."

I laugh. Now I'm the one finding the hard stuff funny.

"Yeah. I think he and I are . . . just on different planes. Right place, wrong time, or whatever. But that's not why we're here. You were telling me about some ceremony you and Tania performed."

"It didn't work," Jude admits. "She was trying to help me make peace with the trauma. To 'bring it in so I could let it out.'" He sounds defeated as he raises and then drops his beautiful shoulders. "I couldn't do it. We stood here, pouring out honey and wine to 'bless this site,' to 'thank it for catching me.' I wrote down what I felt. Then I shouted out into the abyss." He looks at me and winces again.

"What did you shout?"

Jude cups his hands over his mouth. "I'm stuck!" he bellows into the ravine. "Let me move on!"

His voice echoes back to us so clearly, I can hear it a full second time.

"Did you hear that?" I ask, looking across the ravine.

"There's still something missing," Jude says, distracted. "I know it."

I know it, too. What's missing.

"Jude—" I turn to him.

He's already facing me. He takes my hands in his. "When I failed earlier, with Tania, she told me I needed to 'find a light.' The first thing I thought of was you."

"Me?"

"Here's the truth, Fenny. I'm doing this because of you. The things you said about me when we first met—about how I believe in my nightmares—"

"I was angry—"

"It was true. But it didn't use to be. I wasn't always like this." He gestures at himself. "When I lived here, I was so connected to the island. To the world. I was young and dumb, but I was also free. And happy. I think I used to feel like I had a purpose. Nothing dignified—I lived to enjoy the day, and to help others enjoy their days, too."

"That sounds very dignified."

"Yeah. You would have liked the old me more."

I smile at him sadly. "Yes and no."

He inhales, turning to look at the wreckage of the Jeep below. "I was responding to a flare sent up that night. Some campers needing rescue from a storm. After that . . . I don't know. I don't remember." He swallows. "When they used the jaws of life to pull me out, I'd been dead for three and a half minutes. I was in a coma for a month. I did brutal physical therapy every day for two years after that. And I thought I got better. I thought I was healed. But recently, I've been wondering . . . if a part of me didn't die that day. A part of me I'll never recover."

"It's okay," I tell him, near tears.

"No, it isn't."

THE SPIRIT OF LOVE                                    309

"Why?"

"Because I'm not whole like this, Fenny. And you deserve a whole man."

"What do I have to do with it?"

"You're going to make me say it? That I'm falling in love with you?"

My breath hitches, and I can barely speak. Hearing those words feels better than just about anything ever has. Except maybe for Jude's kiss.

"Is it true?" I whisper.

He reaches out and touches my cheek. "I'm falling in love with you, okay? And love has side effects. One of them is that I want to be better—I want to be whole—for you." He closes his eyes. "But it feels out of reach. I'm sorry."

"Jude," I whisper, shivering in the rain. What I want to say feels crazy, but then again, so is what he just told me. Sometimes love can feel so close to crazy that their shadows are the same.

"Fenny."

"Maybe that missing piece of you isn't an abstract idea. Maybe that piece—physically—is here."

"What do you mean?"

I tip my head toward Sam's cabin. "Follow me."

## Chapter Twenty-Seven

I LEAD JUDE THROUGH THE RAIN, ALONG THE wildflower-hedged path, and up the rickety porch stairs of the cabin at the edge of the island and both of our worlds.

"I don't understand," he says, bewildered. "How do you know about this place?"

"Sam."

"Uh-huh?"

I stare at him. I'd only been answering his question, explaining that I know about this place because of Sam. But Jude replied so naturally. As if I'd been addressing him.

"Why did you answer to that name?"

He blinks. "Samuel Jude de Silva. That's my given name. Before the accident, I went by Sam." He touches the front door, his eyes far away. "I went by Sam, and I lived here."

Okay. So this is actually happening. Sam is Jude and Jude is Sam, splintered off by time and trauma. Somehow brought back together by me. But what happens when I open this door and the two of them face off?

"Are you okay?" he asks. "Have I freaked you out?"

"Did Tania mention anything about ghosts?" Saying the word aloud feels true in some ways, and very wrong in other ways. Sam was no ghost when we saw that sunset on the beach.

THE SPIRIT OF LOVE                                    311

He was no ghost when I took off my dress yesterday and he got down on his knees.

"Why do you ask?" Jude says.

"Um."

What if by inviting Jude here, I'm making an irreversible mistake? Will I get stuck in the time loop with him? Will planets wheel out of the sky? But then I think about what Jude said back at the ravine. About the piece of him that's missing. That he needs to be whole. I think about his explanation for why he wants to be whole in first place . . .

Because he's falling in love with me.

He sounded clear. As clear as I suddenly feel right now, standing at his side, at the threshold of a ghost. I've spent the past month wrestling with my feelings for what I assumed were two different men.

But they weren't. They were just one fractured soul.

I don't know if they'll even like each other. I haven't had time to run through all the dozen ways this introduction might go very wrong. But I can't go on knowing what I know right now and not let Jude in on it. Whatever the cost.

I take a deep breath. "I think there's someone you should meet."

I open the door, which requires more hip grease than I expected. I gesture for Jude to walk in first.

"Wow," he whispers. "It's the same."

But when I follow him in, I have to hold back a gasp, because in the space of four hours, everything has changed.

The walls are bare. The furniture is gone. The air is thick with dust. Cobwebs cover all the windows. The bookshelf and the ladder and the handmade bar and the fireplace still stand, but they're shadows of what they'd been before. The cabin looks abandoned to the point of being condemned.

Like no one's been here in ten years.

"What happened?" The words slip out, even though I know. A lump rises in the back of my throat.

*Oh, Sam.*

Jude walks the perimeter of the room, his hands running over Sam's—his—handiwork. He pauses where the couch had been, where a ghost and I once sat, staying up all night and then listening to the sunrise.

I wish I could make this place go back to the way it was. I wish I could have kept them both.

"I was just here this morning, and everything was different." My voice trembles. "He was here."

"Who?"

I turn to look at Jude. "Sam."

"I don't understand."

I step close and put my hands on Jude's shoulders. I look into his eyes. "We deal with the impossible every day. We make fantasies real. We kill people, and we bring them back to life. And I know, like I know you know, that every single thing that's magic on TV is pulled from the collective unconscious because it's also actually real. We use special effects, and tricks of light, and makeup, and editing. But once upon a time, when I was just a kid, I didn't know how to do any of that. But I knew that what made fantasy feel real was the magic of the human heart, which is capable of anything."

"Yes," Jude whispers.

THE SPIRIT OF LOVE                                313

"So right now," I continue, "in the face of some deeply inexplicable, time- and space-defying occurrences, I'm going to lean on what I know. What I guess I've always known." I put my hand over my heart and close my eyes. "The truth I hold in here. One month ago, I met a man on this island in the middle of a storm. He took me to this cabin. He showed me his world. His name was Sam. He was twenty-three." I sniff, but the tears are starting. "He was tall and built and hadn't yet grown into himself. He was thirty-two service hours away from completing his Search and Rescue training certification."

"This can't be possible," Jude whispers.

"He couldn't make toast without burning it, but his boeuf bourguignon rivaled Julia Child's. He loved spearfishing and hummingbirds and listening to the sunrise, right out there." I point out the window facing the sea. "Sometimes while doing shirtless one-armed pull-ups. I could have filmed a two-hour feature film of him doing shirtless one-armed pull-ups."

"That sounds like more of a film-festival-circuit short," Jude jokes, but his eyes are shining with tears, too.

"I don't know how to make this make sense," I say, "and I don't know where Sam is right now. I don't know what happened to this cabin since I left it four hours ago. But I do know that I loved that man." I close my eyes. I sound ridiculous. "Or at least, I was starting to love him. Or if not that, I loved what he was becoming. He was kind and funny and open, and when we slept together on the beach—"

"You *slept* with Sam?"

"I felt like I was touching the core of the earth."

"You slept with my—wow. I'm trying to picture that."

I thwack Jude gently. I'm still crying. "And I miss him. We fought this morning. And I'm scared I did something that made him disappear. I'm scared I'll never see him again. And I really wanted you to meet him. Do you understand?"

He nods. "I'm trying."

"It's a lot."

"What did you and Sam fight about?"

"In the end," I say, "I think it was because he wasn't you."

Jude cups my face in his hands. He closes his eyes now and a tear slips out.

"My doctors were so proud when I recovered," he says quietly. "Of me. Of themselves. I was a medical miracle. No one could believe they brought that shell back to life."

"I didn't mean it when I called you that."

"Yes, you did. And you were right. I changed everything about myself after the accident. I changed my name. I changed my career. I changed my lifestyle and all my plans for my future. I never wanted to look back at the kid who made that reckless mistake. I threw him away. I *let* him die that day." He looks around the cabin sadly. "And the worst part is, I didn't think I missed him. I didn't know I was missing anything—until I met you. This past month. You've got me seeing everything differently. You've got me wanting . . ."

"Wanting what?"

"To reinvent myself yet again. To turn into someone you'd want to be with." He smiles, sadly. "I didn't see you coming, Fenny. I didn't know that the part of me that died that day was the part of me you would have liked best."

THE SPIRIT OF LOVE                                          315

"Jude."

"I came to Catalina to find Sam again. But somehow it seems you found him first."

"Oh, God," I breathe. "And now he's gone because of me?"

"No," Jude says. His fingers brush my cheek. He's smiling. "No, I don't think he's gone."

"But this cabin, this place, it's all so . . ." I look around, and my eyes land on the kitchen counter. Where I'd left Sam that note saying goodbye. Saying we were over. The note is gone, but something else remains.

The adder stone.

"Wait a minute," I say, drawing Jude over to the counter.

Jude studies the necklace and then picks it up. "I used to have one just like this," he says, draping it over my head. "But this one's yours, I think."

"You believe in this stuff?"

"Today I do."

He leaves me with the necklace, walking toward the side door of the cabin, stepping out onto the porch that faces the ocean. It's stopped raining, but it looks like it could start again at any moment. The sky is pocked with blue breaking through thick clouds. In the distance, near the mainland, shimmers an almost invisible rainbow.

Sam's pull-up bar is still here, welded between two wooden posts. Jude reaches up with his left arm, precisely the way I used to love watching Sam reach up. Just before he grabs the bar, he pauses, tosses his head. Then, with his back to me, he whips off his shirt, letting it drop at his feet.

"For continuity," he says as my eyes feast on his back, slightly leaner, ten years older, and quite possibly even more beautiful. "Whenever you're ready," he tells me, "say action."

He's telling me without telling me to frame the shot with magic. I hold up the adder stone to my face and look through the hole at the man who straddled life and death and time and space and ended up whole, right here, with me.

"Action."

Slowly, straining, Jude pulls himself up to the bar. I watch his muscles flex. I watch them swell in size. Jude's chin crests the bar as the sun explodes from behind a cloud. Its rays reach like angels to lift him even higher.

He lowers his body until his feet touch the planks. He turns around to face me. I let go of the stone.

"Wow," I say.

"Did it work?" he asks, touching his arms, his face, his chest.

"I'm not sure," I say. "I think I need to check under the hood."

Jude grins and moves toward me. He gazes down into my eyes. He looks different, but exactly the same. His eyes are open yet discerning. He puts his hands around my waist, and his touch is boyish smooth but also lit with the confidence of a man.

"Samuel Jude de Silva," I whisper, drawing him close.

"Yes, Fenny?"

"Kiss me."

His lips touch mine, and that's when I know. He's everything I want. He's all he's supposed to be. He can reinvent himself as many times as he wants or never again, as long as he doesn't stop kissing me.

# THE SPIRIT OF LOVE                                    317

A blast of horns startles us both. It's coming from the ocean, and we force ourselves to break apart. *The Midlife Crisis* is sailing past Sam's cabin, and ant-sized Olivia and Masha hold binoculars to their eyes, jumping up and down on the deck and waving. A voice calls over the loudspeaker.

"You found the light!" It's Tania at the megaphone in the cockpit.

"More chin-ups, please," Masha calls into the megaphone.

"Was my piña colada better?" Olivia's voice asks.

"Jude, you salty old dog," Captain Dan growls.

"Not a day too soon, man," Jake says.

"I think they're rooting for us," I murmur to Jude as we wave at the ship, sailing onward, around the next cove.

"Question," Jude says, resting his thumb on my lip. "When we kissed just now, did it feel like the earth was splitting open?"

"This is nothing," I assure him. "Wait until I get you horizontal on the secret beach."

"You know about the secret beach?" he asks. "Of course you know about the secret beach."

"I know a zip line that can take us there in thirty seconds."

"No, it hasn't been used in ten years."

"That thing was built to last," I say with a twinkle in my eye.

"When do you think I'll stop being jealous of my ghost?"

"I know how to make it sooner," I tell him with a knowing look.

And then, like so many Hollywood endings, Jude sweeps me off my feet and carries me toward Sam's secret beach and our whole new adventure together.

# Acknowledgments

With thanks to the California Conservatory and the Wrigley family for your stewardship of Catalina Island, my favorite Los Angeles County jewel. To the Banning House for a week of seclusion, inspiration, and pelican-staring. To Becky at the Harbor Reef Bar for the insights into Parson's Landing, for letting my kids play endless games of pool, and for the Buffalo Milk.

To my industry friends who helped me realize *Zombie Hospital* and this story's on-set world: Sarah Carter, Maryam Myika Day, Bayne Gibby, Sallie Patrick, Stephanie Escajeda, and the cast and crew of the *Fallen* TV series.

To Megan Bloom, for trusting me with your first-hand glimpse of the Beyond, which became the key to Fenny's story. Here's to another glorious forty years of friendship. I'm also indebted to Dr. Eben Alexander's stunning memoir of his own near-death experience, *Proof of Heaven*.

To my agent, Laura Rennert, the equivalent of a crisp glass of wine after a long, hot day. To my editor, Tara Singh Carlson, the diamond drill that helps my characters reach their cores. To the excellent team at Putnam: Molly Donovan, Sally Kim, Ashley

Hewlett, Jazmin Miller, Regina Andreoni, Ashley Tucker, and Christy Wagner.

To my readers, to my book clubs, to the Heath on Greenvalley Road, to my parents. To Lhüwanda, Matilda, Venice, and Jason. So much love and beauty and gratitude.

*Photograph of the author © Christina Hultquist*

**Lauren Kate** is the #1 *New York Times* and internationally bestselling author of twelve novels, including *Fallen*, which was made into a major motion picture; *What's in a Kiss?*; and *By Any Other Name*. Her books have sold more than ten million copies and have been translated into more than thirty languages. Kate lives in Los Angeles with her family.

VISIT LAUREN KATE ONLINE

laurenkatebooks.net

LaurenKateAuthor

LaurenKateBooks